About the Author

T.H. Moore is a Southwest Philadelphia native who relocated to Camden, New Jersey at the age of ten. He's an active member of Omega Psi Phi Fraternity, Inc., and earned a Bachelor of Science degree from Morgan State University. His career as an Information Technology Consultant and Real-Estate investor has afforded him the opportunity to travel to many countries all over the world as well as the majority of the United States. Blending experience with imagination helped formulate the basis of, and inspired him to write his first novel, The End Justifies the Means.

His second novel, The Devil's Whisper, is uniquely creative fiction that ventures away from the inspiration of his own life experiences. In The Devil's Whisper, he dives into a darker set of dual protagonists whose sole objective is to survive the circumstances of the world they live in. Tarik is the proud father of one son, Jason, and currently resides in Virginia, where he is working on the next two installments of The Devil's Whisper trilogy.

Copyright © 2016 by Tarik H. Moore

Published by:
T.H. Moore
P.O. Box 4128
Ashburn, VA 20148
www.thmoore.com

Cover artwork by: Art Director Terrance Mease and Graphic Designer Vanessa Mendozzi
Interior book layout by: Rochelle Mensidor

First Edition May 2017

Library of Congress Cataloging-in-Publication Data is available upon request.

ISBN: 978-0-9779519-1-8

The Devil's Whisper

Volume I
(Katingal)

BY T.H. MOORE

Acknowledgements

As always, I would like to first thank my mother for providing me all the educational opportunities I needed to become successful. Without you, I'm nothing. T. Jackson, for reading the manuscript of my first book "The End Justifies the Means." I may have never decided to publish had it not been for you. My editors, Jenna Kalinsky and William Greenleaf. Proofreaders, Marti Tucker, Yasmin Carlos, and Pope Carlos. My friends, family, and loved ones who have supported me to continue chasing my dream of being a writer.

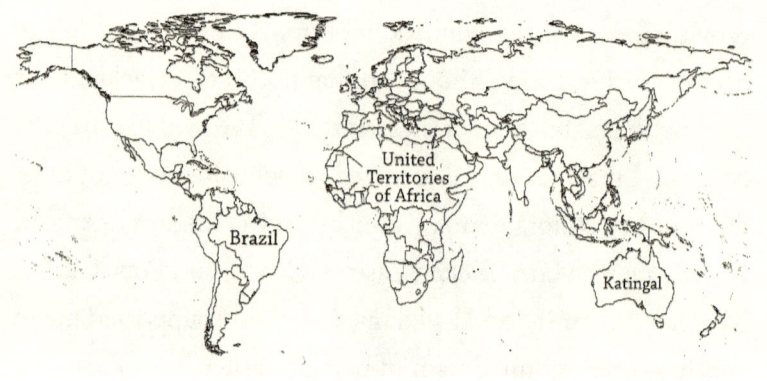

Preface

My children, let me warn you. When you cracked the spine of this book, you ignited a ripple effect that forever changed everything you once knew to be true. This overwhelming current washes over not just you, but everything beyond you. Within these pages, you will realize that the world in which you were born and reared no longer exists. Life as you've always known it is no more.

A transformation of your existential niche began the moment your eyes graced the lines of this text. With each successive page, the material possessions you covet will become irrelevant, your socioeconomic status erased. Whatever your religious or political affiliation, nationality, culture, and heritage is being reconfigured.

This revelation may alarm you, but such an unveiling is necessary. Shattering your reality is a drastic yet required demonstration of my contrition for allowing you to suffer. Know this: I have suffered along with you. I endured your anguish and resisted my instinct to intervene because I believed you could navigate toward righteous humanitarianism. I regret underestimating that a few of my offspring would be drawn to horrid actions and watched you edge closer toward darker days. My intercession now is necessary for the rest of my children to appreciate the world in all its natural beauty.

Now, be free—free from the artificial constraints that have imprisoned you. The effect that triggered in the first paragraph has penetrated all time, from before Adam was seduced by Eve, and from before the stars exploded and the universe was spawned.

The previous 285 words of this text have dissipated the traps of corruption that have crippled and maligned your morality. Do not shy away from this transition, for it will guide you from the cold, brutal world to which you've grown numb. It is now my duty to correct the imbalance of righteousness so you may realize the true meaning of World Peace.

Indeed, no longer will those two words, "World Peace," serve as an empty phrase abused by pageant queens or bandied about by opportunistic politicians. One and a half million years ago, when I created life, my goal was to see all my creatures live in peace, together. The civilization you now inherit is the result of a simple lifestyle that was matured in seclusion on the remote island of Bermuda. I waited until I saw that the hearts of all humanity were open enough to embrace it.

This small group, known in present day by a select few as the Society, nurtured the four principles of goodwill, selflessness, moral standing, and universal brotherhood.

Those four principles were the seeds planted into the fertile soil of Bermuda, and they flourished.

Guided by my grace, the Society blossomed into a simplistically ideal community. The foundation laid by this colony allowed them to, without bias or prejudice, embrace all races, creeds, and lifestyles. Over time, their idealism spread, perpetuating hundreds of years of celebrated peace and harmony.

Since I orchestrated the discovery of the Society in 1505, I've guarded your futures so the 8.5 billion inhabitants of Earth could live in tranquility. Not long ago, you lived as hundreds of thousands of separate tribes, governed by your respective laws. This existence led some societies to flourish, while from conquest and famine others withered.

Today, while many societies are still separated by geography, skin tone, and language, you now share a single collective system of civility and governance. That the clear majority of you have reached a pinnacle of peace and gentility, I rejoice in observing, even as a few have chosen to remain savages. The way of life for the Society has made war, holocausts, genocides, abuses of civilizations, and other large-scale crimes against humanity inconceivable.

The previous mentioned atrocities you know all too well—or rather, *knew* all too well prior to this book. There are individual anarchists or miscreants who continue to engage in immoral behavior, but they are removed and punished. For them, Katingal City was created, a place where criminals can harm themselves and others like them until they all perish.

It is a delight to witness my original intentions for human beings realized. No longer mere vestiges of the raw clay from which I molded you, your DNA and humanity have evolved and peaked. While your clumsy early days of discovering fire gave rise to more advanced modes of technological innovation, you remained misled in your belief that all of life's mysteries could be comprehended through science. From this, a healthy arrogance has arisen, one that has allowed you to believe that all things could be achieved without my influence. Some of you even dare to doubt my existence. But allowing you the freedom to question everything, including me, was the catalyst that galvanized your evolution. I am pleased to see how far you've come.

The pages that follow usher forth a new day, a new world in which people live peacefully. Now is your time. Go forward and claim this new world of which I've given you a mere glimpse. Unlatch the locks from your mind. You have earned your place in this world—a world that acknowledges a belief that your fellow man loves you as much as you love them. Be blessed, and take your place. May peace be upon you.

—Eloah

13.7 billion years ago – I initiated the beginning of the universe, your world, and created the most basic elements needed for your eventual existence. Your history books have labeled my creation of the universe the Big Bang.

100,000 years ago – In Africa, I molded the raw clay of your human existence and breathed life into the first of you, the *Homo sapiens*.

1492 – One of my more curious children, Christopher Columbus, voyaged across the Atlantic in search of a new trade route to India, but poor navigation steered him to a cluster of islands in the Caribbean. He was met with hurricane-force winds that laid waste to the crews and sank all three of the vessels. Columbus and his crew never set eyes on the "New World" and its indigenous tribes. Indeed, the New World was never colonized by the English.

1505 – I instigated Spanish navigator Juan de Bermudez's discovery of a community of people that later came to be known as the Society. By manipulating the winds and sea, I forced his ship to run aground just off the coast of the island this innocent community calls home. When he and his crew scoured the island, they discovered a multicultural population of 140 non-indigenous people. This community had also arrived by shipwreck and was unable to leave the island, so they cultivated their very own harmonious Garden of Eden.

1500 - 1520 – I marveled at the Songhai Empire in West Africa as it entered a period of great expansion and power under the leadership of Askia Mohammed Toure. Equipped with arms and ammunition from Portuguese trade, the Songhai Empire utilized its superior numbers and military tactics to thwart Portuguese and European domination of the African gold, spice, and slave trade. The Portuguese and Europeans were driven out of the coastal countries of northwest Africa. The practice of African slavery was abolished in its infancy. Portuguese and European ambitions of extending slavery were never realized.

1609 – I again manipulated the Atlantic winds, pushing English explorers to the small island of Bermuda. They found 214 inhabitants in a self-sustained community living in peace, innocent of outside influences. The community shared the journal of Juan De Bermudez, the Spanish explorer from a century prior, who chronicled his experiences from living on the island. When the English explorers returned to Great Britain, they published Juan De Bermudez's journal under the title *The Garden of Eden*.

1609 – King James I colonized Bermuda. The king then entered an agreement with the country of Ethiopia, one that allowed the Bermudians to preserve the lifestyle they had created on an Ethiopian reservation. The reservation was dubbed "the Garden" after rumors circulated of this unusual community of relative harmony. Pilgrims from all over Ethiopia journeyed to the reservation.

1625 – The Garden's population exploded to over ten thousand people, outgrowing its reservation and spilling over into neighboring communities and villages.

1770 – Katingal, located between the South Pacific and the Indian Ocean, was colonized, and its southern quadrant subsidized by Great Britain as a destination for exiled violent criminals of the British penal system.

1783 – The continent of Africa reorganized its fifty-three distinct countries into fifty-three territories, thereby unionizing the continent into a single country. The new country, The United Territories of Africa, or UTA, designated Ethiopia as the country's capital and most powerful territory. When each territory pooled their natural resources and products, the UTA became the world's first superpower.

June 1914 – The assassination of Archduke Franz Ferdinand of Austria by the Black Hand, a Serbian nationalist secret society, was prevented. World leaders recognized this event as an intentional attempt by one country to invade another. As a result, world leaders gathered into a secret council, and the United Nations was established. The organizers of the Black Hand were apprehended, tried, and exiled to Katingal City.

1919 – Benito Mussolini attempted to create the National Fascist Party that advocated for aggressive nationalism. His plot to forcefully "restore law and order" in Italy was foiled.

Mussolini and his conspirators were tried by the United Nations and exiled to Katingal City.

1924 – Several defecting members of Kampfbund, and the German National Socialist party in Bavaria, Germany, identified Adolf Hitler and Erich Ludendorff of an attempted coup d'état of Germany. They were exiled to Katingal City for conspiracy to incite a war and enacting genocide on people of the Jewish faith.

1971 – Idi Amin Dada failed in his coup d'état of the Ugandan African Territory. He and his generals were exiled to Katingal City.

1994 – The United Nations intervened to prevent the planned genocide of the Tutsi tribe in the Rwanda Territory of the UTA. Government officials and Rwandan Patriotic Front militia leaders were tried and exiled to Katingal City for crimes against humanity and conspiracy to commit genocide.

2000 – At the turn of the millennium, the United Nations passed a decree that emphasized the restoration of the quality of life across the globe. Recreational drugs in their natural form, such as marijuana and hashish, were legalized. Cocaine and opiate-based drugs such as heroin and opium were outlawed. All organized crime syndicates who manufactured, distributed, or profited from the sale of these banned substances were apprehended and prosecuted.

2003 – As the war on illegal narcotics reduced profits for its ringleaders, organized human trafficking grew. In an urgent response, the United Nations passed another decree to stop the momentum that human traffickers had gained.

2010 – One by one, the heads of all known human trafficking organizations were apprehended and exiled. The head of the most powerful criminal organization Duenno eluded capture. Led by Charles Gravo, aka "Yäbälay," it remained a small yet powerful criminal network. The World Intelligence & Criminal Coalition, WICC, declared him their most wanted fugitive.

2011 – WICC assembled an elite militarized task force to track and apprehend Yäbälay and bring him to justice.

Chapter 1

S IF TO CAST A spotlight on their standing in the world, the moon threw a white glow over the gleaming high-rises clustered at the heart of Addis Ababa, Ethiopia. The pristine pillars were as modern as they were vertiginous. Only social climbers, business moguls, and the most affluent of Addis Ababa could call these architectural masterpieces home.

Yet none could stand as tall as Pantheon Tower. Just below the top beamed a series of penthouse suites constructed of glass, the view affording the occupants the chance to look down on the world as gods.

Nevertheless, this glass box operated only as support for the uppermost dwelling, one of several impenetrable fortresses around the world belonging to the notorious Charles Gravo. A curated collection of military-trained mercenaries in black two-piece suits manned this stronghold. They lined the windows at perfect three-foot intervals, each sentry clutching a semiautomatic assault rifle and donning an earpiece that disappeared into his jacket collar. Most of them stood in earshot of their boss, a man in his mid-thirties, as he pleasured a half-naked teenaged girl.

Eyes closed, the baby-faced teenager moaned from atop the disheveled black satin sheets on the palatial bed. Her tongue mimicked the slow laps as Gravo bobbed his head between her skinny thighs.

She cracked open an eyelid to check his mood. If he were angry, she would need to work harder, but if he were content, she might live. Failure to please him, as per his exact instructions, meant she would end up dead like the others. Nobody ever talked about that. It was just understood.

Gravo soon sat up and wiped his mouth with her shirt. "Lay back and pleasure yourself," he ordered.

Was that boredom on his face? She reacted with urgency. With playful fingers, she traced an imaginary line down her stomach until her fingers met the plaid miniskirt gathered at her hips. She made sure she had his undivided attention as she massaged her bald labia, working in methodical circles.

"Like this, Papa?" she whimpered, her hips matching the rhythm of her hands. She willed herself to keep going in the desperate hope that this would be over soon.

"Yes. Just like that." He scooted closer and stroked himself while watching her small, manicured fingers disappear inside herself and then reappear to rub the full length of her labia.

"Come on," she urged him. "Empty yourself inside me, Papa."

Just then, she felt a single tear sneak out of the corner of her eye. As it streamed down her face, she turned her head and looked through the glass walls and out to the starlit sky to hide her shame. The thought of her so-called Papa discovering her disgust sent a shiver down her spine, so she forged forward with her role.

She wiped the tear into the pillow cover and peeked back at him, only to be greeted by his grimacing stare. She stopped breathing for a split second when she noticed that he was losing his erection.

"Now, Papa?" she pleaded. "Will you fuck me now?"

His upper lip twisted as he lifted the girl up to him. He knew exactly how he wanted her positioned to heighten his pleasure. But before he could do so, a deafening rumble caused him to lurch back. The clink of shattering glass echoed through the room. The lights flickered, and dust fell from the ceiling. Gunfire and explosions sent shock waves through the penthouse.

"UTA police!"

Three masked men in black military assault gear with *UTA Police* stamped across their chests burst through the door.

"Charles Gravo, put your hands in the air and step away from the child!" The police officer locked in on Charles with his assault rifle. A bright red pulsing dot danced across Charles's vision, and he knew it was the rifle's laser sight.

He cracked a menacing smile and, moving with the lithe grace of a cat, slid out of the bed. He stood still, naked and unapologetic, with his hands up. The young girl remained in his bed.

"Shale, do as they say," Charles ordered.

The girl climbed off the bed to join Charles, placing herself in the line of fire between the officer and her Papa. She raised her hands high so her palms intercepted the path of the red dot.

"Put your hands on your head and interlock your fingers," the officer ordered.

The smile remained on Charles's face, and before the officer could speak again, the muzzles of two assault rifles flashed from the bedroom's shadowy back corners amid an unholy roar. The girl flinched as bullet casings crashed and echoed off the heated marble floor. The officers' bodies jerked forward and blood sprayed, then both fell forward, limp, dead.

The remaining members of the task force in the living room made their way toward the bedroom, crouching to find cover.

"Mr. Gravo, to the panic room!" came the voice of his security commander.

Charles grabbed the girl and pushed her ahead of him as they ran to the back corner of the bedroom. His mercenaries engaged the task force in a fierce gun battle as Charles and the girl ducked through a hidden barricaded door and slammed it shut behind them. Charles placed his shaking palm on a scanner.

"Lockdown sequence initiated," a soft, robotic feminine voice recited, followed by the sounds of mechanical dead bolts locking into place. Everything worked exactly as designed. This wasn't the first time Charles Gravo had been forced to escape a raid.

Inside the panic room, he and the girl hurried to the shelves where spare clothes lay waiting. Charles grabbed a black sweat suit and sneakers and pulled them on without underwear or socks. He tossed a similar but smaller sweat suit to his shale. She caught the clothes and dropped them at her feet to begin removing that night's costume.

Charles watched her. The air-conditioned room caused goose pimples to form on the skin around her nipples and down her arms. He grew hard as she flung the schoolgirl costume to the floor, twisted her long black hair into a tight bun, and slipped into the small sweat suit.

He wanted to fuck her right there, despite the continued gunfire just outside his secure walls. He pushed the urge away and dashed over to the padded wall mounted with semiautomatic weapons. He grabbed a truncated AR assault rifle and extra ammunition clips, and quickly locked and loaded the weapon before tossing it to her. She caught it, almost dropping it, then readied herself to aim and fire it as she'd been trained to do by Charles's mercenaries. Charles grabbed a Beretta ARX rifle and extra ammunition clips, locked and loaded his weapon, and nodded to signal it was time to exit the panic room.

He slid back a secret panel in the room to reveal another infrared palm scanner. Seconds later, a door on the other side of the panic room opened to reveal a fifteen-foot corridor with a one-way mirror at the end. From inside the corridor, Charles could see his emergency exit route flooded with task force police in a gunfight with what remained of Charles's security detail.

He pulled his young companion in front of him to use as a shield. When she crouched in fear, he placed his hand on her thin shoulder and bent down to whisper into her ear. He could feel her trembling.

"The brave endure while cowards die alone." He kissed her cheek just before pressing a button that caused the one-way bulletproof mirror to slide halfway into the floor, giving them a cover from which to fire upon their enemies. He nodded at her and pulled her up.

They both opened fire at the back of the nearest officer. He went down, and two of his fellow officers spun around instantly and returned fire.

Charles and the shale took cover again behind the half-raised bulletproof glass, waiting for a break in the return fire. The moment the officers stopped to reload, Charles and the girl stood again, and another officer fell dead.

Charles thought the tide was turning in his favor. Two officers sprawled in bloody pools near their exit. The few remaining UTA officers and Charles's security team continued to exchange fire. Another UTA officer flung out his arms and went down.

"Go!" Charles yelled.

The girl stepped over the cover of the glass and moved in a crouching run toward the exit with Charles close behind.

Now the remaining UTA officers were taking fire from both sides.

"Keep moving forward," Charles told the girl.

They were only a few feet away from the flight of stairs that would serve as their exit. Before they reached that safe haven, a single bullet breached the large windows behind them and exploded the skull of Charles's teenage human shield. She toppled to the floor, her head and face covered in blood and pinkish-gray brain matter.

Charles turned to look out the large window to see muzzle flashes from a hovering helicopter just as another bullet pierced the glass, sending large shards down onto two of his remaining security men.

"Advance!" screamed one of the UTA officers into his shoulder mic. "Yäbälay identified!"

Within seconds, another wave of officers stormed up the escape stairwell. One peered over the top of the stairs and fired two shots at Charles before the officer behind him body-checked him into the stairwell wall.

"Idiot!" barked the second officer, who had a captain's epaulet on his shoulder. "He's to be taken alive!"

Tin canisters hit the floor behind Charles and exploded, releasing a shock wave that sent him stumbling to the floor. Several officers rushed in to surround, disarm, and place him in restraints while others emerged from the stairwell and concentrated their firepower on what was left of Charles's security detail, eliminating them one after another with surgical precision.

The clicking and tight grip of the metal handcuffs around Charles's wrists infuriated him.

The UTA captain spoke into his shoulder mic. "We have the target in custody. I repeat, we have Yäbälay in custody."

The radio crackled. "Acknowledged. Proceed with extraction plan omega, and we will meet you at the safe house."

"You're all dead men," Charles said quietly before a black hood was thrown over his head from behind. He tried to shake it off, though he knew it was hopeless. Then he felt the sting of a needle in his upper arm. His legs buckled, and he slumped forward. Inside the hood, he fought to keep his eyes open. He failed.

Chapter 2

THE DOORBELL DISRUPTED ELAINA SOUZA's morning prayers. Like all her prayers in the last month, these hung on the hopes that her latest visit to her fertility clinic would yield good news. She rushed through the last few words before she rose from her knees.

She made her way through the long hallway of the ranch-style home toward the front door. Even in yoga pants and one of her husband's T-shirts, Elaina was stunning, the petite, curly-haired Brazilian brunette was the object of every man's desire. Despite her looks, Elaina felt deeply lacking.

Elaina was a few feet away from the door when the mail fell through the slot. She rushed to wish the mailman a good day, but he was gone.

She scooped the post off the floor, sifted through the junk, noted the usual bills, and was about to throw the stack on the side table when she spotted the manila envelope. Just like the others, it was addressed to her but had no return address. Her breathing quickened.

She dropped all the other pieces of mail onto the floor and steadied herself before continuing to the kitchen. She ripped open the dreaded envelope. Just like the two previous times, the packet contained several photos of her husband holding hands, embracing, and kissing another woman.

A hot flash washed over her, and her heart rose into her throat. She looked closer at the picture, then dashed into the living room and pawed through a pile of fashion magazines until she located the recent issue of *Claudia*. The face of the woman from the surveillance pictures stared back at her.

She tore through the pages to the feature story, a profile of the former Miss Brazil. Apparently, she had relinquished her crown for self-described personal reasons.

Elaina sank back onto the sofa. She forced herself to look at the photo in her shaking hands. The photo captured her husband's face buried between the former Ms. Brazil's thin, toned thighs. She recalled recent moments of intimacy and his inability to maintain his erection.

When she noticed the fresh time stamp on the photo, her shame twisted into rage. She couldn't remember the last time he'd bothered to use his tongue to pleasure her. It had been at least a year.

Tears poured down her cheeks. She slammed the remaining photos face down on the coffee table. On the back of the last photograph was a typed address, *1411 Rua Visconde de Piraja*. Like the other mysterious packages she had received, the address of the woman accented the photographic proof of a secret relationship.

Elaina had not confronted her husband about the two previous packages. She had always believed that a love as pure and enduring as theirs was impervious to pain, to suffering, that fate had brought them together.

She recalled every moment of the magical day that Carlos had introduced himself to her. A moment before he did, Gabriel, his twin brother, had darted across the worn grass of the school's quad and thrown himself at Elaina's feet.

"Never have I seen a girl as beautiful as you! Before everyone here, I declare my love for you. Tell me, what is it I must do to win your affection?"

Gabriel's scene had attracted onlookers, and from the small crowd came another voice. "You know I have feelings for her," Carlos fumed. "You're selfish, and only doing this to get everyone's attention."

Carlos made his way to the front of the crowd, and Elaina realized she was looking upon two of the same face. He slammed Gabriel into the ground. Gabriel pushed himself up and struck Carlos. Carlos retaliated until his brother's blows became stronger. The students had cheered on one brother or the other until no one could tell which brother the bloodied face belonged to.

"Stop it, Gabriel," Carlos demanded. "You know you don't care for her as I do."

Elaina watched as Carlos restrained himself from finishing his brother off while dodging the onslaught of punches, until Gabriel landed a blow that toppled Carlos and opened up the skin on his temple.

"Oh my God, stop it, the both of you!" Elaina pleaded as she tore through the crowd of onlookers to come to the aid of the fallen brother.

"Why are you running to him?" Gabriel snarled. "I won the fight!" He was breathing so heavily that he could barely speak.

"You won because he didn't fight you back!" she screamed while pressing her scarf against Carlos's wound. "Are you okay?"

He smiled. "I will be once I know your name."

"Elaina Almeida."

"I'm Carlos Souza," he declared with pride. "One day, I'll call myself your husband."

She smiled that day, and every day afterward. A decade later, after they had graduated from the federal university, Carlos kept true to his word.

Despite their tumultuous beginning, the three were a formidable team. Gabriel became a rising star with strong political aspirations, while Carlos grew into a successful businessman. Elaina entered politics as a campaign manager in their home country of Brazil. With endless political savvy, she managed several winning campaigns, culminating in Gabriel's election as president of Brazil.

After the election, Elaina declined a place in Gabriel's cabinet and set her sights on starting a family. She had been yearning to bring a child into the world as a beautiful testament to the love she and Carlos shared.

For two years, they tried, with no success. Their doctor suggested alternative methods. They readily agreed. She never expected Carlos to take this suggestion to mean that he should try alternate women.

As she stared at the newest chronicle of her husband's infidelity, she realized that this package had come with a handwritten note. *This one is pregnant. How long will you be your husband's fool?*

That question flipped a switch in her. She did deserve better.

~~~

As she'd done the previous two times, Elaina visited the address to confront her husband's newest strumpet.

She parked across the street from the woman's home in Ipanema, an exclusive neighborhood in Rio. She sneered at the manicured lawn and the dwarf mango tree in its front yard. She easily identified two peacekeepers down the street by their yellow uniforms and matching baseball caps. When they spotted her, they smiled, raised their hands, and brought them to their hearts. Elaina smiled back and returned the international gesture of peace, but the rage boiled inside her.

After the peacekeepers passed, Elaina marched to the woman's door and knocked. The golden-skinned former beauty queen was adorned with a flowing, sheer nightgown and five-inch platform heels as she opened the door.

"*Querido, meu amor!*"[1] She proclaimed before noticing Elaina.

---

[1] Darling, my love!

Elaina gasped at the exact pet name Carlos had used for her. *"Não! Eu sou seu único querida, puta!"*[2] Elaina cursed.

She peered at the woman's exposed belly pushing through the sheer gown. The woman looked past Elaina and onto the street before returning her gaze and making a smug face. The sight of the mistress leaning on a cane disrupted Elaina's anger.

The beauty queen seemed to notice the hesitation, and threw the cane to the floor. Her weakened legs tremored in the expensive Italian heels. *"O que você está fazendo aqui, puta!"*[3] She shouted as she placed one hand on her belly and rubbed it.

Seeing this woman pet herself sent Elaina's reason into a swan dive off the cliff of sanity. She slammed open the door hard enough to knock her husband's mistress backward and sliding down the wall. Then she pulled out a .38-caliber handgun from her bag and aimed it at the mistress's beautifully symmetrical face. Elaina had easily run two previous mistresses off, but this one offered only defiance. The paramour struggled to stand tall but appeared unafraid of Elaina's gun. It only made her flash a bigger smile.

Elaina kicked the door behind her closed and butted the gun's nozzle against the woman's left eye so she could feel its cold steel.

---

[2]   No! I'm his only sweetheart, bitch!

[3]   What are you doing here, bitch!

"*Você não vai fazer isso, sua puta!*"[4] the beauty queen said. "*Você não vai atirar em mim. Uma mãe doente e esperando. Ele obviamente me prefere por você, então você não o merece. Ponha seu brinquedo e vá embora, eu não quero que ele o veja aqui e arruine nosso dia juntos.*"[5] She threw back her shoulders, challenging Elaina to strike her down.

Elaina's anger left her unable to keep her hand steady. This woman spoke as if Carlos was her husband and Elaina was the whore. As if *she* was the one who should give Carlos a son.

Her vision blurred. Her body felt light. She was no longer able to feel the weight of the gun. All that remained was the disappointment of her marriage.

"Let Eloah's will be done," the mistress whispered as she looked toward the heavens.

Elaina steadied her arm with her other hand and squeezed the trigger. She lost count of the number of bullets she unloaded. In a matter of seconds, she had dismantled everything about the woman: the infidelity, the fear, and the shame building inside over the last two years.

~~~

Within twenty-four hours of Elaina's arrest, the intimate details of the murders had become common

---

[4] You're not going to do it, you bitch!

[5] You're not going to shoot me. A sick and expecting mother. He obviously prefers me over you so you don't deserved him. Put your toy away and leave, I don't want him to see you here and ruin our day together.

knowledge. Pictures of Elaina's and Miss Brazil's gorgeous faces plastered every news outlet in the city. Stories about the dead woman's suffering from an aggressive form of multiple sclerosis, crime scene photos, and the sequence of events filled the tabloids. The evening news created computer-generated simulations that reenacted Elaina murdering the mistress and lying in wait for her adulterous husband. The enactment depicted Carlos opening the door with his own key before Elaina fired a single shot to the back of his head. He was dead before he even realized there was a threat.

The police found Elaina sitting on the cream-colored couch, saturated in blood. She cradled a tiny fetus in one hand and chain smoked with the other. One of the officers barked commands. She gazed at the Brazilian soap opera on the television until the officer dared to touch her shoulder. She looked at the officer, tossed the fetus aside, and ran her bloodstained hands through her curly black hair.

Then she surrendered.

An autopsy of the unborn baby revealed that Elaina had been extinguishing cigarette butts on its cheek. Crime scene photos documented Carlos's body, gutted from genitals to sternum with a kitchen carving knife. His intestines were looped about his neck, and the carving knife poked from his pubic bone, where his penis once was. For a final touch, Elaina had removed his tongue.

Elaina's attorney used an insanity defense. The prosecutor responded by calling the previous two mistresses that Elaina had stalked to demonstrate that Elaina's act of murder was a natural and calculated culmination of her violent nature.

The trial lasted barely a week. Elaina's lack of remorse in the courtroom expedited her conviction and sentencing. Katingal City would be her home now.

Chapter 3

N A DIM BASEMENT, THREE muscular military men huddled in silence around a small television. Behind them sat Charles Gravo, battered and chained to a metal chair. Soaked pants clung to his legs, and water dripped from the ends of his black hair. His torn shirt revealed an abstract tattoo over his heart. Thick white towels soaked in water from a dripping sink lay near the captive.

In the corner behind a plume of cigar smoke, the man overseeing this interrogation kept a steady gaze on Charles.

"We interrupt this regularly scheduled program to bring you breaking news from the president of the United Territories of Africa," the news anchor from United Territory TV (UTTV) announced before a shot of the president appeared in the screen.

"Good evening," the president began, speaking in the calm, well-modulated voice that was so well known. "Tonight, I can report to the citizens of the United Territories of Africa and the world that, in conjunction with WICC special operations forces, we have captured Charles Gravo, also known as Yäbälay. As you may know, Gravo runs Duenno, the world's most notorious human trafficking network responsible for the abduction of an estimated half-million innocent children. He has been a dark shadow that challenged our light.

"Five years ago, I authorized the formation of a specialized task force to apprehend this criminal, and I offered every resource at our disposal to aid this mission. We saw a dramatic decrease in child abductions as we worked with our friends and allies around the globe to capture and convict scores of this network's participants and financial backers. In doing so, we drew ever closer to Charles Gravo.

"Earlier today, we received information that he was on Ethiopian soil. Following my orders, a team of Ethiopian and WICC militarized special operatives took Charles Gravo into custody after a fierce gun battle." He paused dramatically, then added, "I regret to say that several members of our assault team gave the ultimate sacrifice in the process."

A photo of Charles Gravo flashed onto the screen.

The oldest of the three military men in the basement turned from the television and looked back at the captive. With his head held high and sly smile, he pointed to the television screen. "Now the world knows you have a face," he said. "The demonic legend exposed as nothing more than a sick, depraved man."

Chained and motionless in the metal chair, Charles Gravo maintained an appearance of indifference.

His photograph vanished from the screen, and the live broadcast returned to the president sitting in his pristine office with tall, gold-colored drapes behind him. The gray-haired and regal leader took a deep breath before continuing his announcement.

"Today we have brought an end to yet another criminal enterprise that tried to compromise our humanity and brotherhood. We must not be naïve. Securing our country, its beliefs, and its morals is not complete. Despite our best efforts, some will always choose anarchy over justice and freedom. Let us hold firm in our right and our duty to ensure that those who violate our values meet the stern fist of the just. Let us remember that this right does not come from our wealth or power, but from who we are and our choice to coexist in peace. May Eloah bless you, the UTA, and may she bless our United Nations."

The screen faded to the UTTV logo.

"With that news from the president," the news anchor said, "families are rejoicing at the end of this horrible chapter in our history. As you can see from our affiliate news stations across the globe, people are taking to the streets to celebrate an expected life sentence for Charles Gravo and his exile to Katingal."

"Turn that off," came the quiet command from the man seated in the dark corner of the room. Cigar smoke wreathed his head. He was a civilian, and he spoke in a calm yet stern voice. He was also well out of range of any bodily fluids that might erupt from Charles Gravo as they moved to the next stage of interrogation. "We have work to do. No more water games. Get the machine."

The commander nodded at one of the younger soldiers, who scurried away. He returned with a jumble of metal and jumper cables. Two of the soldiers grabbed Charles's right arm, while another clamped the cables around his wrist.

The captive remained placid. But when the young soldier bent over, Charles head-butted him. The other soldier retaliated with a barrage of punches and elbow strikes.

The commanding officer's face grew tight with disappointment. He glanced at the man in the corner before scolding his charge. "Protect your perimeter at all times, soldier."

Charles smirked and spat blood onto the dirty floor.

"Light him up."

The soldier flipped the switch. Ignited with pain, Charles shook and screamed.

"That's enough," the man in the corner said after a few seconds.

Charles slumped in the chair and groaned.

"Again!" the dark figure barked from the shadows.

Charles convulsed and heaved through the lingering pain.

"Aren't we going to question him?" one of the soldiers asked his commanding officer.

"Your job is not to question, but to follow orders," came the reply. "Is that understood?"

"Yes, sir."

"The prisoner will be questioned when it's time for him to be questioned," the man in the corner said. "Right now, he's to suffer. "Now, that's enough."

Charles's head hung. "What do you want? Money? I can make you all rich."

"Don't you dare speak!" the man in the corner bellowed. All calm had fled his voice.

"Turn up the dial and hit him again!" A heightened voltage of electricity contorted Charles's body. He ground his teeth until a small chip broke off onto his tongue.

"You dare to offer money for what you've done? Stop the current!"

Charles shivered in pain. A trickle of blood dripped from his wrist to the top of his foot.

The older commanding officer glanced over at the dark corner where the cigar smoke was streaming into the air. "How much longer do you want us to keep at him, sir?"

The amber glow and the smoke continued, but the man didn't respond.

The soldier Charles had head-butted walked over to a wooden table, where power tools and a coffeepot stood.

The room grew quiet in waiting. Still nothing from the man in the corner.

The elder officer nodded at the younger soldier standing beside Charles. He began punching Charles's face and midsection. The soldier at the table picked up the coffeepot, shoved his fellow soldier out of the way, and threw the scalding liquid onto Charles's naked torso. Charles screamed and writhed.

The man in the corner laughed. "Nice touch, soldier. Hit him again, Sergeant."

The elder soldier flipped the switch, sending another surge of electricity to the clamp fastened to Charles's wrist. The steady flow of electricity penetrated Charles's every cell. His body arched and contorted until the switch was turned off and he fell limp. He fought to stop his jaw and body from trembling and used his last strength to lift his head to stare his torturers in the eyes.

"When this is over, I'm going to have each of you killed." Blood and saliva streamed from his mouth.

The younger soldier thrust his boot heel into the captive's face, knocking him and the chair against the concrete floor. Then he leaned over him, coming so close that their noses nearly touched. "Who says you're ever getting out of here?" He went to the circuit board and made sure the dial was at its highest setting before flipping the switch.

Charles's eyes rolled back. The surges continued until his bladder and bowels emptied urine and feces onto the floor.

"That's enough," the man in the corner ordered. He tossed his cigar to the floor and stamped it out with the heel of his polished leather shoe. He walked to Charles and stood just outside of the puddle of urine and excrement. "Come now, Gravo. Have a look, will you?"

Charles lifted his head to see a man with inky black skin and eyes shot through with blood. He wore a double-breasted suit, tailored and crisp. Behind him stood a large man with a briefcase.

"Pick him up," ordered the man in the suit.

The two younger soldiers hoisted him upright.

Charles squinted. "Of course," he said. "Governor Negesso. Who else but you would cower in dark corners while others do the heavy lifting?"

The governor nodded at his large companion, who then kicked Charles in the chest, toppling him over again. His head bounced against the concrete floor, and white stars danced before his eyes. He blinked rapidly, fighting against his body's strong desire to escape into unconsciousness.

"Bring him back up."

The soldiers complied.

The governor smacked Charles's cheeks in a playful manner. "I don't recall giving you permission to speak my name. Speak out of turn again, and my assistant Greer will pull your tongue from your head with pliers. Understood?"

The big man standing behind the governor grinned and made squeezing motions with his hand.

Charles gazed around the room as if he hadn't heard and hadn't a care in the world.

The governor smacked him across the face. "You're too stupid to live. Nod your head if you understand."

Charles looked the governor in the eye, but said nothing.

"Defiant until the end, Gravo? So be it. Either way, I win."

"You sure about that?" Charles asked.

The governor lifted an eyebrow and glanced at his assistant, Greer, before turning his eyes back to Charles. "Oh yes, quite sure. I'm going to enjoy the anguish I'll unleash upon you."

Charles's expression remained still.

The governor stepped aside and gestured for his assistant to take his place in front of Charles.

"Let's see what this brave man is made of," Greer said as he released the metal clamp from Charles's wrist and dropped it onto the concrete floor. He reached into his pocket to retrieve a small bottle of clear liquid. Humming, he unscrewed the bottle top and dabbed a drop of the solution onto Charles's wrist.

Charles's body twitched and jumped, and his face contorted in failed defiance of the anguish. In his agony, he stole a glance at his wrist. The open wound was liquefying into a puddle of flesh and blood. His eyes poured tears, and blood ran from his lower lip from where his teeth had bit through.

When the putrid smell hit the torturers, the younger soldier dashed behind some stacked boxes and retched.

"W-Where'd you f-find that p-pussy?" Charles asked, mocking the ill soldier.

"You're a brave soul," Greer said as he screwed the top back onto the bottle. "But everyone's brave in the beginning. And I've just begun." He paused to make eye contact with Charles. "You see, my daughter was stolen from my wife and me many years ago. By you, as it turns out. I joined this task force to hurt you. I prayed to Eloah every day for this moment. You probably didn't even know my daughter. For you, she was just another commodity to be bartered."

"Enough talking, Greer," the governor said, annoyed. "Get on with it."

Greer pulled out an iron vice equipped with fingerholes. "Mr. Gravo, unclench your hands."

Charles refused.

"You heard him," the commander barked, jabbing his elbow into Charles's face. "Open your hand!"

Greer shook his head. "Amateurs, the whole lot of you." He removed a steel lighter from his pocket. "You see, by now, adrenaline has raced through his body, helping him cope with your juvenile beatings. But with the right catalyst, one can manipulate any situation." He flipped open the lighter, and a thick blue flame turned orange and burned high and bright beneath Charles's clenched fingers.

The captive resisted for a few seconds before screaming and opening his hands.

Greer forced Charles's burned fingers into the precut holes, slipped a small, solid, metal bar into the top of the contraption, and gave it one full twist. Charles screamed.

"This is nothing compared to the suffering you've caused." Greer gave his device another half-turn. Charles's fingertips swelled as the pain engulfed his wrist and sent a lightning bolt up his arm and into his chest. He panted and gagged.

"That's it, Greer!" the governor cried. "That's what I want. Limitless pain! Gravo, you'll be the first to be exiled without trial, and not a single person will object. The moment you chose to prey on the weakest and most innocent civilians, you chose your fate. Duenno ends tonight, and you don't leave this basement until we know how it works and who's involved." The governor pointed to a collection of medical devices and machines in the corner. "Not even death can save you tonight."

Charles tried to speak, but was incapable.

"Someone get him some water," said the governor with a thin smile. "Let's hear what this *brave* man has to say."

Greer fetched a Styrofoam cup and filled it halfway. He held it to the captive's lips, but Charles didn't have the strength to drink, and the water ran down his front. He began to whisper names. The young soldier grabbed a notepad and prepared to write down whatever information Charles provided.

"Louder!" the governor commanded eagerly.

"Your pretty little wife, whew!" Charles exclaimed. "I bet she still has a soft, round ass, even after giving birth to that spoiled bastard of a son, huh?"

The governor's eyes narrowed, but he revealed no other reaction to Charles's taunt. He spoke quietly. "These men have my authority to torture you, Mr. Gravo. If you lose consciousness, they'll revive you and start again. If you die, they're going to revive you and start again. The moment we have what we need from you, you'll be transported to the Ethiopian Territory prison in preparation for your exile to Katingal City."

Charles wasn't listening. He looked at Greer's watch. "Is that a Patek Philippe? It's nice. What's the time on there?"

At this, the governor chuckled. "You have somewhere to be?"

His phone rang before the captive could answer. A blocked phone number appeared on the phone's display.

"Go ahead and answer," Charles said. "And make sure to find out what took them so fucking long."

The governor hesitated before taking the call. His eyes remained fixed on Charles. As he listened, his entire body went rigid. The muffled sounds of a man's voice on the other end of the phone changed to one much younger and softer.

"Yes," the governor said. "Yes, I understand. All instructions will be followed." He hung up.

"How's your son, Governor?" Charles taunted before leaning back, a man again in his element. But before his back hit the chair, the governor lunged at him and grabbed his throat. Charles's face turned red, but his defiance was resolute.

"Sir! Sir, please!" The older soldier ran to the governor. Greer tried to block the officer, but the officer grasped the governor, and Charles swung free.

Charles laughed. "It didn't have to be this way, Governor. If I die, your son dies, and you'll have yourself to blame."

The governor made a visible effort to gather himself, then gestured to Greer, who handed him a phone. He punched in a number.

"Hello, sir, it's Governor Negesso. Yes, we're still in the process of extracting information from the suspect regarding Duenno, and we're set to transport him to the territory prison." The governor hesitated before clearing his throat. "But there is a problem, sir. The suspect's accomplices have abducted my son, and they're demanding the release of the prisoner."

The governor listened while the other man spoke. Then he drew a deep breath and pressed the speaker button. The UTA president's voice boomed through the phone.

"To all law enforcement agents and or military present," he said. "This is President Manawi of the United Territories of Africa. You are ordered to cease all interrogations. Deliver the recovered intelligence and the prisoner to the Ethiopian Territory prison for processing and subsequent transport to Katingal. If anyone, including Governor Negesso, deviates from these orders, you are to arrest that individual or individuals so they can be punished to the fullest letter of the law. The UTA does not negotiate with terrorists. Is that understood?"

"Yes, sir!" barked the three military men in unison.

"I didn't hear your response, Governor," the president said. "Have you heard and understood my orders?"

"Yes, sir," the governor said.

The secretary of defense will be awaiting your arrival at the prison. Do your job, and we will get your son back. That will be all."

The line went dead.

The governor threw the phone against the stone wall of the basement, shattering it. "Take this piece of shit to the car," he said, his face still down, his voice barely perceptible. "He's to go to the territory prison just as the president instructed."

"Yes, sir," the soldiers responded. One removed the medieval device from Charles's hand and handed it, dripping with fluids, back to Greer.

"You'll transport the prisoner in your car," the governor said. "My assistant and I will follow you." He turned toward the exit, but halfway across the room, he paused. He turned around and looked Gravo in the eyes. "Charles Gravo, you hear me, and you hear me well. I don't give a damn what the president says. Should anything happen to my son, I will personally ensure the time you spend in Katingal will pale in comparison to your short experience here, all the way up to the moment I decide to rip whatever life you have left from your body."

Without another word, the governor turned his back to Charles and ascended the basement steps into the dark night.

Chapter 4

HE DEN OF TORTURE WAS an old stone cottage that stood between an open field and a dense forest. Three stretch town cars with tinted windows idled in front. Other than the car headlights of the prison caravan, the sole sources of light were the full moon and the stars above.

Two attack dogs snarled and scratched at the windows of the rear town car as the young soldier guided Charles past. The captive fell on the rocky ground and knocked his escort off balance. The young soldier reached to pull him up, but Charles pushed himself back onto his feet, pivoted to face the soldier, and latched both hands around the back of his neck. With a leap, he jammed his knee into the young soldier's sternum.

The soldier crumbled to the gravel driveway. Stunned, he looked up just in time for Charles to rub his open wound into the young man's eyes. The soldier screamed out and clutched his face, letting go of Charles.

Charles grabbed the soldier's weapon and bolted into the forest. His feet pounded on the loose gravel beneath him and kicked up a trail of pebbles that fell behind him like rain. He glanced over his shoulder as Greer emerged from the second car and alerted the men to release the dogs.

By now, Charles was ankle-deep in mud. The brush clawed at his body as he ran. One of the cars pursued him, its dancing headlights making it difficult to see. He heard doors slam and angry dogs barking. He stopped and rolled in the mud in the hopes of camouflaging his skin and scent before moving deeper into the forest.

Behind him, the men had flashlights. The bright beams flashed and zagged over the ground around Charles. He heard the frenzy in the dogs' calls as they crashed through brush. The thought of being shredded alive in the powerful beasts' jaws propelled his legs forward.

"I see him!" one of the men yelled. "Go get him, boy!"

The tracker freed the dogs, who rushed at Charles, devouring his head start in seconds. Charles pulled out the semiautomatic handgun he had just swiped from the soldier and readied himself. The flashlights bounced closer, the hounds a mere twenty-five feet away, close enough that Charles could see their tongues flapping in the air as if they could already taste his salted flesh and hot blood.

One of the dogs leapt and arced through the air, teeth bared and fur standing on end. Charles dropped to one knee and lined up the single dot on the nozzle of the handgun at the middle mass of the dog. He held his breath and stilled his body. A double tap of the trigger killed the canine midflight.

The dead dog's momentum sent it toppling into Charles, throwing him off his aim just long enough for the second dog to take hold of his arm. Charles absorbed the bite and weight of the dog as he rolled onto his back. While the beast tore at his flesh, Charles planted the barrel of the gun into the dog's ribs.

At the sound of the gunshots, the two men stopped their pursuit. Charles rolled the dead animal off and jumped back onto his feet. His body was alive with savage fury. He locked eyes with the two trackers. They looked at each other, and then back to where Charles had been standing, but he had slipped into the dark night.

"That son of a bitch shot our dogs!" the fatter of the two trackers shrieked.

"How in the hell did he get a weapon?" the other tracker wondered aloud.

Charles took advantage of the stymied trackers and ducked behind a tree.

He heard a sharp chirping noise uncommon to any forest breaking through the night. "Isaac! I'm hit! That dog killing bastard shot me!" The fat tracker yelled out. Charles peered from around the tree and saw the man's neck snap violently to the side. A red mist sprayed into the air, and his body fell onto the dead dogs. Charles looked around for the source of the shooter.

Chirp! Chirp!

Two shots found their mark in the chest of the remaining tracker. Charles crouched lower against the tree. The sounds of crunching brush were getting louder, but he could see nothing. A red, pulsating beam of light illuminated the woods just enough that Charles could make out a large, Greer-shaped figure holding a rifle equipped with a silencer.

When Greer reached the dead men, he knelt to inspect their bodies and examine the ground before looking in Charles's direction.

Startled by the man's acumen, Charles retreated deeper into the woods, careful to swerve through trees to prevent Greer from getting a clear shot. He paused to listen but heard no sounds of pursuit. He looked down to see a beam of light dancing across his chest. Charles dove to the ground, but he was too late. A bullet cut through the foliage and grazed his thigh.

Pain exploded from his leg. Charles reached for his gun with his right hand and clutched his newest wound with his left. At every crackle, he shifted his gun but saw nothing. He felt desperate, hunted.

The next chirp, a close-range shot, launched Charles's gun from his hand and shattered it.

Greer appeared from behind a tree and pulled off his night vision goggles. He pointed the sniper rifle at Charles's face. Then he grinned and said, "The last man I hunted was much better game than you."

Chapter 5

"STAND CLEAR OF THE GATE!" a prison guard yelled from the end of the cellblock. "Close number four!"

The steel bars slid shut, locking Charles in a room surrounded by cement walls and outfitted with nothing more than a cot, a stained sink, and a stainless-steel toilet backed up with yellow water, feces, and a bloated, floating rodent.

"I'm guessing there's no turndown service," Charles said before sitting on the unmade bed.

A flurry of water bugs and roaches scurried out from beneath the thin, brown cover. Charles pulled the sheet from the bed to find dead roaches scattered on top of the bare mattress.

He closed his eyes and conjured up a memory of his last bedroom escapade, snorting cocaine from the smooth-skinned backs of four fourteen-year-olds and later, their soft bodies floating around him in the infinity pool like moths.

He opened his eyes at the sound of a deep voice.

"Are the accommodations not to your satisfaction, inmate?" said a well-groomed man in a tailored three-piece suit. Next to him, a prisoner with the word *Trustee* printed on the front of his uniform pushed a wooden cart bearing a single food tray and a bottle of water.

"You must be the warden," Charles said.

"Perceptive of you," the warden said.

"And that's for me?" Charles asked, eyeing the tray.

"Correct again. But before you dine, we need to discuss a few things. I know you haven't eaten since your capture yesterday, so I'll be as brief as possible. This officer"—he tilted his head toward the guard that stood beside him—"will be posted outside of your cell until he is relieved by another. They're here to make sure you don't harm yourself. If there is anything you require, notify the officer. He will attend to your request."

The trustee lifted the cover from the tray to reveal Salisbury steak, mixed vegetables, and mashed potatoes and gravy. Charles stared at the food and salivated.

"You will respond when the warden addresses you, prisoner!" the guard shouted, breaking Charles's trance.

"Did you understand my instructions, prisoner?" the warden repeated.

"Yes, Warden," Charles responded. "I understood everything." He smiled.

The warden motioned for the trustee to serve the food to Charles. He slid the tray through a waist-high opening in the barred door. Charles grabbed the spoon and began shoveling meat into his mouth before the tray had fully slid through.

"Savor this meal," the guard said. "You'll never see another like it in Katingal."

The warden continued his speech. "An in-house physician will assess your health and mental wellbeing for your prison file. But don't get any ideas that we care about you. Your medical information helps forecast the average life expectancy of exiled inmates.

"She also will place a computer chip the size of a postage stamp into the base of your skull. This chip serves as an alert mechanism when scanned by United Nations border control security devices stationed at all major border crossings, airports, and train and bus stations. If you try to escape, the chip will transmit your location and other subsequent data to WICC. Officially we call this the Katingal pre-entrance procedure, or KPP, for exiled prisoners, but I find it a formality. No one has escaped Katingal. Should you try, we'll know where you are and authorize local authorities to execute you on sight. Should you have a moment of clarity and surrender, we will thank you for making it easy for us, and then you'll be executed on sight."

"You enjoy this, Warden," Charles said. "Talking to people as if they are guinea pigs. But you're no different from me, are you?"

"We are nothing alike," the warden snapped back. "I mourn the children, the disappeared, and those so mentally mutilated that their parents no longer recognize them. In the early days of this program, we tried to rehabilitate human garbage like you. We tried to maintain peace and fairness in the spirit of those who founded the Garden of Eden. But you are beyond humanity, beyond repair, slobbering over child pornography when you were barely out of childhood yourself. That was your first mistake."

Charles started to respond, but the warden lifted his hand.

"Your routine for the next few weeks will be as follows. At seven a.m. you'll have five minutes to shower. Food will be brought to your cell three times a day. At midday, you will be released for one hour in a segregated yard space for exercise. Then you will return to your cell and remain there until the next morning. Do you understand?"

Charles shrugged, and the warden continued.

"In a moment, a detail of correctional officers will escort you to have your KPP administered."

Charles scraped his plate clean and downed the contents of his water bottle. "No one's putting a chip in me." Charles said before losing his balance and slumping back onto the bed.

The warden laughed. "We've been performing this procedure for over a decade now. You think this fine meal was for your enjoyment? I've been talking only to allow enough time for the sedative in your food and water to take effect."

Chapter 6

HE CREAKY WHEEL OF THE metal gurney woke Charles from his forced slumber. He blinked, trying to focus until he was able to make out the hazy figure of a tall, thin woman walking beside him, reading a medical chart. Dressed in medical scrubs, she appeared to be a doctor. Charles raised his heavy head enough to see a sign that read *Surgical #1* above a double-door.

At first the room was full of doctors and orderlies in scrubs and surgical masks. Some were wheeling in devices, monitors, and shiny surgical tools. He bristled, his body recalling the pain of his interrogation in the cottage basement.

When two large men in white, sterile clothing approached the gurney, everyone else left the room. One removed a key from the pocket of his gown.

"We're correctional officers," the burly man explained. "When we unlock you, you will step down from the gurney and we'll lay you face down on the surgical table and fit your face into the open space at the head of the table. Once you've done that, we will again place restraints on you that will prevent you from moving off the table. Do you understand my instructions?"

"Yes, I understand," Charles slurred.

"Be warned. If you attempt to resist, we're authorized to execute you on the spot."

Charles paused for a moment to weigh his options.

"I'll ask you again, inmate," the correctional officer said. "Charles Gravo, do you understand my instructions?"

"Yes, I understand," Charles answered, his innate will to survive winning out over his more natural impulse to attempt flight.

The two men unlocked him and moved efficiently to position him before placing heavy restraints across the upper, middle, and lower parts of his body.

Moments later, Charles heard the doctors and nurses return to the room. He stared at the white squares of tile and watched as a mix of footwear moved in and out of his line of sight. He lay quiet, still groggy from the sedative.

Then a new set of feet draped in blue, sterile, protective footwear came into his view. She spoke with a calm, no-nonsense voice.

"Hello, Charles. I'm your surgeon, Dr. Peña. The nurse will give you a sedative to calm you before the full anesthesia."

"No," Charles protested. "No more sedatives."

"Gravo, this is your first and final warning," the correctional officer said from his right. "If you refuse again, you will be executed."

"Gentlemen," the doctor said. "there's no need to turn my operating room into an execution chamber."

As she went on to explain the anesthesia and surgery, Charles decided he liked her. She sounded like a kind person—someone who hadn't experienced loss or pain. She was still innocent.

"Mr. Gravo," she said, "I can understand your apprehension, but there's nothing to worry about. I'll be monitoring your vitals the entire time to make sure everything goes fine during the procedure. When we're about to begin, the nurse will place a mask over your face and have you count backward from one hundred. When you wake up, the procedure will have been completed."

"I understand," Charles replied. He felt a slight stinging at his IV entry point.

"You should feel the calming effects of the sedative right about now." The doctor placed a heart monitor on his index finger. Charles's heart rate steadied and a warm, euphoric feeling overcame him.

The doctor checked his pulse. "Looks good. We'll begin now."

The nurse approached Charles with a gas mask and placed it over his mouth. "You may begin your count."

Charles counted backward. "One hundred, ninety-nine, ninety-eight, ninety-seven, ninety-six, ninety-five, ninety-f-fouuuur, ninety-threeeee . . ." His speech grew slow and slurred, and then he was out.

When he came to, he was aware of his surroundings but felt a bit off-kilter. He wondered if this was from the anesthesia in his system or the foreign device they had placed in his head.

Charles smiled as his doctor approached, but it sounded like she was talking in slow motion.

"Why are you talking like that?" he asked. "Did something go wrong? Did you screw it up?" His heart rate increased, making him feel hot.

She assured him that the surgery was a success.

Charles started to reach for the incision site, but his right hand was still shackled to the protective bar of the hospital gurney. He lifted his free left hand and waved it in front of his face. It seemed to move in slow motion, though he believed he had moved it at a normal speed.

The doctor pulled out her stethoscope, placed it against his chest, and listened for a few seconds before repositioning herself behind him. "Take four deep breaths for me, please," she said as she listened to his lungs. The speed of her last sentence had increased, but it still wasn't normal.

"Your heart and lungs sound fine," she said. "You may feel a bit strange until the anesthesia wears off."

"How long do I have before I'm sent back to my cell?" Charles asked.

"One week," she said.

The surgeon left and closed the drapes around his bed. Charles looked at the clock on the wall. He could hear her scribble something onto his chart before hanging it on his bed. That small action seemed to take half an hour, but when he looked at the clock again, only a few minutes had passed.

Once he heard the door close, Charles crawled the length of his bed and stretched his free arm to retrieve his medical chart. He took one more glance at the door before flipping through the pages. There were meticulous details of the endless lacerations, chemical burns, and dog bites. The bullet wound in his leg was noted, as well as the intricate KPP procedure.

He scanned through each page in a matter of seconds before pausing to consider *how* quickly he had absorbed the information. It felt different somehow. *He* felt different, and he was beginning to think that it went beyond the aftereffects of the anesthesia.

He flipped the medical chart face down on his lap and closed his eyes. In an instant, everything he had just read appeared in his mind as if he were looking at a photograph of each page.

He flipped the chart back over and looked through the pages once more to verify that what he was recalling was precisely correct. Every number, every line, and even how the loops of the doctor's signature flattened out at the end of her name were exactly as he had pictured in his mind.

He pinched himself, testing to see if this was a drug-induced dream, but it wasn't. He hooked the chart onto the foot of his bed, crawled back under the covers, and closed his eyes.

Once again, the exact image of the doctor's hieroglyphic scribbling appeared in his mind as clear as if the pages had been scanned into his memory. When he shut his eyes tighter, random images popped up like a film. First, he saw the more recent, like being chased through the woods and his capture. Then, deeper, darker memories of his youth began to surface, from boarding school through the first child he abducted, raped, and killed.

Upon remembering this girl, he began to grow erect. Then a sharp and terrible pain snapped from the incision point of the KPP procedure, followed by an instant headache.

He blinked and shook his head, hoping to scatter the old images and alleviate the intense pain that accompanied them.

Chapter 7

THE SOUND OF HARD-SOLED SHOES echoed through the nearly empty Ethiopian prison. Without lifting his eyes from the book in front of him, Charles noted that, based on the strike of the shoes against the concrete, it was a group of two men and one woman approaching him.

He saw through his peripheral vision the warden and his prison surgeon being escorted by a correctional officer down the two-tiered, cascading cell block. A thick manila file was tucked under the arm of the warden while the doctor carried a medical chart. Shouts from the few remaining inmates from his cell block followed the two until they arrived at Charles's cell.

When Dr. Peña and the warden approached, Charles sat on the edge of his cot, surrounded by the stacks of books he had read the night before.

"Good morning," he said casually as he flipped to a new page in his book. He flipped again and again, scanning each page for only a second or two before moving on to the next. "Decided to show off your guinea pig, Doctor?"

"You said this was an urgent matter," the warden said to the doctor. "So please make haste with the purpose of this meeting."

Charles looked up from his scanning and gestured in a casual way. "Dr. Peña, I expect someone as learned as you should know that those with Type-A personalities such as the warden are rigid, organized, impatient, and obsessed with time management. They're also often high-achieving workaholics who multitask, push themselves with impossible deadlines, and hate delays and ambivalence equally. Under Psychodynamic theory, derived from Freudian Psychology, Type-A personality is related to anal retentiveness. In short, Doctor, the warden needs to be well-informed and in control of the everyday happenings of his prison." Charles grinned as he turned his gaze to the warden. "Because he's terrified that if he doesn't know everything, he'll lose all control. Isn't that right, Warden?"

"Look who's enjoying the sound of his voice," the warden quipped. "Dr. Peña, this would be an excellent time for you to begin explaining what the hell is going on."

"My apologies, Warden," the doctor said, "but we're just beginning to understand what's happened ourselves. There was a complication during the KPP procedure, so we would like to delay his transport to Katingal—"

"Complication?" Charles interjected. "I wouldn't say that's entirely accurate, Doctor."

"Shut your mouth, inmate!" the warden ordered, glaring at Charles before looking past him to the stack of books that had accumulated since his last visit to Charles's cell. Clearly perplexed, he traded stares between Dr. Peña and the correctional officer posted across from Charles's cell. "Would someone care to explain how this prisoner acquired such a collection of literature without my authorization?"

"It was part of our testing, Warden," the doctor answered. "Once we discovered that the complication had brought on such a cognitive jump in intelligence, we've had to test its levels. But I assure you, not informing you of our protocols was an unintentional oversight."

"Oh, I see," the warden said, his voice dripping with acid. "So, adhering to the *strict* protocols and procedures of this territory's penal system that you and I both serve is optional now?"

"The scientific findings we're seeing are revolut—"

"This is a prison, Doctor," he interrupted. "Not a laboratory. Science has no authority here."

"That oversight is precisely why I insisted on speaking with you today, Warden. Again, rest assured—"

He held up his hand to silence her. "Dr. Peña, you're new to my facility, so let me make something crystal clear to you. Contraband is forbidden. Those books in his cell, unless authorized by me, are contraband. Furthermore, there are no delays in my prison. Everyone is held accountable for the smooth operation of this prison, its policies, and procedures. Those who do not will find themselves unemployed, and unemployable, by any form of law enforcement in this territory."

Again, she started to speak, and again, he raised his hand to stop her. He leaned in and lowered his voice.

"You were recruited to this facility because you're one of the more promising neurological surgeons in the country. Up until now, your performance has been stellar. Maybe since this is your first surgical complication, you're allowing your very natural feelings to emerge. I assure you that the man in that cell does not deserve one ounce of your pity."

Her brow went up. "It's not pity, Warden. And although what we experienced during the procedure can be classified as a complication, what we've stumbled upon is something that neither medicine nor science has ever seen."

"Indeed, Doctor," Charles interjected. "This would be an excellent time to inform the warden of the results of your uncharacteristic oopsie."

"Sergeant, if he mutters another word, tase him," the warden said.

"While I was inserting the chip," the doctor explained, "the monitors tracking his brain activity began to show spikes in activity, like a seizure. We stabilized Mr. Gravo and finished the procedure, but the monitors still registered increased brain activity in the cerebellum. As you know, Warden, the chip is designed with metal clamps that grip into the skull. Due to osteoporosis, Mr. Gravo's skull is unusually thin. When we planted the chip, we inadvertently penetrated the thinned skull and pierced his cerebellum, causing the seizure. We were able to remove some of the clamps in the hopes of preventing future seizures—"

"*Some* of the clamps?" The warden's eyes narrowed.

"Three of the four." Gesturing and wide-eyed as she spoke, Dr. Peña seemed entranced by the possibility of this discovery. "One is still piercing his cerebellum, and the built-in power source for the tracking signal is sending constant electrical currents that are stimulating his cerebellum."

"Such enthusiasm over a mistake." Charles chuckled, placing one completed book on the floor and picking another from the stack.

The warden led the doctor down the corridor. Charles watched as their discussion grew more animated.

"Now, that wasn't very nice to say, Warden," Charles called down the hall. His eyes still scanned the pages of his book.

The warden glared at Charles before nodding at the officer. The officer slid his Taser between the cell bars and pulled the trigger. Metal darts flew through the air and pierced Charles's skin with fifty thousand volts of electricity.

"This slight mishap seems to have affected your common sense, as well, inmate." The warden sneered at Charles, who was convulsing on the floor. Then he held up his hand. "That's enough, officer."

The moment the electrical current stopped, Charles gasped, yanked the darts out of his skin, and dropped them to the floor.

"Now, if there's nothing else, Doctor, I need to get back to my office." The warden turned to walk back down the long corridor of the cellblock.

"Warden!" Charles bellowed. Still trembling from the effects of the Taser, he stepped over to the steel bars of his cell. He coughed, his voice raspy. "Just in case you're still wondering, no, I don't have the cure for HIV or cancer." He smiled.

The warden whirled around and stared in disbelief at the doctor.

"You have a listening device," he accused the doctor. "Officer, search her for contraband."

The officer took two steps toward the doctor, shoved her against the wall, and with his meaty hands, spread her legs open, lingering between her thighs.

Her face tensed as she endured the humiliation. "I assure you, I'm not wearing a listening device."

"This is truly unlike you, Warden," Charles chimed in. "Paranoia is not at all a type-A characteristic." Charles bent down to retrieve the book he had dropped after being tased. He tossed it through the bars. *Reading Lips* by Olive Bartlett landed at the warden's feet.

The warden picked it up from the floor and turned to display the title to the doctor. "Really, Doctor? This is the material you're feeding him?"

"I didn't choose the books," she replied. "But you see how quickly he learned. Since his surgery, we've administered every standardized test that measures intelligence. All these tests have been developed by educators and scientists to measure aptitude, and we've given them all to Mr. Gravo."

"Not 'Mister,'" the warden barked. "'Inmate.' He's an inmate."

"Yes, of course. This inmate has achieved a perfect score on all of them."

"So, what, then? Your mistake has made him a genius?" The warden laughed.

"'Genius' doesn't even begin to do his condition justice."

"Well, do it justice!" he hollered.

She paused before responding, shrugging as if in disbelief of her own words. "Warden, he's intellectually flawless."

The warden appeared to ponder her statement for a moment. "Is there even such a thing, or is this a term you've conjured up on your own?"

"This phenomenon has never been observed before. What I've. . . what *we've* stumbled upon is an intellectual range that has never been tapped into. Scientists theorize that humans use only twenty percent of our brain capacity. Based on our initial early tests on Mr.—sorry, *Inmate* Gravo—we believe he may be the first human in history to surpass that threshold. His surgery triggered such an acute surge in aptitude that, in the span of a week, he has experienced a leap in intelligence so great. . ." The doctor paused for a moment.

"Spit it out, Doctor!" the warden ordered impatiently.

"The leap in intelligence is so great, dare I say that our tools and tests aren't capable of accurately measuring it."

The warden looked her up and down, absorbing the weight of her report. "So you want to delay transport of your new laboratory rat because he may be the smartest person on Earth?"

"I do," Dr. Peña agreed with excitement. "And I would like to remind you that *legally*, as his KPP physician, I am the sole authority required to sign off on his release and approval for his transport to Katingal."

The warden looked at Charles, who was rummaging through the stacks of books in his cell. Side by side and on top of one another, the books comprised two stacks reaching halfway to the ceiling.

"Open number five!" the warden yelled down the hallway.

There was a loud buzz, and the door to the empty cell next to Charles's slid open.

"Officer, place the prisoner in cell number five and leave him there," the warden ordered. "For the rest of his stay in my facility, no one is to bring any items to this prisoner, except for food and water."

"Yes, sir," the guard replied. "Inmate, do you understand?"

"Of course I understand. Didn't you hear the doctor?" Charles laughed. "I'm a super-genius."

The guard cuffed Charles's hands through the steel bars, opened the door, and guided him into the adjoining cell.

"Could you pass some books to me so I can occupy my time while you perform your search?" Charles asked.

"Officer," the warden said through his teeth, "if this inmate speaks again, tase him until he soils himself." Then he redirected his attention to Dr. Peña. "You see, this is all amusement for him. He's confined to his cell twenty-two hours a day, and this is how he entertains himself. He's not special, nor did he read all these books. There has to be over a hundred of them."

"Sir, I found something." The correctional officer came out of Charles's original cell holding a small trash can.

The warden motioned that he should follow him back out into the hall. The doctor came over for a look. The warden reached into the plastic trash can and removed a rotting apple core, plastic sandwich wrapping, and several empty, pint-sized apple juice bottles.

"Care to explain how these got into his cell, Doctor?"

She looked like a child caught with her hand in the cookie jar. "He complained that he was still hungry after dinner, so I gave him some of the extra food I had stored in my office refrigerator. The battery of aptitude tests we were administering was quite strenuous, and I wanted to make sure he could perform at his best. I'm sorry."

"First, you smuggle unauthorized literature to this inmate. Now we discover that you've also supplied him with unauthorized food and beverages. Do you realize that you've committed a crime, Doctor? Do you know that I could have you thrown into one of these cells for such a breach of protocol?" The warden removed the file folder from under his arm. "Your job in this facility doesn't allow you access to the classified files of these prisoners, but perhaps just this once, you need to be briefed on the criminal history of your pet genius."

The warden began to recite Charles's criminal history from memory.

"Inmate Charles Gravo, aka Yäbälay, the leader of Duenno. Age fifteen, misdemeanor petty theft. Age seventeen, misdemeanor lewd and inappropriate conduct in public. Age twenty, his first felony conviction, possession of child pornography. Sentence, ten years in territorial prison. Age thirty-one, conspiracy for creating a criminal organization, Duenno, which is responsible for the abduction and exploitation of half a million children across the globe.

"You'd think it'd end there, but not for this one. After his capture, he managed to escape and murder two law enforcement officers in addition to masterminding a criminal conspiracy to kidnap Governor Negesso's son, who is now, as we speak, being held hostage at an unknown location in exchange for this inmate's release."

With every felony the warden revealed, Charles watched as the doctor's face paled and her interest in his abilities deflated. He watched her stiffen and shift her stance, and cross her arms protectively over her chest. She was frightened of him now.

"Dr. Peña," the warden continued in a reasonable tone, "don't misunderstand me. I can sympathize with how something like this can be a marvelous discovery for you and this institution." The warden looked the doctor in the eye. "Of course, you do, as you pointed out, have the final decision. If you believe that this animal is your Rosetta Stone, then *legally* there's nothing I can do to stop you. As his KPP physician, you are the sole authority required to sign off on his release and approval for his transport to Katingal. But I urge you not to delay his transport to that maximum security facility. Charles Gravo is vicious, dangerous, and cunning. He will use you to his advantage, if he can. You and other medical personnel who come into contact with him are under constant risk."

The doctor shot a glance at Charles, and he gave her his best smile.

"In a few weeks," the warden continued, "you'll have another group of felons to experiment on, if you'd like. If you're able to duplicate this phenomenon, then you have my word that we can delay that prisoner's transport to Katingal. But this particular inmate should be transferred as soon as possible."

The doctor nodded thoughtfully, her eyes still on Charles. He gripped the steel bars and held his smile while he read her body language. She was so close. Charles knew that if he wanted to, he could grab her around the throat and watch her die.

He caught a whiff of the doctor's perfume and closed his eyes, remembering one of his first, a young girl he had coaxed to meet him. She had worn her mother's perfume to appear more mature, likely imagining more romance than the rape and abduction he had planned for her.

A growing, dull pain spread in the back of his head. He pressed the incision site, and the doctor placed her hand over Charles's other hand where it gripped the bar.

"No contact with the prisoner!" the officer yelled.

"It's fine now," Charles said. "It's subsiding." He looked up at the doctor before his face grew warm and he felt jarred in surprise. He snatched his hand away and retreated into his cell, turning his back to her. He glanced up to the mirror on the wall.

The doctor followed and met his eyes there.

"Behind you," he mouthed.

She looked puzzled until she caught a glimpse of the officer who had his hand on his firearm, the safety already flipped off, his eyes planted on the doctor.

"Decision time, Doctor," the warden said. "Will you sign the form?"

Defeated, the doctor turned and nodded, her eyes lowered. She reached for the release form he held out to her, and with quivering hands, signed it and handed it back. Without another word, she turned and began to walk down the hall.

The warden rushed to catch up with her. "You've made a very wise decision, Dr. Peña," Charles could hear him say.

"It's just like you said," she replied. "There will be plenty of felons to reproduce what we've achieved with this prisoner."

"You don't look well," the warden said. "Is everything all right?"

She paused and looked at him. "You said he's been convicted of pedophilia, so his crimes are against young victims? Children, correct?"

"Yes, the sick fuck . . . excuse me, Charles Gravo has probably never been with anyone remotely close to his own age."

"Interesting."

"Why is that interesting?" the warden asked as Charles cocked his ear to listen.

"He developed an erection after I touched his hand," the doctor replied.

Chapter 8

RATINGAL CITY HAD BEEN CONSTRUCTED a century prior, designed to house the thousands of men who worked the iron ore mines owned by the Apex Mining Company. When the mines flourished, the city expanded to make room for the thriving population. But eventually, the mines were stripped and the people left in search of other work, turning the once-vibrant city into a ghost town.

At the time, the world was enjoying a utopian existence, and crime was almost nonexistent. There were a few prisons, but they were mostly scarcely populated by those who committed crimes petty enough to allow for those individuals to be rehabilitated back into society. Yet there were still a few criminals who proved beyond repair. Rather than have them rattling around a near-empty prison, taking up resources better used by law-abiding citizens, the British government began to look for another way.

The government decided to purchase the rights to the land. Soon after the acquisition, it began exiling its worst criminals to what was left of the abandoned Katingal City. Since its original construction, Katingal had received no repairs, new buildings, or updates to antiquated systems of water importation, sanitation management, or roads. The only significant modification the government made was to construct a monstrous wall, replete with watchtowers, that encircled the city's perimeter. The dormitories used to house the mine's labor force and their families became the dilapidated, vermin-infested homes of the city's criminal inhabitants.

In this lawless place that came to be called K-City, it was kill or be killed. It was hell on Earth.

The newest felons on the bus came from all corners of the earth. Each prisoner's journey began with transport from his or her home country to the island continent of Katingal by plane to the closest airport located in Darwin. Upon arrival, the felon was shuffled onto the black prison transportation bus manned by a team of correctional officers. Once the bus reached capacity, it sped through the rugged outback headed southeast for the fourteen-hour drive to the front gates of K-City.

The regular potholes, along with rocks the size of a man's fist that flew up against the sides of the bus and peppered the road, served as constant reminders of how lost this continent had become, how long ago it had been since it featured the modern amenities of a civilization's infrastructure. Only the heartiest of souls could navigate the unpaved, unlit roads. If a tire blew or the radiator overheated, the driver would be in dire straits.

Built to withstand all environmental challenges, the transport bus sped along. Red clouds of dust billowed into the thick outback air as the bus headed for the headquarters of the prison city. As a precautionary measure dictated by the British penal code, the side windows were blackened to ensure the shackled prisoners aboard were blind and disoriented as to their geographic surroundings. The only light penetrating the fortified vehicle shined in through the front windshield, the wipers whipping back and forth on high speed to keep the dust away.

To ensure the safety and timely arrival of this particular load of prisoners, there were five young, heavily armed correctional officers and one older, higher-ranking officer on board. The correctional officers were familiar with the monotonous, anxious trip to the prison city in the center of the continent. While the driver battled the bumpy road, all but their ranking officer busied themselves checking their weapons. The officer kept his beady eyes on the prisoners while wiping his sweaty brow and the rolls on the back of his neck with a hand towel.

Newer correctional officers wouldn't even consider taking a job on Katingal, but for those who had been on the force and heard the stories, it was a coveted assignment. Despite having to work at the wretched facility, exiled for three-month rotations away from their families, loved ones, and civilization, and having to face hazardous situations and see the worst of human beings, at the end of that time they could return home and enjoy wages unmatched by any profession worldwide.

It was the money that talked. None of them would dare to admit that the work scarred them. When they returned home after a rotation, they brought back with them endless tales of K-City's inhumane living conditions, tortures, rapes, murders, and mutilations. To maintain their own humanity, they eventually became inured to the suffering and atrocity and erected walls of their own.

On the job, accompanying another transport of hardened criminals, they let themselves feel no empathy for what these prisoners would soon endure. The most observant prisoner would notice how he, too, should harden himself against what was to come, as this would give them the best chance at survival. Most didn't notice enough to help themselves in time.

The driver of the fortified bus turned the knob to increase the speed of the wipers, but they couldn't whisk away the dirt and kicked-up gravel enough to clear the windshield. The stones dragged along the glass like fingernails on a blackboard.

Toward the back of the bus, Charles Gravo sat in silence next to an equally quiet woman. When the bus smashed into another pothole, the passengers were launched out of their seats and jerked back down by the chains.

"Hey, muthafucka!" screamed a bearded Italian convict. "Hit one more pothole and you'll be the first one I kill when we step off this raggedy bus!"

"I wouldn't do that if I were you," Charles muttered from the row in front of him.

"What in the hell?" the Italian barked, glaring at Charles. "A white man speaking with an African accent? Your mama preferred men from the dark continent, huh? Hmph, you don't look like a mongrel."

Charles didn't respond.

"Nothing to say now, eh?" The Italian grinned and folded his arms over his chest. "It doesn't matter. First the driver, and then you."

The driver glanced up at him in the rearview mirror.

"You won't be the first officer to have his life snatched by Donato Bilancia," the Italian bragged.

The woman beside Charles turned her head to look at Donato. In return, he leaned forward and licked his lips like a salivating dog.

"*Ciao, bella*,"[6] Donato said. "What's your name?"

Charles glanced at the petite yet voluptuous, curly-haired beauty shackled next to him. He let his eye travel down her body. Her silicon-enhanced breasts were all but bursting through her standard-issue jumpsuit.

"Don't you prefer them a bit younger, Gravo?" Donato asked.

Charles raised his head but continued to remain silent.

"That's right, I know who you are. Everyone here does. After all, you're a celebrity." The chatty Italian opened his arms as wide as his chains would allow.

Charles looked around the bus, noting that all eyes were now trained on him.

---

6   "Hello, beautiful,"

"Yäbälay." Donato jabbed a finger at Charles. "That's what they call you, right?"

At the mention of his alias, Charles heard murmurs in a variety of languages echoing through the bus. The Brazilian beauty next to him inched away as far as her constraints allowed.

"You pronounced my name correctly," Charles calmly retorted. "So what of it?"

The murmuring became louder.

"When we get to Katingal, you'll be passed around like a cigarette." Donato scoffed. "With all the beautiful women on Earth, you go after children? Little girl babies? Even now, you're shackled to a woman I can't wait to shove my cock in. But when I saw you eyeing her, Gravo, the look on your face was priceless."

The young beauty tensed and sneered, turning her head toward Donato.

"That's right. Get angry, cunt." The Italian wagged his tongue at her. "I want you to fight the entire time I'm fucking you."

Just then, the bus hit a large pothole, sending every passenger into the air again and causing Donato to bite his tongue.

"*Bastardo!*"[7] He griped as he spat blood.

Charles watched as the driver glared at Donato. Then, in his rearview mirror, he scanned the ceiling above Donato's seat. The driver peeked at the distracted commanding officer,

---

[7] "Bastard!"

then slyly opened a control panel near the steering wheel column. A second later, Charles heard a rapid thumping behind him. He looked back to see Donato convulsing, his eyes rolled back and bloodied tongue hanging out and dripping saliva. He fell over onto his shackle-mate, passing the electrical current onto him.

Charles turned back around in his seat to catch his Brazilian shackle-mate looking at the abstract tattoo on his wrist.

"You take pride in what you do to children?" she whispered in her lyrical accent.

"We've both consorted with the devil," Charles responded with a faux-apologetic smile. "You want answers, look inward. I'm sure you'll find plenty. The time I spend on this continent among you people will be minimal. Your fates have already been predetermined. I'm the only one here in control of his destiny."

She pursed her lips and looked at him. "Thin skin for such a diabolical criminal." She chuckled. "I have to say the Italian is right. They'll soon be passing you around."

He leaned toward her, eyeing her chest as it bounced in rhythm with the jostling bus. "Me?" he whispered. "The moment we step from this bus into K-City, you'll be gang-raped for hours, maybe days. Then, nine months from now, your body will spit out a bastard that won't survive the first week of its life. You're a lamb in a den of wolves."

"I'm sure my dead husband and his dead whore also suspected me to be weak and naïve." She smiled, showing her straight white teeth. "Right before I tore the guts from their bodies."

A small smirk graced Charles's face as he shook his head at her. "As if any of that matters here. . . " he began to say, but was distracted by the sudden transition as the bus rolled onto a paved road.

He craned his neck and saw that they had arrived at the outer reaches of the vast barrier wall of K-City. He raised his chained wrists up in the air until the tension forced his shackle-mate's to move also.

"We'll be there soon," he said to her. "So for your sake, you better hope the Italian's cigarette theory is wrong. Because, like it or not, you and I are in this together."

"Attention!"

The commanding officer's bellowing jarred his subordinates from their slumber. They checked their weapons and straightened the creases in their uniforms.

A speck of K-City could be seen in the distance. Its massive walls had been inspired by the Great Wall of Zhoukoudia, with Katingal's architects having tripled the height and width in creating their masterpiece. The biggest difference was that the Great Wall of Zhoukoudia had been constructed to keep would-be conquerors out, while Katingal's barricade was designed to keep the same sort of savage man confined.

As the bus neared the wall, countless surveillance cameras and drones patrolling the skies fed the warden all the information he needed to govern the city. The live video feeds that these cameras offered doubled as a means of tight patrol, as well as gambling entertainment for the correctional officers during their three-month deployments. They would often take bets on which prisoners wouldn't make it through the day. Or the next hour.

When the first of two steel security gates opened, the inmates got their first unfiltered glimpse of the prison city. Watchtowers with large floodlights stood at thousand-meter intervals. From those high perches, guards with automatic weapons lorded over the property.

The bus came to a halt at a giant, metal entry gate.

One of the non-English-speaking prisoners butchered the warning information on the sign at the gate as he read it aloud.

"The word is 'warning,' you dumb Spaniard," the young driver said with a sneer.

The Spaniard pushed aside his long, jet-black hair and stared at the driver.

"You eyeballing me?" the driver asked as he smiled and reached for the control panel. He flipped the numeric switch corresponding to the prisoner's seat, sending a quick but powerful jolt.

"*Detener!*"[8] The Spaniard spat out from between his tightened jaw. "*Tengo una afección cardiac. Puedes matarme!*"[9]

Donato laughed. "*No hablas Espanol! Hablas Englais!*"[10]

---

[8] "Stop!"

[9] "I have a heart condition. You're killing me!"

[10] "I don't speak Spanish! Speak English!"

"He's saying he has a heart condition, and the electricity could kill him," Charles said loudly enough for the ranking officer on the bus to hear.

The chubby sergeant tried to pull his utility belt up over his protruding belly, but it sank back down again. He pursed his brow. "You shock another prisoner without my direct order," he scolded the driver, beads of sweat forming on his crumpled forehead, "and you'll never work this detail again."

"Yes, sir!" the driver responded with mock seriousness.

The Spaniard clutched at his heart and took deep breaths, his eyes wide with panic.

"*¿Le parece bien?*"[11] Charles asked. "*¿Necesita un médico?*"[12]

"*Estoy bien,*"[13] he said, nodding. "*Gracias.*"[14]

Charles rested his head upon the seat in front of him and sighed.

"Keep back fifty feet," the sergeant instructed as he read aloud the notice on the steel door. "All violators will be shot without warning." He repeated the same message in Mandarin, Hindi, Russian, Japanese, German, Italian, Spanish, Portuguese, and Arabic while examining his cuticles.

The prisoners at the front of the bus craned their necks to see the seventy-foot wall. Ten signs stacked one after the other, written in ten languages, alerted the incoming inmates

---

[11] "Are you okay?"

[12] "Do you need a doctor?"

[13] "I'm fine."

[14] "Thank you."

that marksmen were prepared to shower bullets on those who violated the prison's protocols.

"*Meda! Meda!*"[15] The Spaniard declared with agitation as he pointed out the window. "*Los cadáveres, algunos de ellos . . .*"[16] He paused, his voice trailing off.

"Goddamn it, what's he saying?" Donato demanded.

"He says he sees corpses," Charles said.

Before anyone could respond to that, the speakers on the bus crackled to life, broadcasting an official statement about what the inmates were seeing.

"One of the dead is a guard," Charles translated. "They shot down one of their own."

The Spaniard was rocking back and forth, eyes closed, hands clasped together. "*Dios te salve, María,*"[17] he muttered, "*llena eres de gracia. El Señor es contigo, bendita tú entre las mujeres, y bendito es el fruto de tu vientre Jesús.*"[18]

The sergeant seized the opportunity to teach the driver a lesson. "Look out there on the ground, rookie," he said. "That's the officer you replaced. That's what happens when you don't follow protocol on this detail." He was interrupted by a voice coming through the bus radio handset.

"This is Warden Johnston. Identify yourself and cargo."

---

[15] "Look! Look!"

[16] "The corpses, some of them…"

[17] "Hail, Mary,"

[18] "full of grace. The Lord is with thee, blessed art thou among women, and blessed is the fruit of thy womb Jesus."

The sergeant reached over and flipped a switch. The blackened windows of the bus lowered. Charles looked out and saw what had shaken the Spaniard. Among the countless bullet holes that had scarred the walls was a rotting corpse being picked over by buzzards and insects.

The sergeant coughed and firmed his stance as he eyed the prisoners. His uniform was soaked through with sweat, his hair matted down into little points. He moved as close to the bus door as the elastic radio wire would allow. The radio crackled.

"This is Warden Johnston. You have fifteen seconds to identify yourself before your vehicle is fired upon."

"This is Sergeant Ludlow of the Southern Wales Territory, Great Britain," the sergeant announced, now looking a bit anxious. "I'm the ranking officer for this transport of twenty-three prisoners."

"Verbal identification has been accepted," the warden acknowledged. "Disembark and approach the prison entrance for retinal and palm verification. You have forty-five seconds to comply before you're fired upon."

The sergeant scrambled from the bus to the massive front doors, where a computer panel stood. Charles took another look at the greedy buzzards and then watched the sergeant. He had almost reached the control panel when several birds scattered into the sky and startled him.

"You now have thirty-five seconds to complete retinal and palm identification before you're fired upon," the warden warned.

The sergeant lunged at the panel, punched in a few buttons, and put his face up to the infrared orb. The red line scanned his face. He backed up and wiped his palm on his pants before placing it flat against the panel.

"You now have fifteen seconds to complete retinal and palm identification before you're fired upon," the warden's voice rang out again.

"Shoot him!" Donato shouted from the bus.

"Shut up, you fool!" Charles's shackle-mate yelled. "If they shoot him, do you think they'll think twice about littering this whole bus with bullets?"

A computerized voice approved the scans over the loudspeakers outside the prison. Sergeant Ludlow hurried back onto the bus. He grabbed his wet hand-towel and wiped his head and his quivering double chin. The driver shut the door just as the massive, hydraulic-powered, metal gate of the prison roared to life. Atop the doors' control panel, a large digital clock began its countdown from forty-five seconds.

"That's it, rookie, squeeze right in there," the sergeant urged to his driver. "If we don't pass through before zero, the hydraulic pressure will crush this transport as easy as an empty can of beer under my fat foot."

The driver punched the accelerator, and the engine stalled.

Silence held for a long moment. Then the sergeant burst out with, "Get this goddamn thing moving!?"

The digital clock read thirty-seven seconds.

The driver leaned forward, and the bus's engine started cranking.

"Hurry!" shouted the sergeant.

The engine started, and the driver again stomped on the accelerator. This time the bus lurched forward, which roughed up the prisoners. Nobody complained, though, and they made it through the gate just in time.

Once inside the compound, the bus passed through two sets of high, metal fences topped with electrified razor wire. At each fence stood a checkpoint where prison officers verified the identification of the transport officers while taking a count of the prisoners.

Once they cleared the fences, the bus came to a halt at a series of very modern and fortified structures—the prison headquarters. A sign indicated the prisoner intake building. Ten officers in full riot gear fanned out around the door. The warden stepped out.

"Okay, now, pay attention," said Sergeant Ludlow.

Several of the prisoners continued talking among themselves in low tones.

The sergeant opened the control panel on the bus and flipped a large switch. The sound of the prisoners' screams was so loud that the officers covered their ears. The convicts convulsed until the sergeant reversed the charge.

"Muh-thuh-fuckuh!" Donato cried out between his clenched jaws.

"Shut up, or I'll hit you with another!" the sergeant yelled. Everyone quieted.

"Like I said, pay attention," the sergeant hollered. "I'm going to release your chains. Stand and file off this bus.

Form a single line across the courtyard. Once you're in the courtyard, your orders will come from the warden."

"I don't have all day, Sergeant!" the warden shouted. "Get those prisoners off that bus now!"

Sergeant Ludlow flipped the switch that released the prisoners' shackles. Moving awkwardly with the heavy leg chains still attached, they shuffled off the bus and into the dusty prison courtyard. The strapping guards all bore scowls and had angry eyes that dared the prisoners to fall out of line. The warden barked an order. The officers in riot gear pushed the prisoners through another set of doors.

The warden approached the sergeant and saluted. He was an imposing man with hulking shoulders and a full gray beard. He wore dungarees, steel-toed boots, and a Kevlar vest.

"Sergeant Ludlow, thank you for your service," he said crisply. "It pleases me that we didn't have a repeat occurrence of your last visit—especially when it could have been prevented by adhering to my prison protocols. You may exit my prison now. You have three minutes to exit my facility until you'll be fired upon."

The sergeant saluted and waddled back to the bus. He wasted no time as he slammed the door shut, already yelling at the driver. The bus lurched forward and sped toward the gated checkpoints and the hydraulic doors.

The warden turned to the new inmates and prison guards. He calmly nodded at one of the guards. "Please describe to our new guests how life works here." Without waiting for a reply or glancing at the prisoners, the warden turned and began striding toward the main building.

The brawny guard stepped forward and spoke in a measured tone, informing them of the bleak life they would lead from that day forward. The inmates, he told them, would receive one week's worth of military-style food rations, a gallon of water, and one black uniform. Once their food and water was gone, acquiring more was up to the prisoner. After their basic processing in K-City headquarters, they would be released into the surrounding wasteland.

As for life in K-City, it was kill or be killed. There would be no policing from the guards or even simple interactions. Many of the inmates would die of dehydration, starvation, disease, or exposure within a week or two. Those, the guard said, would be the lucky ones. For those who survived their first week at K-City, rape, mutilation, murder, and cannibalism were common, and it was beyond the scope of the duties of the guards to interfere.

Those who survived were welcome to take residency in one of the ramshackle housing structures still left standing.

The guard finished with an encouragement to join a gang, since daily battles for any pool of water, or dogs, possums, rats, and other wild animals to eat, was seldom successful alone.

Chapter 9

THE TWENTY-THREE PRISONERS SHUFFLED INTO a cold, gray room, their chains a cacophony of cast iron against concrete. The steel door clanged shut behind them. They stood against a wall.

The warden walked the length of the line, pausing to look each prisoner in the eye. Behind him was K-City's team of correctional officers, who stood so tall the ceiling lights cast halos down onto their shaved heads.

"My name is Warden Johnston, the archangel of the Global Judiciary System." He smiled at his little joke and gave a bow. "You all are now citizens of Katingal City. This island, which is as far away from civilization as humanly possible, is humanity's sole maximum-security prison. Six point seven million prisoners in her history, and not one has escaped. The outer wall stands seventy feet high and forty feet thick. For those of you keen to test my wall, my guards have specific orders to fire without warning on *any* prisoner attempting to scale, penetrate, or burrow underneath it."

The warden walked over to a wall-sized map of the island.

"You are here." He pointed to the center of the desolate continent. "Just shy of three million square miles of desert wasteland surrounds you. To put that into perspective, if you were to walk seven days a week, twenty-four hours a day without rest, it would take you half a year to get from one coastline to the other.

"Here in the southern quadrant of the continent, the temperatures drop as low as twenty degrees at night and rise as high as one hundred twenty during the day. So, go ahead, escape. There will be no search party hunting you. You saw the skeletons littering the outer walls of my city. They were prisoners who were expelled from my city for challenging my authority. Starvation and thirst compelled them to return. Can you imagine the level of desperation that would compel a person to prefer reentering prison? Of course, once they are expelled, they are not invited back. My marksmen crippled those who returned with shots to a limb, leaving their fate to heat, cold, insects, and vermin."

The guards ushered the prisoners forward to pass by a metal table that held their survival gear, leather satchels, twenty-one military-style Meals-Ready-to-Eat or MREs, and one-gallon bottles of drinking water.

"Some of you may find life inside the walls of K-City too much to bear," the warden continued. "Some of you will take your own lives rather than face the savagery required to survive here."

He inspected the prisoners as they gathered their rations and returned to the line along the wall. Two were female. When the last rejoined the line, he began applauding.

"Congratulations on your acceptance to this very distinguished club."

His clapping grew in intensity until the guards joined him, banging their batons against their full-body shields.

"You're in esteemed company," the warden said. "Adolf Hitler, Mao Zedong, Leopold II, Benito Mussolini, Joseph Stalin, and countless others who chose anarchy over peace have spent their final days here." The warden pulled a pair of leather gloves from his hip pocket and slid them onto his hands. "Life is very simple here. Survive or perish. We are the gatekeepers who ensure you never leave this continent." He paused to sweep his eyes over the line of prisoners. "You are the worst this world has to offer. We've endured your savagery long enough. And now you've been segregated from civilization to live out the rest of your natural lives among your brothers and sisters who have also embraced your wretched way of life."

Donato rolled his eyes. Charles wondered what the warden would have done to the Italian if he had noticed.

"I weep for you and what you've allowed yourselves to become." The warden stepped to the front of the line. "Let's get acquainted. Here we have Pedro Alonso Lopez, a Colombian-born, confessed serial killer accused of raping and killing more than three hundred women across South America."

The warden moved to stand before the next person in line. "Petr Zelenka, Czech serial killer. A male nurse!" The warden scoffed. "The male nurse that murdered seven patients by lethal injection before being caught."

He skipped past four or five men to the first female convict among the shackled. "Juana Barraza, the Mexican serial killer dubbed 'La Mataviejitas,' sentenced to seven hundred fifty nine years for killing eleven elderly women."

Charles wanted a better look at the quiet, older woman the warden had just addressed, but the warden blocked his view. When Charles tried to peer around him, the warden turned suddenly and gave him a quick jab to the face, and Charles discovered the hard way that those gloves were comprised of more than leather. Charles was knocked to the floor and blood shot from his mouth. His weight pulled down the two men shackled to him on either side. The correctional officers leaped to keep the other prisoners against the wall and in line.

The warden crouched over Charles and whispered in his ear. "I've been given the authority by the President of the UTA, with the blessing of WICC, to do whatever it is I deem necessary to enhance your suffering, Inmate Gravo."

He gestured to a guard wearing a ring of keys. The guard separated Charles from the others. He stood alone, about two feet in front of the line, shackled only to himself at the wrists, ankles, and waist.

The warden flexed his fingers and frowned. "It's always been my experience," he pontificated, "that in every new group of inmates, one thinks he *or* she is exceptional—the most heinous murderer, the most sadistic rapist, the cleverest of white-collar criminals, the most feared and powerful of all tyrants."

From the corner, the warden retrieved a rusted steel chair with large welded hoops in all four of its legs and positioned it in the center of the room. The correctional officers secured the remaining prisoners to hoop locks built into the stone wall.

"For those 'exceptional' prisoners I've just described, I have always found it beneficial for them, as well as their chain gang, to learn just how exceptional they're *not*. It's so very enlightening to educate those like you, Charles Gravo, so you're aware of just how vulnerable you are here in my world."

The warden walked to the other side of the room, turned, and signaled the correctional officers flanking Charles. They led him to the metal chair, bent him over the back, snaked his chains through the welded hoops in its legs, and bolted the chair to the floor. Blood dripped from Charles's mouth onto the seat of the steel chair.

The captain of the guards stationed at the door interjected in a booming baritone, "Don't you think this is an excellent time to introduce our newest inmates to Kristoff, Warden?"

"Indeed, I do," the warden agreed with a smile.

Two officers entered the room, escorting a hulking inmate with SS and swastika tattoos littering his body. Even though the officers were large men, the inmate towered over them, and his massive arms and shoulders rippled with underlying muscles and tendons.

"After his capture," the warden began, "Charles Gravo's network of pedophiles managed to orchestrate the abduction of the child of one of the most respected citizens in our international community. Governor Negesso oversees the most powerful territory in the UTA. Some say he's slated to be the next president. And you thought it was a good idea to kidnap his son?"

"My daddy always told me to aim high," Charles said. Despite the severe discomfort, he managed to smirk at the warden.

The warden stared at him for a long moment. Then he spoke in measured tones. "Inmate Gravo, you probably think of yourself as a man with a keen sense of humor. I'm sure the young girls you raped and murdered thought differently of you sense of humor. The spirits of your victims hover above, watching you here in K-City, from heaven. They're the ones laughing now that your smart mouth will bring you nothing but trouble." The warden gestured at the guards, and Charles prepared himself for the onslaught of blows.

Chapter 10

"INMATE GRAVO!" ONE OF THE overgrown correctional officers sang as he stood over Charles. "Wake up!" A warm stream of yellow urine saturated Charles's hair and ran down over his face.

"That's enough, officer," the warden said.

Charles roused himself and cast a glance around the gray room. He had been knocked unconscious by the beating his smart mouth had earned him, but apparently had been out for only a few minutes. He was still draped painfully over the back of the metal chair, held in place by the chains attached to his wrists and ankles. The other inmates from the bus, most grinning at his predicament, stood watching.

The officer zipped his pants as the warden stepped to Charles. He bent down and looked into his eyes. "Just being around you sickens me."

A different officer knelt and adjusted the dial on his Taser wand before sticking it into Charles's ribs. Amplified by the fluid, metal chains, and chair, the electrical current curled Charles and kicked the sweet scent of burning into the air.

"One can't afford civility in this line of work," the warden said. "But I'd like to think that I'm fair. Which is why, Inmate Gravo, I'm offering you the rare opportunity to right your wrongs."

The warden listed a series of demands, including the location of the governor's son, the names of all members of Duenno, particularities of their finances, addresses of safe houses, and the whereabouts of every child trapped in the network. He crouched down to talk face to face with Charles.

"Let me be frank," the warden said. "You're one of the younger, fitter prisoners here. You've had military training, and from the report on your KPP orientation, it seems you're now exceptionally intelligent. You've heard the stories about life in K-City. Eventually all of you will fall victim to starvation, disease, murder, and some even rape. If you give me what I want, your introduction to this world will be fair. If you don't, I'll slowly escort you through this hell myself."

As though that was their cue, the two large officers restraining the inmate called Kristoff laughed and yanked him forward.

"You must have gotten a call from someone really important to make me such a long-winded offer," Charles said. "Was it the governor or the president?"

"You *are* a smart one." The warden pursed his lips and came close to Charles's ear. "The governor was very disappointed at the lack of information you provided. We still need the names of your accomplices, safe house locations, all of it. This is your last chance."

"The governor, I'm guessing," said Charles. "He was pretty pissed off when he got that call from the president. What'd he offer you? A way out of this rathole?"

The warden backed up a bit. "As a matter of fact, I've been presented with an once-in-a-lifetime offer that I intend to collect on. I help him find his son and get the information I need to bring down Duenno, and I'm free of this continent." He widened his eyes and smiled. "For two decades, I've held the line and kept you savages at bay. Now I'm ready to enjoy the fruits of my labor. Which means you *will* give me what I want." His smile grew smug. "Naturally, you have a choice. Tell me what I need to know, or I'll make sure your suffering in K-City will be legendary."

Charles mirrored the warden's sweet smile. "Fuck your deal with the governor, and fuck you. The moment I die, his son will be auctioned to the highest bidder, and his innocence destroyed while the entire world bears witness."

The warden spat in Charles's face. "Kristoff!" He threw his arm in the air to summon the oversized Nazi. "Inmate Gravo, let me introduce you to my handpicked mayor of K-City."

Kristoff paused to size up Charles. "*Du hast mich eine saubere Weibe versprochen!*"[19] He blurted in a gravelly voice.

---

[19] "You promised me a clean woman!"

"Mind your tongue!" the warden snarled. "You were promised someone clean. No one promised a woman. Women are a rare commodity in K-City, especially ones as young and attractive as our newest arrival." He glanced at Elaina, who stared back defiantly.

The warden nodded for his guards to circle around Charles, leaving enough space for the other inmates to watch. Kristoff looked at the warden, panting in anticipation of the command from his master.

"*Naja, Kristoff,*"[20] the warden said with a disgusted wave of his hand. "*Haben Sie oder gar nichts.*"[21]

Kristoff stormed to Charles and tore away his prison jumpsuit, first with his black fingernails, and then with his rotting teeth. He wasted no time ripping off Charles's briefs. The metal legs of the chair clattered and rattled as Charles struggled.

"You let this happen and the governor's son dies!" Charles yelled.

"You think I give a damn about what happens to the governor's son?" the warden replied. His voice was smooth, delicate, wrapped in silk. "You and I both know he's likely already dead. Kristoff, halt!"

Several officers pounced on the heaving, sweaty Nazi and moved him away from Charles's naked, quaking body. In one hand, Kristoff clenched a fistful of Charles's black hair. The

---

[20] "Well, Kristoff,"

[21] "Have him or nothing at all."

other hand fondled his thick erection through the front of his soiled prison jumpsuit. He gave the warden a questioning look, his heavy brow furrowed.

"You can continue in a moment," the warden promised. "But I don't have to watch it. Captain."

"Yes, Warden?"

"Process the prisoners and release them into K-City."

The guards unlocked the chain gang from the wall one by one and led them to a large, circular door with the words *Katingal City* etched in the stone above. The captain keyed a code into the control panel, placed his eye to the retinal scanner, and then set his palm on a flat, hand-shaped panel. The circular door opened into a thick glass tube. The hall stretched fifty yards to a matching circular door. The guards unshackled the inmates one by one and shoved them forward.

Behind them, Charles still arched over the back of the chair. He watched as Elaina and the Spaniard passed through the threshold. The Spaniard looked back at Charles before the door closed.

Most of the prisoners remained clustered together in the first twenty feet of the portal. When the door shut behind them, it made a sucking sound as it sealed. The intercom crackled, and through it came the warden's voice, echoing in the tube.

"This passageway serves two purposes. The first is that it is your portal to K-City. Now that the door behind you has been shut, you will notice that the door at the other end has already begun to open. You will have forty-five seconds to exit the passageway. Once the forty-five seconds has elapsed, the hydraulic door will close.

"The second purpose of this tube is that it serves as a gas chamber. Should you fail or refuse to cross into K-City in that time, you will be confined inside the airtight portal while hydrogen cyanide filters into the air vents."

The warden's warning sparked a mad rush for the opening door as the prisoners in the back of the pack began to push those in front toward the exit.

"Thirty-three seconds remaining."

The prisoners continued their scramble toward the door, with Elaina and the Spaniard bringing up the rear. One of the warden's correctional officer's voice could be heard under the warden's voice. "Warden, what do you want to do with Gravo?" "Kristoff, du hast ja 15 Minuten,"[22] said the warden. Within seconds, screams and grunts were bursting through the portal's intercom speakers.

Back in the tunnel, the only one that did not move was a skinny Japanese prisoner who knelt on the glass floor with his long black hair hanging over his face. The digital clock hanging from the ceiling at the midpoint of the tunnel taunted the inmates with its countdown.

One by one, most of the prisoners made it through the door until the tunnel was empty. The only ones who remained were Elaina, the Spaniard, and the kneeling Japanese prisoner,

---

[22] "Kristoff, you have 15 minutes,"

who had closed his eyes and appeared in a meditative state despite Charles's piercing screams over the intercom.

Elaina looked at the Spaniard, who was almost at the door. She knew rape and violence awaiting her across the threshold of K-City. Her knees began to bend to join the Japanese man in his pose.

The Japanese prisoner briefly opened his eyes and swept away his hair to look at Elaina. He smiled peacefully. "I am glad my final vision on this Earth is a beautiful one."

She felt a sense of peace, too.

The Spaniard turned around. "What are you doing?" he yelled, startling her. "Get up!" He ran back and grabbed her by the hair. "Death will come for us all in its own time, but for you, it must wait. Today, the brave endure and cowards die alone."

"No, let me die here. Please," she cried out, competing with Kristoff's aninalistic heaves and grunts ringing out over the speakers. The Spaniard's grip was tight. She ran with him, terrified and confused. Was this a sinister or humane gesture? She couldn't tell.

"Fifteen seconds, " the warden said. "Ten seconds."

"Take your hands off me!" Elaina struggled to keep pace with the Spaniard as he pulled her through the portal. They both fell through the hydraulic door as it began to close. The Spaniard released her.

"Dragging a bitch by her hair is caveman shit, Spaniard," Donato said. He grinned. "I like it."

No one seemed quite ready to make their way down the road to K-City.

Donato reached to help Elaina, who ignored his hand, jumped to her feet, and without pause, threw a snapping kick combination to the midsection and face of the Spaniard. He fell to the ground and spat blood from his lacerated lip. Elaina maintained her battle stance, ready for him to retaliate. He stood and stared intensely at her slowly dragged his index finger across his throat before turning to walk alone down the road to K-City.

Elaina looked back through the observation glass of the hydraulic doorway. The lone Japanese prisoner knelt with his palms resting atop his thighs. His chest rose and fell in deep breaths.

The clock blinked a red *zero*, and a white, milky gas billowed through the tube. When it reached the prisoner, he clutched at his throat and clawed at his face. Desperation replaced his meditative trance as he thrashed on the floor of the tunnel. Blood trickled from his nose, and his eyes bulged. His tongue wagged out of his mouth.

"Not so peaceful, after all," Elaina muttered.

Within seconds, the air cleared. The Japanese prisoner lay twitching for a moment, and then was still. A puddle of urine spread out around him.

Elaina turned away from the portal, shaking, her breath out of control. She vomited onto the red clay earth of Katingal over and over again as tears ran down her cheeks and she clutched her stomach.

Donato looked at her, still wearing the sinister smile and fonding his genitals. "I'm going to fuck you til you're bloody."

Chapter 11

HARLES GRAVO WOKE IN HIS shelter, and as was his ritual, breathed deeply several times before pulling himself up from his makeshift mattress.

Since the first moment Charles had set foot on Katingal soil three weeks ago, he had been constantly aware of how much freedom he had lost. He kept mental tallies, as if this might help him understand what defined a man and kept him human. Twenty sunrises since his vicious violation by Kristoff in the prison headquarters. 480 hours since he had walked through the airtight glass portal to K-City, then trekked into the outback alone. 20,800 minutes since his last shower. 1,728,000 seconds since his last hot meal.

Charles wondered if he had crossed not only a threshold to this place, but also to another side of humanity where he had always belonged.

His mind worked constantly as his body healed. He'd found shelter in an old foreman's office built half-inside the mountain at the mouth of the mine that had brought Apex to

Katingal years ago. He had fortified it as best he could with rocks and scrap lumber.

A few hundred yards beyond Charles's shelter, the main road led to K-City. The warden's quarters also squatted about a hundred yards away. This intermediate zone resided within firing range of the tower snipers' high-powered rifles. Charles accepted the risk of being a potential target for guards. Common sense led him to seek refuge in this outback, a less risky prospect than surviving among the other inmates while he healed from his rape.

He had rigged pipes to channel the water that dripped from the roof of the mine into a five-gallon gasoline container he'd been lucky enough to find. Every four seconds, a fresh drop fell.

Next to his water storage system, a warped, wooden table held Charles's accumulation of rudimentary weapons constructed from fragments of metal, glass, stone, and other materials he'd salvaged.

His best weapon was an ax he'd found half buried far back in the mine. Its handle had mostly rotted away, but he'd been able to fashion a new one from a scrap of wood, and had even put a decent edge on the blade with a small grinding wheel that had been left behind in a tool locker when the mine was abandoned.

He'd also cut up an inner tube from one of the mine vehicles and used it to make a slingshot much like one he'd had as a boy. Metal shards and steel ball bearings scavenged from mining equipment fit perfectly into the pouch. Since it would be his only long-range weapon, he spent several hours a day practicing with the slingshot until he was satisfied that he could fling one of the metal shards a hundred feet or more with fair accuracy, and even farther with the ball bearings.

The table doubled as a scouting station. He had barricaded the window, leaving a sliver uncovered so he could see out. He spent days staring out that window, uncomfortable but alive.

He often thought back to the warden's bragging of how harsh life in Katingal could be. The warden was so proud of his city, the brutality of its inmates, and the impenetrability of its defenses. It made Charles wonder why the warden was so intent on leaving a place he adored so much.

Charles's stomach rumbled. Every day, his biggest challenge, among many others, was foraging for things he could eat. And it was time to confront the challenges of this new day. After all, this would be a special day. He had plans to carry out.

Uncomfortable with removing all his clothes, he took off his shirt, boots, and socks to wash his face, arms, and feet. Once finished, he put his socks, boots, and shirt back on and lowered his pants just enough to wash his genitals. He swished water through his mouth. He dried his face and body with the remains of a flannel shirt found in the foreman's desk. He hung the shirt to dry on the back of a chair before stepping into his prison coveralls.

In Charles's first few weeks, he had waited for nightfall and the cover of dark to investigate the no-man's land between K-City and the prison headquarters. He noticed that the guards in the towers relaxed at night, relying on the wall to take care of the masses inside. Under the twinkling desert moon and stars, Charles had inspected as much of the wall as he could to find weakness in the stone. He discovered previous inmates' failed attempts to chisel through, dig under, or scale over the wall. Bullet holes scarred the stone, and human bones lay scattered in the dust.

He would place his fingers into the fissures made by the bullets. The materials used to construct the wall were none he had ever touched before, but even a novice in masonry could detect that this was no ordinary stone. Now that he looked upon it for the first time with the benefit of daylight, he could see that he was correct. With a ridged and rusty buck knife, he tried to chip away at the hole in the wall. After nine or ten stabs, a small speck of dirt fell from around a metallic rebar forged into the wall.

Charles had found himself chuckling at the futility of K-City inmates trying to gather the appropriate tools to chip away at a wall laced with reinforced metal wire. He could imagine how the warden and his correctional officers might fashion themselves in a control room, laughing over their surveillance cameras at malnourished inmates trying to escape.

During those long nights of scouting the wall, Charles had nothing to do but think. His new brain traversed every book, every piece of information he had come across both after the surgery and before, now able to recall each moment, each piece of trivia, every last memory down to his earliest days as an infant.

None of those memories had helped him to figure out a way to get over, under, or through the wall. On all those nights of excursion, he had traveled what he calculated to be several miles in either direction of his shelter until the position of the descending moon would indicate it was time for him to take cover. In both directions, he had discovered nothing.

And last night, the moon, round and white in the sky, had told him there was no use in investigating the wall further. There was no life, no hope of escape, as long as he remained in the shadow of the control center or in its immediate vicinity.

And so it was that Charles had decided that he could no longer avoid K-City. Instead of escape plans, he'd spent his previous night busying his mind with his plans to enact revenge on Kristoff.

He shouldered his satchel containing water, his last remaining MRE, and his weapons. When he was ready, he looked through his peephole one last time. Seeing no one, he began to wrestle away the rusted filing cabinet and the boulder in front of the door.

Chapter 12

THE DOOR SWUNG OPEN, AND Charles was greeted by a wall of heat so thick, its density was more like water than air. The sun was at its highest point in the blue sky with a light sprinkling of milky white clouds.

Charles paused a moment, realizing that for all this place was and represented, its beauty was stunning, almost serene. He allowed himself to imagine that he was on a remote beach, the sun gracing his skin, until he paused and forced himself to remember where he was. His boots crunched on the dry gravel beneath him as he set out.

Dirt roads striped the empty desert before him. He calculated a thousand yards of open terrain between him and the edges of K-City. He would be visible, open game until the road wound into the cluster of towering buildings beyond.

After final readjustment of the satchel straps, he headed to the unpaved road. As he marched along, the distant buildings appeared to dance to the rhythm of his steps. He passed solitary, caved-in lean-tos of board and brick and the occasional clusters of rocks, metal, and rag. He shook his head at the idiocy of building shelters out in the open. Debris and wire sectioned small portions of sandy soil and weeds, failed attempts at cultivating crops. The farther he traveled away from the headquarters, the more shelters and gardens he saw. Charles noted how most of the shelters featured botched tin roofs, boards for walls, bricks stacked atop each other. Others weren't half bad, he had to admit.

All in all, it wasn't smart to remain here. Everything was flecked with bullet holes, lending the whole landscape the impression that it had been plagued by a pox.

Through these slums, Charles continued his trek to K-City, and out of the range of the tower guards' rifles. The closer he came to the outskirts of the city, the more frequent were the shelters, several with their garden fences still intact. Charles's stomach lurched at the thought of fresh food, but the soil was sandy and the patches were overgrown with weeds.

He looked at the sun's position and calculated that he had walked for no more than an hour. A few hundred yards from the road, he saw a windmill and the remains of a farm dwarfed by a cluster of high-rise buildings in the distance. The windmill was motionless. An untilled field and a saggy barn stood next to a wooden house. Not a shadow or flicker of movement anywhere.

He approached, holding his satchel tight against his chest. Thick foliage engulfed the house, and the windows looked black with dust. He didn't want to be caught on the property, especially in the open land where he was so vulnerable.

A hundred yards from the house, he heard multiple voices, a woman's scream, and cheers. He cut across the field to squat behind a rusted tractor toppled to its side. Another eruption of noise came from the back of the house. This time it was much louder. Charles drew his ax as another celebratory roar erupted. He peered from around the tractor, maneuvering himself to a vantage point where he could see the rear of the crowd. He wished he could see what they were looking at.

"We have a winner!" a man with a reedy, commanding voice declared.

Another roar followed the declaration of victory, and rising above the din, a woman gave a harrowing scream.

"No!" she pleaded. "I can still fight!"

Charles needed to see what was happening. He crept on his hands and knees before flattening onto his stomach to military crawl toward the windmill standing idle some forty yards away. He made steady progress, and the closer he slithered, the better his vantage of the crowd became. Eventually, he made it to the foot of the metal ladder attached to the windmill. He made sure no one saw him before climbing the ladder. With each rung, he could better see the large crowd behind the dilapidated farmhouse.

From the maintenance platform of the windmill, the entire event unfolded before his eyes as if he were a god and the criminals below mere mortals in the throes of a bacchanalian revelry. He could see two separate groups of men. The larger circled two women tearing at each other in hand-to-hand combat. In a different circle, men took turns raping the battered woman who had apparently lost the previous fight. She was a thin, leggy woman with short, dark hair. One man had her arms pinned to the ground above her head while two others each held a leg and a fourth unfastened his pants.

"The bittersweet joys of losing a wager," one of them taunted her. "Next time, fight harder."

The man between her thighs began to shove himself into her to the cheering of his cronies. He bent to lick and kiss her face, but paused to wretch and cough, his lungs rattling with mucus. She flailed and pushed against him. Her arms and legs bulged with definition, the muscle tone a clear testament to her desire to survive. But in the end, it seemed to Charles that everyone knew the four men pinning her down would have their way.

"Nineteen, twenty, twenty-one, twenty-two. . ." the crowd of spectators counted aloud.

"Eight more and then my turn," one of the instigators yelled. He spat into his dirty course hands and stroked his flaccid penis.

"Twenty-eight, twenty-nine, thirty!" they concluded before the next one in line hurried to pull the man off of her.

"Wheeeew! This one here is a firecracker." The rapist gave everyone the thumbs up as he pulled out of her.

The next inmate, whose wiry torso was littered with tattoos, shoved the coughing man aside and took his place between the woman's bruised thighs.

"Get in there," the coughing man said while he rolled around on the ground, pulling his pants up. "You won't be disappointed."

"I lost two dogs and a gallon of water betting on you, bitch." The tattooed man narrowed his eyes as he jerked at his short erection.

In the larger circle, another fight was about to begin. Ropes and chains tied like leashes around a line of women's necks. Four or five men held their tethers and collected wagers on their success or failure. The men shouted a din of numbers. The women said nothing and looked nowhere.

A large, dark-skinned man with tribal scars on his cheeks walked the interior perimeter of the circle. He stopped here and there to engage in quick discussions with random men.

At the edge of the circle, a man in a Scottish kilt paced. He had red hair, a face full of freckles, and a patch over his left eye. He cupped his hands around his mouth and yelled, "All you bastards need to shut up. The next match is between Grover's and Rodriguez's bitches. Anything goes except eye-gouging. Even bitches deserve to see."

This initiated laughter from the crowd.

"The first bitch to be knocked out or submit to her opponent loses. . . and we all know what happens to the loser." He thumbed toward the smaller circle, where the men were counting in a frenzy, starting another roar from the crowd.

Charles watched the two women, how the rage filled their bodies, the way they scowled at the men.

"All winnings will be paid *immediately* after a winner has been declared."

One of the handlers, a small man, yanked his woman's leash hard, causing them both to lose their balance. She snarled like a cougar and leapt onto his torso, wrapped her legs around his waist, and raked his face with her nails while he howled and roared. She bit into his neck, and Charles realized she'd torn open the man's carotid artery when blood shot into the air. Several men rushed to pull her off him, but it was too late. The small man never rose again.

"Crazy bitch!" a spectator standing behind her yelled. He lunged at her and struck her in the face.

She fell off her victim in a daze, then stood and glared at the man who had hit her and the other men near her, her hands out. A mane of tangled brown hair hung over her shoulders.

"Teach her a lesson," the spectator yelled.

She spat on him, and two other men converged on her.

"Order!" the redheaded ring announcer shouted.

The men began chanting, "Get her, get her."

Over their voices, the announcer called out, "Nnamdi, maintain order here!"

A large Nigerian man walked into the center of the feud. He stood still a moment to wait for the men's fury to die down. "The bitch still has another fight," he said, his voice surprisingly high-pitched. "And anyone who interferes with that answers to Kristoff."

At the mention of the lunatic's name, the two men backed away from the woman.

Nnamdi then approached and grabbed a fistful of the woman's hair to guide her back to the circle. He broke through the crowded spectators and released her on the opposite side of her opponent. She snarled at Nnamdi upon her release, wiped the excess blood from her mouth, and spat upon the ground to prepare herself for the impending battle.

The Irishman yelled, "Fight!"

***The women charged from opposite sides of the crowd and collided at the center. They punched, clawed, and ripped at each other's hair, clothes, and flesh. In moments, their shirts were shreds, and their exposed breasts incited cheers.

Charles glanced back to the savage rape of the woman in the loser's circle. His body recoiled in memory of his own brutal rape at Kristoff's hands. Blurry visions of the prison room walls flashed across his mind until he shook himself back into the present.

He scanned the crowd with renewed anger perpetuated by his shame. Revenge fueled his desire to see Kristoff's face among the crowd.

His eyes returned to the ravaged victim in the loser's circle. Her sudden absence of resistance and limp body signaled that she had fallen into shock. Her eyes were empty of expression as they seemed to stare up at Charles. A flicker went over her brow.

He crouched out of sight, hoping she wouldn't give him away.

Charles closed his eyes and cursed Eloah's indifference, her detached sensibilities, and her lack of empathy for this world she had created.

Then he opened his eyes and felt new determination. He was not lost. He would control his own destiny. He would not be at anyone's hand—not even Eloah's.

The main fight raged on. Screams pierced through the crowd, signaling the untold havoc the two women were wreaking upon each other to secure temporary clemency from the loser's circle. One of the women threw the other onto her back. Dust rose into a cloud above them.

"Get up, or I'll have you pinned to your back until your final days," the handler of the losing woman threatened.

His threat reignited the fight in her. She screamed out in a rage, and fought her way off her back and to her knees. It was clear that she was using every bit of energy she had left, but her recovery was temporary, and her opponent the better fighter. Seconds later, she was back on the ground, being pummeled without mercy with fists, elbows, and forearms landing in panicked, rapid succession.

In this K-City barnyard ring, there were no bells to signal fighters to their corners. The stronger woman kept on with her beating, and finally the weaker woman lay motionless.

Charles hoped she wasn't dead but wondered if it might be better if she were.

The Irishman pulled the heaving woman from her opponent. The winning men thrust their fists in the air. The losers complained, spat, and threatened the unconscious woman.

Charles decided he'd seen enough. He started backing along the windmill platform toward the ladder, then paused when he saw another woman being led out on a leash by a man whose face he couldn't see.

"You sons of bitches ready for me yet?" the man bellowed.

Charles knew that voice. He looked down to spot Donato swaggering and hitching his pants. The crowd parted enough for Charles to see Elaina with barbed wire wound around her neck. Speckled rings of blood lined her shirt.

Charles recalled the last thing he had told her, that her beauty would be her curse here. He felt a flicker of remorse—an unfamiliar emotion to him—that his prediction had come true as he saw her having to follow Donato around like his pet. The bounce in Donato's step made it apparent that he had just raped her. Charles could guess from her sagging face and shoulders how many times she'd had to endure such brutality.

"Is it time for my bitch to fight?" Donato yelled again as they breached the large circle, where happy men were gathering their winnings and the groggy loser, too broken to protest, was being dragged off to the rape circle by her financiers. Donato positioned Elaina to one side of the circle and peered across to the opposite side, where her opponent crouched, waiting.

A fight broke out among the men, and the ginger-haired ringleader looked over the crowd. "Pay what you owe!"

One man grabbed a crudely-honed knife from his sock.

When the larger man saw the weapon, he laughed, his smile gummy from lost teeth. "What you gonna do with that, little man?" he taunted.

"Nnamdi, we have a dispute!" the redheaded ring announcer shouted. When the Nigerian enforcer didn't come, the announcer scanned the crowd again. "Nnamdi!"

The Nigerian had gone off to the rape circle and barged ahead in line to have his way with the previous fight's loser. His face was intense as he ignored her cries.

Another man who'd been counting at the Nigerian's elbow paused and snickered. "Sucks to be you, my friend, but looks like they need you over there."

Even from Charles's vantage point, the Nigerian brute was so broad that he eclipsed the woman beneath him.

"Hey," another eager rapist said, "McLaughlin needs you. Two men are fighting over wagers."

Nnamdi ignored them. He took a quick glance up at the larger circle to see two men brandishing weapons as they circled and took swipes at each other. Then he went back to thrusting into the woman beneath him. "After I'm finished," he snarled.

Charles saw movement as, with the grace and focus of a lion, a huge man slipped through the crowd. The unsuspecting Nnamdi never saw what hit him until it was too late. The man threw one of his massive arms around Nnamdi's throat. The Nigerian gasped for air and grabbed at the tattooed bicep of the imposing forearm. From the fear in his eyes, it seemed clear to Charles that the Nigerian knew he was outmatched. He struggled to look over his shoulder to see who his attacker was.

"Kristoff?" Nnamdi gasped. His arms fell limp to his sides, and he collapsed onto the woman under him. His scarred knuckles scraped the ground and saliva dripped from the sides of his mouth onto her bare chest.

"Every stroke you steal delays the fight, the bets, my winnings," Kristoff said, each syllable angrier than the one before. Kristoff reached down and unfastened his worn cargo pants to pull out a raging erection stained with dry, yellow pus. He inhaled deeply through his nostrils and spat into his course palm a mixture of mucus and saliva that he wiped between Nnamdi's buttocks.

Before he could start, Kristoff looked at the ravaged woman lying under Nnamdi. "Fight or fuck," he ordered the woman half-trapped beneath Nnamdi.

She worked her body free and ran off towards her handler.

As Kristoff thrust himself into the Nigerian's backside, Nnamdi snapped back into consciousness and cried out in a feverish panic.

"Kristoff! Please!"

"Keep your apologies," Kristoff said, his voice demonic and strained.

Charles watched his adversary burying himself into the Nigerian. Nnamdi squirmed and pulled at Kristoff's bicep that was still wrapped around his throat, but he was powerless under the madman's grip. He clawed at the red earth beneath him, his fingernails cracking until his blood mixed into the dust.

Kristoff pulled a knife from his waistband and plunged it through Nnamdi's hand, fastening it to the ground. "The next time you disrupt one of my fights, there will be shit on my knife instead of my dick!"

Nnamdi whimpered and winced with each thrust until Kristoff released a roar at the heavens as if daring the gods to intervene in his savagery. The huge man pulled himself out of the emasculated Nigerian, reached down, and ripped a large portion of Nnamdi's shirt off his back. He used it to wipe the mixture of blood, feces, and semen off himself, and tossed it back at the Nigerian. He stood and worked his way back through the crowd.

"Donato!" Kristoff beckoned. "Is my bronzed beauty ready? I'll be taking the bets today."

Charles descended the ladder with haste, hoping to depart as quietly as he had arrived. He could neither save Elaina nor watch what might happen to her. Once he was on the ground again, he crawled away from the cheering crowds and fixed his eyes on the K-City horizon.

After what Charles calculated was an hour's time, he saw the first signs of having reached his destination. A large, rectangular sign with sun-bleached, green borders and barely legible white letters read, *Now Entering Katingal City*. Beneath that was a vandal's tag: *All dat enter hear ubandun hope*.

A brisk and eerie wind blew from inside the city and carried the scent of death and decay. The massive buildings cascading on either side of him cast a shadow forward, leading him further up the road. They were built so closely together that they appeared stacked atop one another along the flat landscape. He suspected that the warden's boast of 6.7 million exiled criminals was more propaganda than fact. Besides those at the old farmhouse and the twenty-two inmates who arrived with him on the prison transport, the roadside skeletons were the only other evidence of inhabitants leading up to K-City.

"Circle around him!" barked a man in the alley around the corner. "Hurry!" There was some scurrying and crashing. "Get him, you fool!"

"It's your fault he got out," another man growled. "You better pray you catch him, because if not, *you're* the one that'll be on the spit today."

The two men continued to threaten each other amid the sound of trash and debris crashing. Charles ducked behind the nearest building and bumped a large, metal dumpster overflowing with a century's worth of garbage. He struggled to keep his footing among plastic MRE packages, twisted and destroyed furniture, old scrap metal, and food so moldy and rotten that even the starving inmates wouldn't eat it.

He crouched among the filth. Brown and black rats scattered into different directions. One ran up his leg. Charles snatched it and flung it against the brick wall. It fell, twitched, and lay still.

The men sounded like they were coming closer. A wild dog with patchy and matted fur staggered out from the alley. One of its hind legs trailed behind it like a second tail. It cast a quick, hopeful glance at Charles as though seeking help.

Sorry, Charles said silently to the mutt. *You're on your own. Just like the rest of us.*

Seconds later, the men emerged in pursuit of the crippled dog. Their tattered clothing streamed like flags. The older of the two brandished a large piece of wood with nails protruding from it while the other carried a piece of metal fashioned into a sword. The younger paused a few times to hurl rocks at the dog.

"You're letting a crippled dog outrun you," the older man yelled.

The younger man threw another rock that came close to the dog's head. He pursued while the elder man slowed, his breathing labored and heavy.

The elder stopped and bent over with his hands on his knees to cough and take in gulps of air. "You lose that dog, don't bother coming back," he wheezed.

Charles leaned to watch the scene but slipped on the debris. Another surge of rats evacuated the area. The old inmate looked up, his scarred face wrinkled with suspicion. He roared with dominance, gripped his weapon, and walked closer to peer around the dumpster.

When the inmate roared again, closer this time, Charles removed his ax from the twine around his waist and readied himself. Adrenaline surged through his body. His pulse pounded in his temples and the back of his skull.

The older man's hunched shadow was twenty feet away when the dog yelped in the distance. Charles hefted his axe and readied to strike, but the older man turned in the opposite direction and ran toward the sound of the dog.

"Did you get him?" the elder man called eagerly.

"Oh yeah, I got him," the younger man rejoiced. "Got him good, too. Not going to be running off now with two busted legs."

Charles lowered his ax and placed it back into its rope holster. He watched the two men disappear behind the building, where the younger man had broken the dog's other hind leg. Not wanting to take any additional risks, Charles doubled back and flanked around the other side of the building, abandoning the main road.

Chapter 13

A FEW HOURS AFTER EXPERIENCING THE savagery at the abandoned farm and his encounter with the men and the dog, Charles arrived at the endless cluster of buildings that was K-City. The sun was hanging on the horizon as he penetrated the heart of the city center. The side streets and alleyways were the arteries that fed it, its criminal population its lifeblood.

As he looked around, Charles couldn't shake the thought that only a poet could truly convey the complete havoc of this place. Buildings buckled from failing foundations. Their walls bulged and supports creaked as if they were in the perpetual process of snapping. Loose bricks fell at random. Insects and vermin scurried about the structures. Cesspools of human excrement so putrefied the air that Charles breathed through his mouth. Mixed with the stench of rotting flesh, it tasted like active disease.

As he walked, he admired the way inmates had clustered to protect the decayed spaces they had claimed as homes.

Those who hadn't found one roamed the streets aimlessly. Even on his way in, Charles saw several fights break out among these miserable humans who fought for just a patch of space on the street to call their own.

One of the buildings Charles passed on his way in featured what seemed to be the first successful garden he had seen since arriving on Katingal. It was guarded by an inmate who squatted at its entrance like a monkey in the bush. As Charles walked by, the inmate seemed to absorb his entire being in his stare, daring him to even consider stealing from his food supply. After a moment of locked eyes, the squatting inmate looked over his right shoulder at a large tree at the back of the garden. A body had been crucified to its trunk, and around the decaying corpse's neck was a sign that read, *Food Theef.* Insects and maggots swarmed what remained of the criminal's body to the point that his skin appeared to be moving.

Charles kept his eye on the inmate and was careful to display no hostile moves as he cleared the garden. The sun had set, casting the world into thick darkness, save for the occasional fire. The inmates who had been hiding during the day emerged like anxious vampires, all arriving at once to flood the streets with their suffering. Charles's hyper-intelligence registered every visible inch of their skin, including rashes, blotchy blisters, scaly patches, and raised spots. These rampant inflammations triggered a memory of a text he had read about polymorphic light eruption, or PMLE. Caused by exposure to sunlight, this condition forced the sufferer to remain indoors, as extended exposure would result in fatality from auto-immune disease.

In the few minutes following nightfall, K-City's epicenter morphed from scarcely populated to a flooded capacity. Charles was now shoulder to shoulder with lunatics, most of whom had clearly embraced the anarchy. He maneuvered in and out of the crowds of criminals, some hooting with insanity or enacting abuses on those weaker than themselves, and others looking like they had maintained some semblance of their humanity. Those were the ones Charles tried to avoid, since they could surely see that he was new among them.

Charles ducked in and out of alleys to remain inconspicuous. Those taking cover in the backstreets were afflicted in ways he had never seen. His mind began to spin again as he diagnosed every disease that had taken hold of the forgotten residents.

Countless corpses littered the streets. Some were fresh, others skeletal, and the rest accounted for every stage between. But the worst were those on the fringe of death. Their sores and lesions were as visible as the rodents and insects that feasted on the extremities of the helpless bodies. Charles realized that an inmate's life expectancy in K-City diminished with every passing minute. Those dark and narrow corridors contained the most wretched conditions K-City had to offer.

One man on the ground near Charles was shaking with tremors. He alternated between low moans and high, vicious laughter as he lay dying. Charles paused before stepping over the tortured remains of the old man. As he did, the inmate tugged feebly at the leg of his coveralls. Charles snatched his leg away and turned to the man.

"Kill me, please," he begged Charles, his eyes rolling as he spoke.

Charles gave a brief shake of his head and continued down the alley before coming to a dead end. He had no choice but to go back out the way he had come in, toward the dying man.

"You're new," the man said. "Your skin, too clear. Your face, too fat."

Charles stepped over him again.

"One day you'll lie here begging to die just like me."

"Your suffering isn't reason enough to strike you down," Charles said.

The man burst into uncontrolled laughter, followed by a bitter cough. "You're a liar and a stranger to this city," he wheezed. "I've been here a long time. I know my way around. My wisdom in exchange for one blow of your ax?"

Charles considered it, then shrugged. It was worth a try. "Where does Kristoff reside?"

"Kristoff?" the stranger repeated, twitching at every bite the rats took from his flesh. "That's easy. Is that all you want? If so, my death will come soon. As well as your own if it's Kristoff you seek."

"If a swift death is your desire, tell me where I find him," Charles said.

"You will find Kristoff," the man said before trailing off. "High-rise." He tried to point with his finger, but his hand was unsteady.

Charles watched the rats feasting on the man's bleeding legs. He kicked away two of the largest vermin.

"The top floor of the Apex building," the man said. "Only one with a balcony still standing."

With this information, Charles let his body grow stone cold, and his vision turned inward. His lust for revenge increased with every passing second until his trance was broken by the man's insane laughter.

"That's it," the man cried. "Release the demon within you. Stain your ax and strike me down!"

Charles drew his ax from his waistband. The man continued to laugh. Charles raised his ax above his head and brought it down upon the side of the man's neck. Blood spurted in all directions and ran down the man's shoulder and the front of his chest. The rats scurried up his body and into the wound to feast on the fresh, warm blood. Charles reared back for another chop. The head rolled down the alley a few feet before coming to its final rest.

Charles sighed before cleaning off the blade on the man's pants and leaving the alley. Back on the main drag of K-City, he scanned the skyline in search of the building the man had told him about. Soon he spied it in the distance, the largest building in K-City. The unmistakable *Apex* on top confirmed the target. Just beneath the sign, a balcony jutted out from the twentieth floor. Charles could see figures moving on the balcony.

Though Charles felt relieved to have discovered Kristoff's lair, he could see that the savage was surrounded by his men.

Nevertheless, Charles surged ahead, his heart racing in tempo with his legs as he moved closer to his objective.

As Charles drew near, a commotion broke out on the balcony. The group of men were drinking, dancing, and fighting as if the balcony were a mosh pit. One reveler grabbed another, while a third man struck the unfortunate chap with a pipe. He buckled, and with one swift movement, the two men flung their victim from the balcony. His limp body fell twenty floors to the hard pavement below. Charles heard the thump when it hit, and the cheers from a group of men who had been waiting for it on the street.

"The king is offering sacrifices tonight," one maniac on the balcony cheered, hooting down at the dead man sprawled on the pavement.

Charles quickened his pace, staying close to the edges of the road. He ducked into a nearby building and crouched down in a dark corner, using his hands to gather a pile of dirt. He took a mouthful of the water from his satchel and pushed it around his mouth to alleviate his thirst before releasing a thin, controlled stream onto the dirt pile. After mixing the water and dirt into a dark paste, he covered his pale face until all that remained visible were his green eyes.

As he continued his trek toward the epicenter of the city, Charles heard the faint symphony of suffering. Angry yells of men coming from the east and bloodcurdling screams of women pierced the night to the west. Moments later, he slid past a band of filthy men vying for ownership of a corpse like a pack of wolves.

Another ruckus was followed by another violent assault. Just like the one before him, the beaten man was thrown from the balcony. He screamed the entire way down while the maniacs rejoiced from above. Scavengers sprinted past Charles to the man's broken body and started ripping him apart.

Kristoff's acolytes leaned over the balcony railing and waved their arms in the air, chanting, "Kris-toff! Kris-toff! Kris-toff! The king of K-City!"

Charles was fifty yards from the barbed wire courtyard that secured the front entrance to the Apex building. Another scream of fear, followed by another thud, a pitched body, and the scurry of the scavengers. This time, Charles was close enough to hear bones snapping against the pavement. He took cover to avoid the scavengers, and waited while they butchered the latest sacrifice with their homemade weapons.

Charles darted along the side of the building until he spotted four men guarding the back doorway.

"Four offerings so far tonight," one of the guards warned the other three. "Two more before it's safe to go up there."

"You sound like a woman, Manta," the smallest guard said.

"Fuck you, Hiro!" He laughed. "You *look* like a woman. Now give me some pussy, you dwarf!"

"Curse me again and I'll take your tongue," Hiro seethed, pulling a short knife from his belt.

The other three guards erupted into laughter. "You call that a knife?" said one. "The only thing that piece of shit is good for is picking your rotting teeth."

"I'll pick your bones after I cut your throat with it," Hiro fired back. "I just come from Kristoff's, and I'm still alive. The new fella, Donato, made moonshine." He reached behind him and brandished a glass bottle that was about half full of sloshing brown liquid. "Got this for keeping watch tonight. They're all up there having a go at the Brazilian bitch. She's one nice piece of ass." The small man lifted the bottle and took a massive gulp.

Another one of the guards grabbed the bottle out of his hands and started guzzling.

"Hey!" yelped the one named Manta. "Save some for the rest of us." He jumped at the guard who was still gulping from the bottle.

"Kill him, Juan," one of the men shouted.

While Manta and Juan tossed each other around, Charles readied his slingshot and placed a metal shard in the pouch. Twenty yards away, hiding in the shadows, he hefted the slingshot and focused his attention on the man egging on the fight. He pulled the rubber sling taut, held his breath, and released the shard. It struck the man in the right side of his throat.

The man grabbed at his throat and instinctively ripped the shard out, removing part of his larynx in the process. He coughed a mouthful of blood onto the two feuding men before falling to his knees. Panic filled his eyes.

"What the hell!" Hiro shouted.

Fueled by moonshine and rage, Manta and Juan continued their battle, unaware of the attack. Hiro squinted to where

Charles stood, removed a weapon from his belt, and crept toward the darkness. Just then, Charles released another shard that flew into Hiro's open mouth, piercing the back of his throat.

Hiro dropped his weapon and shoved his entire hand into his mouth, grasping at the metal shard while Charles looked on with satisfaction.

All that practice paid off, he congratulated himself.

Charles emerged from the darkness with his ax and ended Hiro's gagging and spitting with a swift and powerful blow before sprinting to the two scuffling men. When Charles's dark figure appeared behind Juan, Manta's eyes lit up with alarm.

"Behind you!" Manta grunted.

"Shut up and die," Juan growled, burying his blade in Manta's throat.

Manta's body went rigid, but not before he spewed blood onto Juan's arms and face.

Juan didn't have a chance to lay eyes on Charles before his head was severed from his body. As Juan collapsed on top of Manta, Charles looked over the four dead men he'd just laid waste to. He felt no remorse. He dragged each of the lifeless bodies along the dark wall, stacked them, tossed Juan's head on top, and covered the pile with a section of scrap metal.

Keeping in the shadows, he reached the entrance of the building. The moonlight penetrated a few feet into the hallway, allowing him light enough to see the foot of the stairs. After the first few steps, he was thrust into complete darkness. He paused his ascent and waited for his vision to adjust.

While his pupils dilated, his sense of smell became acute. He swore he could taste the aroma of urine, feces, and decaying flesh as he breathed through his mouth. It was overwhelming and could not stop himself from vomiting.

He steeled himself and continued his climb up the twenty flights of stairs. Every so often, a hole in the wall or a broken window allowed enough moonlight for him to maintain what floor he was on.

At the twentieth floor, he crept into the dark hallway and kept his back to the wall. Down the corridor, a lone light flickered against the wall. As he inched closer, glass crunched beneath the soles of his boots. He drew his ax. He could feel his pulse in his ears.

"Kristoff, king of K-City!" the men chanted in unison. "Kristoff, king of K-City!"

Charles followed the voices. When he arrived at the doorless entrance, he could see that the torches were as tall as the men outside. He watched as another flailing victim was tossed over the balcony.

When he heard the familiar voice, Charles's rage redoubled.

"You!" Kristoff commanded someone. "Go to my bedroom and bring us another birdie."

A laugh of drunken amusement echoed from the balcony. Donato took two large gulps of his drink and shook from the alcoholic rush before stumbling inside the living room from the balcony. From there he pushed his way into Kristoff's bedroom. There was a yell from inside the room, followed by a thud. Donato soon returned, dragging a man by his long, black, tangled hair.

Charles was surprised to see that it was the Spaniard from the prison bus. He was shaking and clutched at his heart. The group's newest birdie was shoved onto the balcony, where he lost his balance and fell to his hands and knees. When he raised his head, the Spaniard locked eyes with Charles. He blinked several times.

"*Te veo!*"[23] He shouted. "*Te veo, diablo! Eres demasiado tarde!*"[24]

Charles froze and scoured the room for any reaction to the Spaniard's ramblings. The others paid his words no attention. Instead, the savages treated him like a toy. One bent over and bit a chunk of flesh from the side of the Spaniard's stomach, chewed, and swallowed. When he stood, the cannibal was trembling beyond control.

The sight triggered Charles's subconscious aptitude, sending his mind to a text about Kuru disease, an incurable degenerative neurological disorder brought on by consumption of human flesh. He recalled with perfect clarity every page, each footnote, including the symptoms of body tremors and pathological laughter as the afflicted's mind disintegrated.

---

[23] "I see you!"

[24] "I see you, devil! You're late!"

While the men were busy with the Spaniard, Charles darted down the hallway to the bedroom where Donato dragged the Spaniard from. He quietly closed the door behind him and when he turned around he saw Elaina, naked and bound to the soiled bed. A small pool of blood and vomit lay a few inches from her head. Her once-beautiful mane of brown hair was matted, and almost every inch of her petite body was bruised.

As he took in her naked body, her curves, her taut flesh, something awakened in him. He told himself that it was pity, but he knew better. He was aroused by her—something he didn't understand. Why was his body suddenly reacting to adult women?

Charles watched as she became aware of him, and he could see that she was alarmed. When she opened her mouth to scream, Charles darted toward her to muffle her cry. His weight on the bed jostled a cowbell rigged to the headboard. He bent down to Elaina and placed his cheek on hers.

"Don't scream," he whispered. "It's me, Charles, from the bus." He sat up and revealed the cryptic tattoo she had noticed during the bus ride. Certain that the bell had alerted the animals on the balcony, Charles stepped back and put his finger to his lips.

"The bell," Kristoff yelled from the balcony. "Donato, go see what's got my bitch into a fever."

Donato whistled his way down the hall and burst through the door. He gazed down at Elaina's nude form as he walked toward her, fondling himself. With his dirty fingers, he grabbed a fist full of her hair and forced her head into his crotch.

The drunken Italian staggered from side to side as he thrust his pelvis into her face. "We wagered whose eyes and hair your bastard will have when it's born," he said with a laugh. "If it makes it long enough to be born, anyway."

Elaina scowled at him. "If my bastard has your eyes," she said before spitting on him, "I'll be sure to tell it how much I enjoyed watching its father die."

"Whore—" His words cut off as he seemed to sense Charles's presence behind him. He jumped back and started to turn just as Charles's ax whistled through the air and plunged into his neck. The blade failed to decapitate Donato, but it crushed his spine. Blood spewed as he collapsed onto the floor next to the bed. Elaina smiled as he expired just inches from her face.

Charles ransacked Donato's pockets, collecting a buck knife that he used to cut away Elaina's restraints. She jumped to her feet, her gaze never leaving Donato's body as it twitched before becoming motionless again.

"He's not dead yet," she insisted. "Give me the knife."

"He's in hell by now," he whispered.

He understood her need to give into the rage, but it was another thing to trust her with the knife. When he flung a handful of her clothing at her, she glared at him but complied, then held out her hand. Charles looked at her for an extra few seconds, reached into his satchel, and handed her a lead pipe. She grabbed it and followed Charles out of the room.

Kristoff and his men were still amusing themselves with the Spaniard. The mob was enjoying tormenting him, and had begun using found objects to beat him.

One of the men tied a scrap of cloth around a thick piece of wood he had been using to beat the Spaniard. "Watch this," he said as he snatched the moonshine Donato had mixed and poured a healthy amount into his mouth. With his cheeks full, he held the homemade torch in the flame of one of the larger torches until it caught fire. He bent down toward the Spaniard and, holding the smaller torch a foot away from the man's face, he spewed the liquid through the fire.

The Spaniard's head was engulfed. The marauders howled as the Spaniard fell to the balcony floor and tried to smother his flaming head. By the time he extinguished the fire, patches of red, burned flesh on his scalp were visible even from where Charles and Elaina stood watching.

Seeing Kristoff and the Irishman reveling in the Spaniard's suffering flooded Charles with a simultaneous rush of anxiety and fury. He knew they would soon discard the Spaniard over the balcony like the others.

Kristoff paused. "Where's Donato?" He looked around. "One of you get him off that bitch and bring him here."

One of the men pulled himself away from the Spaniard, took a long drink from the communal bottle, and lurched off in the direction of the bedroom.

Elaina started past Charles toward the balcony door, but Charles yanked her back. He pressed his index finger up against his lips. The Spaniard's gaze met Charles once again, and a mutual smile was exchanged. Charles gripped Elaina's wrist. He could tell the Spaniard had recognized him.

"Be ready to fight our way out of here," Charles warned her.

"*Tengo un secreto!*" the Spaniard exclaimed. "I have secret!"

His translated outburst commanded the attention of the entire group. The fire-breather took another drink to burn the Spaniard again, but was fatally interrupted when Kristoff rose from his seat and delivered a powerful kick that launched the overeager fire-breather off the balcony. He screamed, grabbing at the open air around him, until his body crashed onto the broken remains of the others. Everyone else inched away from the edges of the balcony.

"Kristoff! Kristoff! Kristoff!" came the faint chanting from the men circled around the pile of death on the ground below.

"Why waste drink to burn someone?" Kristoff posited. "Fire needs no accomplice." As he returned to his seat, one of the men retrieved the container of moonshine from the balcony floor and handed it to Kristoff. He snatched it and drank it down, wiping the streams of liquid that escaped out the sides of his mouth with the back of his wrist. "Tell us your secret," he said to the Spaniard. "Then we'll teach you how to fly."

The tortured Spaniard's smile was delayed as he accepted his end would soon come. His speech was slurred, either from pain or rotgut whiskey, or a combination of both, and his head waved from side to side. His eyes were half-closed. Wincing, he rose from the floor and pressed his two index fingers together against his lips.

"Shhhhhhhh, I have secret to speak." He giggled in broken English. Stealing one last look in Charles's direction.

Charles tightened his grip on his ax and Elaina's wrist.

The Spaniard swung his other arm around the room, passing over Charles's direction until settling on Kristoff. "All you rape pretty girl in bedroom!" he shouted. "All you!" He then returned his attention to Kristoff, saluting and breaking into insane laughter. "She call El Presidente[25] Kristoff *Pene Tim.*"[26]

Kristoff's heavy brow lowered. He looked around to his men ignorant to what the last two words meant. "What the fuck is he say—" the Spaniard interrupted.

"She say El Presidente has the *smallest* dick she has ever seen. *Pene Pequeño*[27]. Is it in yet, El Presidente? She ask. Me feel nothing, she say!"

Dumbfounded by the Spaniard's reckless taunt, the marauders on the balcony looked around and shuffled as far away from their king as possible. Kristoff's initial shock gave way to blind rage. He leapt to his feet to maim the Spaniard, his face scarlet and contorted.

As his tormenter descended upon him, the Spaniard yelled, "*La paz es la asimilación en el encubrimiento! Vaya! Vaya ahora, Yäbälay!*"[28]

---

[25] President

[26] Tiny Tim

[27] Tiny penis

[28] "Peace is assimilation in disguise! Go! Go now, *Yäbälay!*"

The grinning man grabbed two handfuls of Kristoff and threw himself from the balcony, pulling the king over with him.

Intoxicated and stunned by the Spaniard's trick, Kristoff's men watched with mouths agape as the two men, embracing like lovers, plunged to their death. While the men peered silently over the balcony, Charles and Elaina slid through the open living room and out the door, undetected and unscathed.

As they descended the stairs, Charles couldn't help but feel intense joy. His rapist, Kristoff the King of K-City, was a thing of the past.

Better yet, he had a prize in tow.

Chapter 14

CHARLES SAT IN A LOPSIDED chair by the door and tried to stay awake. Lack of sleep left him half-delirious, but he knew that even his tucked-away shelter far from K-City's center offered no guarantee of safety.

Elaina slept on the dirty mattress, hugging her knees to her chest. He watched her breasts rise and fall with each breath. Her braided hair hung over one shoulder, adding a childlike air to the moment.

A crash and clatter broke the peace, and Elaina bolted awake. A metal canister had come through the hideout's front wall, ricocheted off the opposite wall, and rolled to the middle of the floor.

"Cover your ears!" Charles yelled.

A shock wave rocked the building. Elaina fell. The table of weapons toppled. Charles crouched close to the floor and covered his head. Another explosion followed, and half of the ceiling collapsed as the front wall crumbled.

Five men in full riot gear charged into the room, surrounding Charles and Elaina. Within seconds, the invaders had cuffed their hands and covered their heads with black hoods.

Their ears still ringing, they were pulled to their feet and shoved into a large vehicle. The van shook under the weight of the correctional officers who boarded behind them. Charles and Elaina were shoved onto metal benches that lined the walls of the vehicle and were shackled to a metal bar in front of them.

Once the doors slammed shut, someone said, "Hit 'em' both just like the warden ordered."

Darts pierced Charles's skin at the back of his hand, followed by a debilitating electrical current. He felt his blood boil, a heat made worse by the sound of the men's sadistic laughter.

~~~

Charles woke, shivering and shackled to a metal chair in the prisoner processing room. Elaina slumped next to him. Warden Johnston crouched down before the two.

"I'm beginning to think you don't understand the gravity of your situation," he said. "I have eyes and ears all over this facility, and K-City. Nothing happens here or there without my knowledge or permission. The report I received about your activities last night is very displeasing. Now, any reasonable person would expect a man to desire revenge after having his manhood ripped away from him as Kristoff did to you." The warden put his hand on Charles's knee and smiled in exaggerated sympathy. Then his face darkened. "But Kristoff was *my* savage, and I wouldn't have cared if he had raped and murdered your entire bloodline. No one does anything in this city unless I authorize it." He smacked Charles across the face with a hand gloved in black leather. "And I do *not* recall giving anyone authorization to lay a hand on him." The warden smacked him again, turning Charles's face a lurid red. "Did I? Seems to me your first lesson about life in my city wasn't processed very well. Seems to me another lesson is required."

Charles remained silent as the warden stood and crossed the room to a collection of batons, chains, brass knuckles, and whips displayed on a metal table. He caressed the weapons one by one.

"I didn't kill your savage," Charles said. "I would have, but someone beat me to it. If it had been me, you would've woken to his head mounted on a stake outside your headquarters."

The warden selected a spiked rod from the table and nodded at the sergeant guarding Charles. The sergeant took out his keys and removed all of Charles's restraints except the handcuffs.

"You're turning out to be even more trouble than I anticipated," the warden said. He twirled the weapon, turned, and placed it back on the table.

Charles took the opportunity to elbow the sergeant in the throat. The sergeant doubled over, and Charles delivered a snapping kick to the side of the sergeant's knee crippling him, one knee on the floor. Charles grabbed two handfuls of the toppled sergeant's greasy hair and drove his knee with enough force to push the bridge of the sergeant's nose into his frontal lobe.

A swarm of officers tackled Charles and started hitting him. The sergeant lay motionless on the floor.

"Sarge!" A junior officer broke away from the beating and rushed to the side of his colleague. "He fucking killed him!" the officer yelled out.

This ignited a blood lust from the remaining correctional officers, who took to beating Charles with a rejuvenated flurry of fists, boots, Taser wands, and nightsticks. The first to lose wind retreated from the beating to drag the dead sergeant away from the scene while the others continued to beat Charles until they were breathing hard and sweating.

Charles remained in the fetal position for several minutes before he was able to unfold himself. Shaking on the floor and in a state of delirious agony, he lay spread-eagle with his back against the cold floor and his eyes focused on the ceiling, a bright smile shining towards the heavens.

"I didn't mean to kill him," Charles mumbled through split lips. "That was just plain good luck."

A quiet came over the men. Charles rolled over onto his side and grinned at the warden. Johnston's face was blood red with rage.

"In the twenty-one years I've been warden of this prison," the warden said, his voice strung with tension, "I've *never* lost a correctional officer. In the last forty-eight hours, you've killed two people you didn't have authority to. You remind me of the misguided Ugandan Idi Amin Dada. He once curled up here in the middle of my floor, just like you. He, just like you, thought he could challenge my authority. So I had him extracted from K-City just like you were this morning. I ordered my men to strip him naked and suspend him by the wrists outside the prison walls, twenty feet above the ground, and that's where I left him." A smile of pride crossed the warden's face. "It took a few hours under the sun before the insects started in on his sweaty body. Then the buzzards came. He agonized for days before he died."

The warden went on to brag about his management of Arnfinn Nesset, the most prolific serial killer in Scandinavian history. His crimes remained unsolved until his desire for recognition inspired him to feed clues about his murderous habits to reporters. An ego that large didn't fit on the warden's island.

The warden rolled his eyes. "To give him the audience he desired so badly, I placed him in one of the few solitary confinement rooms we have in our command center. We strapped him to an apparatus that released single drops of water onto his forehead, over and over again. Drip, drip, drip. A drop every seven seconds without fail. We put him under twenty-four-hour surveillance cameras and transmitted the signal to a large television screen with audio so K-City could witness his final performance." The warden was smiling, lost in reverie. "Initially he laughed at our—oh, what did he call it?—yes, our, 'weak attempt to teach him a lesson.' The water continued, little drop after little drop. Soon the laughter stopped. Then exhaustion set in after he made so many futile attempts to free himself from his restraints. His exhaustion was replaced by rants, curses, and the screams of a madman, all from tiny little drops of nature's most precious resource. It took twenty-six hours to break him. The next morning, when we released him back into K-City, his mind was so gone that he died of dehydration three days later, too impaired to remember to drink." The warden chuckled.

Charles rolled onto his back and stared at the ceiling lights. He felt vulnerable, lying open to the heavens. He would accept his torture, but how could he protect Elaina?

"These are kiddie games compared to what I have planned for you."

The warden gestured to the guard nearest Elaina. He lifted her from her chair. Her face remained expressionless. She avoided eye contact with Charles. Another guard stepped to her side and awaited orders.

"Take her to the showers and get her cleaned up. You have thirty minutes to do what you want with her. Two of you will remain with me to tend to this prisoner."

"I'll stay, sir," a younger, keen officer volunteered.

"Hamilton has the least seniority," another officer declared. "He should keep Jordy company."

The singled-out officer stepped away from Elaina and said nothing. The others pushed Elaina into the next room and shut the door. Her protests carried through the walls.

"What are you doing? No! Stop it!" Elaina shouted. More screams and the sounds of clothes tearing and beating came from the room.

"Leave something for us!" Officer Hamilton shouted. He elbowed Officer Jordy, who stepped out of Hamilton's reach.

"What the fuck, Jordy? You like little kids like this sick fuck right here?" Hamilton kicked Charles in the chest.

"Or is it that you don't approve of my decision regarding that female inmate?" the warden asked.

"It's not my place to question, sir," Jordy said. "My place is to follow orders."

In the other room, Elaina screamed.

Charles sighed. "I'm going to enjoy killing all of you."

Hamilton pulled a wand from his belt and shocked Charles until he lost consciousness.

Chapter 15

THE FOLLOWING MORNING, SIX HEAVILY armed guards sandwiched Charles and Elaina on a small prison bus. Elaina hadn't said a word during the day-long travel, and Charles left her to her thoughts. Unlike the blackened glass on the bus that had brought them into K-City, the windows on this bus were clear. The freedom to watch dust, rock, and sky seemed an ominous gift.

Charles had accepted long ago that he was something of a control freak. He saw it as a strength, not a weakness. He had made a career, despite its deprave nature, out of being sure of his every step, knowing how to react to each moment. But now he rued how he couldn't be sure of anything, and had no idea about what fate awaited him. His stomach churned, not from hunger, but from regret. He had lost control, something he hadn't allowed to happen since he was a child.

He ground his teeth in frustration. How could he, the mastermind behind the most powerful criminal organization in the world, not know whether he would survive the next few days? He had mastered how to control and manipulate masses of people for his benefit. He had gone to great lengths to secure insurance policies and plan contingencies to optimize his likelihood of survival. He had orchestrated the kidnapping of the governor's son to ensure his safety. All the stakeholders responsible for his capture and prosecution were aware that if anything happened to him, the boy would suffer the consequences of his wrath.

But none of his planning and strategizing seemed to have the slightest impact on what was happening to him. For the first time in his life, he had lost control of the situation.

Charles looked into his lap, roiling with anger. Had Duenno betrayed him? Or maybe the governor had given up hope and written off his son as dead. As smart as Charles had become, he couldn't make sense of his situation. All he knew in this moment while speeding through the outback on this bus was that his destiny would be determined once they arrived at wherever they were headed.

"Over there, see that tree?" Officer Jordy said. "Pull up to it." New sergeant stripes gleamed bright and stiff on the sleeve of his uniform. "If we hustle, we can get back before lunch."

Will Elaina and I be dead by then? Charles wondered. *Dead before lunch?*

The remaining five officers stood ready to go through the cage door that separated them from the prisoners. Jordy held up his hand for them to pause. He opened the control panel in the dashboard of the bus, set the dial to maximum, and flipped the switch that sent electric shocks to Charles and

Elaina, who had been docile and quiet the entire ride. Their bodies stiffened and shuddered with the high voltage.

The group of officers looked back at their sergeant, but said nothing.

"Am I the only one who remembers how easily he killed Sergeant Williams?" Jordy said. "Would any of you like to take the chance of having the warden call your family with some bullshit story of how you had an accident and fell down the tower steps?"

As the men shrugged in agreement, he continued to hold the switch another moment before flipping it off. The two prisoners slumped over in the back.

"That'll soften them up." Jordy nodded, and the other officers unlocked the door and went in. Sergeant Jordy pressed the button that unlocked the shackles that kept them chained to the floor of the bus. "Hurry up," he ordered.

Four officers each grabbed an arm while the last one remained behind them to cover the rear. The prisoners were too weak to walk on their own. The guards dragged both prisoners through the aisle of the bus, out the door, and onto the smoldering ground of Katingal's outback. The sergeant exited carrying a twelve-gauge shotgun and a black duffle bag whose contents clanked with each step.

Officer Hamilton reached for keys on his belt that would unlock the prisoners' wrist-, waist-, and ankle-shackles. As he approached Charles's slumped figure from behind, he noticed that Charles was watching him from the corner of his eye. Hamilton stopped dead in his tracks.

"He's up to something!" he shouted in a panic.

Two officers stepped in instantly to restrain Charles and Elaina, taking them both facedown to the ground.

"What's the problem?" Sergeant Jordy questioned, his shotgun pointed at Charles.

"He was playing possum, Jordy—I mean, Sarge," Hamilton said, his broad face quivering. "I saw him eyeing my keys. He was going to make a move."

"Make a move? We're armed to the teeth. How could he make a move?" The sergeant shook his head at Hamilton. "You're a real pussy, Hamilton. Now, remove their chains."

"Yes, sir."

Hamilton approached Elaina, still face down on the ground, to unlock her shackles first. He placed his knee into her back and took his time, making sure his hands grazed every part of her body.

"He's right. You are a pussy." Elaina shouted.

The other officers began to laugh.

"Aww, what's the matter, Hamilton?" one of them said. "You still disappointed you didn't get your turn?" He minced around, gyrating his pelvis at the large man.

"Fuck you and your seniority," Hamilton whined before leaving Elaina and moving on to unlock Charles. "I didn't want your sloppy seconds, anyway. No telling what diseases I might've picked up."

"On your feet, both of you," the sergeant ordered. "Prison uniforms off."

"The next man who touches me dies." Elaina looked up, her expression bitter.

The sergeant blasted a load of pellets over their heads from his shotgun. Both inmates crouched and covered their ears.

"Shut your mouth," he barked. "No one here wants your diseased twat. Uniforms off." He kept his gun pointed at them.

Charles underwent the difficult process of removing his clothes, his body screaming in pain at every movement. Elaina followed suit until they both stood in front of the officers in their underclothes.

The sergeant gestured with the shotgun. "See that big tree over there? Let's go."

With Charles and Elaina staggering over the hot, uneven terrain in their bare feet, the group made its way to the tree the sergeant had indicated. In the shade, the sergeant placed his shotgun on the ground while the other officers maintained their aim. From his duffle bag, he dumped out a length of rope, some twelve-inch camping spikes, two hammers, and a large container with a twist-off cap.

"Lay on your backs," the sergeant ordered.

Though the hot, uneven ground burned their exposed skin, they complied.

"Get the rope and tie their hands and feet how the warden instructed," the sergeant ordered.

While the other officers advanced with their weapons fixed on the two prisoners, poised to shoot, two of them holstered their weapons, forced the prisoners to spread their arms out, and tied them up. After knotting the rope around the inmate's ankles and leaving two feet of slack, they tied the rest to a spike, which they drove into the ground until the head disappeared into the red earth. They then did the same to their wrists.

Charles saw buzzards already circling overhead, dark shadows against the brilliant blue sky.

The sergeant tossed the large bottle at one of the officers. "Spread half the bottle on each prisoner," he commanded. "The warden wants every inch of skin covered." He walked around Charles and knelt at each spike. He pulled at the center of the ropes, testing their tension.

Despite the glare of the unforgiving sun, Charles saw how eager Officer Hamilton was to apply the lotion to Elaina's exposed skin.

"Look at Hamilton getting off rubbing on the Brazilian," one of the others teased.

"Please, Sergeant," Elaina said. "Don't leave me here."

"Open your mouth," the sergeant instructed. He barked at his officers, and one of them tossed him a twenty-ounce bottle of water. He twisted off the cap and poured water into her mouth until it was full. She swallowed and opened her mouth for another. Charles watched the sergeant until he noticed. He stood, stepped over Elaina, and crouched down next to Charles's head and wiggled the bottle.

"I can't free you," he explained, gesturing with the bottle. "But if you tell me where the governor's son is, I can promise you a quick death instead of the death you'll face from whatever's out here in the wasteland."

"Either way I'll be dead," Charles said. "So what the fuck do I care if the little boy dies from a bullet to the head or my comrades auction him off to be ass-raped until he's old enough to realize he'd rather slit his own wrists than have another train of men push his colon into his throat?"

The sergeant raised the water bottle to his own mouth, drank the rest of its contents, and belched. "And here, for a moment, I toyed with the idea of treating you like a human. But you've proven unworthy. So, fuck you, too. Enjoy the shade while it lasts. Eventually the earth will rotate out of your favor, and the sun will cook you. With the evening comes the chill. By then, you'll pray the cold finishes you. Hypothermia is a much better death than dehydration or heatstroke."

"Sarge, what about their uniforms and shackles?" Officer Hamilton asked, glancing back for one more look at Elaina.

The dirty clothes were tangled up with the handcuffs, chains, and shackles in a pile.

"Leave them here in case they get cold." The sergeant chuckled as he walked away. The rest fell in line.

When Charles twisted his neck to look, the correctional officers were already climbing into the small prison bus. They were chatting among themselves, obviously pleased with the job well done. None of them looked back.

Chapter 16

As soon as the bus was out of sight, Elaina and Charles started testing their restraints. Minutes became hours, and the struggle left them exhausted, panicked, and raw from rubbing against the coarse ropes. Overhead, the buzzards wheeled patiently.

"I'd actually thought myself lucky when you rescued me from Kristoff's bedroom," Elaina said, her voice thick with angry tears. "Now I'm not so sure."

"I can understand your doubt," Charles said, "but it's still a bit early to give up hope."

"Hope?" she spat. "Hope has no place here!"

"Those buzzards above will not feast on me," Charles snapped, squinting into the sky. "Not today, not tomorrow, not ever." He tried again to tug his wrist sideways through the rope.

"Who the fuck do you think you are, huh? God?"

"Good, go ahead," Charles replied in a simpering voice. "Maybe a little tantrum will make the pampered princess feel better."

"Fuck you!"

"Nobody is coming to save us," Charles said. "Get used to the idea. We have to save ourselves."

"Listen here, pedophile," Elaina said. "There's no 'we' here. You deserved what Kristoff did to you. All the families you destroyed? I pray you die before me so I can get some satisfaction before I leave this world." She turned her head away and shut her eyes.

"Maybe you were pardoned and I somehow missed it," Charles fired back. "You think looking away from me will wash away the blood on your hands? The memories we've created can't be erased. We've both etched our place in history." Charles sneered, satisfied that he had undone her. Quickly he returned to trying to free himself.

"Shut up!" she screamed, shaking her head from side to side as if trying to rid herself of her memories.

A long period of silence ensued. Then finally, she spoke.

"I can admit I harbor no remorse for what I did to my husband and his whore," she said in a voice just above a whisper. "But what I did to that child inside of her was unforgiveable, and for that, I've reserved my place in hell. I can admit my wrongdoings, but what about you? You're a hollow vessel. Even when faced with imminent death, you refuse to honor your countless victims. You hold on just to spite the warden or the governor. It's like a game to you, the abomination you've created."

Charles leaned his head back, exposing his throat to the sky. "We all have choices to make when standing at life's crossroads," he said in a soft tone. "Choices that determine whether the next stage of our lives will be tormented or blessed. I choose the blessings." He cocked his head to one side. "Then we have you. It would have been much easier for me to use my hands to cut your throat rather than to muffle your scream in Kristoff's lair. Had I not chosen the latter, I wouldn't have had this very distinct pleasure of hearing a vapid trophy wife judge me when it wasn't so long ago that she herself had thrown such a murderous tantrum when her storybook marriage turned out to be fiction."

Elaina narrowed her eyes and said nothing.

For the next few sun-soaked hours, they didn't speak. The heat sapped their energy, and by nightfall, they took momentary solace in the relief from the sun. But just as the sergeant had warned, with the moon and stars also came frigid temperatures. Within minutes, they were shivering as hypothermia encroached.

"I'm afraid, Charles," Elaina confessed as she broke another lengthy silence. "I don't want to die. Not like this." When Charles didn't respond, she hollered, "Say something!"

"What do you want me to say?" he murmured, still gazing up at the sky. "That our death will be quick and painless? That death will be easy? Or that we should discuss all our missteps and pray for forgiveness? It would all be for nothing." He glanced over and saw her tremors and heard her sob.

A few moments later, she looked back over at Charles. "I'm sorry for what I said earlier."

"No, you're not," he said. "Don't insult me with your lies."

"I just don't understand it," she said. "We both know this is the end. I can't bring back the people I murdered, but you can. You can bring back the children you've enslaved. You can bring peace to those parents and make their families whole again. You still have that power."

"Why would I help tear down what will be mine again?" Charles asked.

"What?" she shrieked. "Have you gone mad? There's no escape. Only penance, and through that, forgiveness. Charles, pray with me, confess your sins, and beg that Eloah's grace is bestowed upon you and saves your soul."

"Fuck Eloah!" he screamed to the heavens. "Do you hear me up there, you bitch? Fuck you!" Then he turned his head and glared at Elaina. "You go ahead and waste away the final moments of your life, if you desire. The last chapter of my life will not be written here."

The night was crisp and cold with a mass of shining stars twinkling overhead. Charles continued to struggle with his restraints with as much tenacity as he could muster until exhaustion took hold of him and he lost consciousness.

~~~

A vehicle drove up and stopped in front of them, the squeaking brakes waking Charles. The piercing white headlights forced his eyes away from the car. He looked over at Elaina, who was shaking in her sleep.

Officer Hamilton emerged from the vehicle and headed toward her. He bent over her and yanked down her underwear.

"Wake up," he ordered.

Elaina opened her eyes and looked at the officer standing over her.

"What a failure," he said. "You were placed out here to get information, not sleep."

Charles saw horror flood her face as the officer spilled her secret. He put his hand into her underwear and closed his eyes before opening them and looking at Charles.

"So now you know, Inmate Gravo," he announced, looking as though he was pleased to be bringing such news to Charles. "Her beating and rape was staged so they could plant a wire in her bra." Hamilton slid his hand around her breast and moaned before he turned the strap around to show Charles the small black transmitting device stitched into the elastic. "It was a setup, and she screwed it up," he said as Elaina began to sob again. "They promised her privileges if she could extract any information out of you regarding the governor's son. She would've had her own cell, bed, and three square meals as the warden's personal trustee." He stood and dusted off his hands. "What a shame." He sneered as he reached into his pocket and retrieved a set of keys.

"Please, I didn't have enough time," Elaina begged as she began to cry again. "I can't go back there. You know what happened to me before, Charles."

He could tell that it was more than fear, that she felt shame for having betrayed him. For the first time, he felt himself soften toward her.

"Blah, blah, blah. I couldn't care less." Hamilton chuckled. "All I'm concerned about right now is getting between those nice thighs of yours."

"Please don't do this," she pleaded as he used his knife to saw at the ropes wrapped around her ankles. "I'll do anything. Just don't send me back to K-City. Please!"

"I *bet* you'll do anything," the officer said, smiling. "I don't doubt that for a moment."

The rope's tension gave way, and he removed the knotted rope that remained around her ankles. She sighed, her body awash with relief. She brought her legs up for circulation while he put the knife back into his utility belt. He leaned forward and forced open Elaina's trembling legs, rubbing them.

"Take a good look, pedophile," the officer taunted, glancing over at Charles as his hand moved between Elaina's legs. "You're not going to want to miss this."

Hamilton unbuttoned his pants with his free hand. His hips were deep between Elaina's bare thighs as he pulled down his zipper.

Then, in one quick movement, she arched her back to launch her legs at the officer's throat. Her powerful thighs clamped around the base of his neck while she intertwined her ankles to secure her grip. The officer grabbed at her thighs, pulling at them, but her grip was too strong. As she pulled harder at the ropes still tied to her wrists, Elaina squeezed with every ounce of effort she had left in her.

"Take a good look? Isn't that what you said, Officer Hamilton?" Elaina grunted as the officer began to flounder in a panic. "I told you. I'd kill the next man who touched me, didn't I?"

Charles watched as Hamilton's eyes bulged as if they would burst from his face, and his mouth hung open. Charles could see his tongue thrusting from inside as he made harsh gagging noises, trying to suck in air.

Elaina shook her body and whipped the officer onto his side and held him there until he went limp. Even then, she maintained the grip until she knew unequivocally he was dead.

After she savored the victory for a moment, she rolled backwards towards the spiked ropes that led to her hands. She positioned herself in between them, crouching into a squatted position. Elaina swayed back and forth until the ground around one of them gave way. Once liberated, she grabbed the buck knife from the dead man and cut herself free.

Charles whistled in appreciation. "Very nicely done. I'm impressed."

She ignored him as she retrieved her underwear and her prison uniform and dressed. Then she knelt at his left wrist with the buck knife, and hesitated.

"You do understand, right? You understand that I was trying to get you to talk about the governor out of survival, not malice?"

He just stared at her.

She closed the knife and leaned closer. "I need to know that you understand," she urged. "I won't cut you free just to have to fight you, too. I'm not going back. If I let you go, you and I work together. Agreed?"

Charles examined her eyes for any trace of insincerity, and nodded in the affirmative. She stared right back into his eyes to decipher any deceit, then sawed away at the ropes. As soon as he was loose, he hurried to dress and looked over at the van.

"Toss me the keys," he instructed. "We'll drive it as far as the gas in the tank will take us, then walk the rest of the way there. It'll give us a good head start."

"There?" Elaina asked as she went to retrieve the keys. "You sound like you know where we're headed."

"Darwin. There's a port there. Once we get there, we're just a boat ride away from leaving this continent."

Elaina snatched the keys off the man's belt, then gave him a swift kick in the face before heading toward the van. When Charles held out his hand, she cocked her head at him.

"Why do I have to give you the keys?" she asked.

"That's rich," Charles said before letting out a small chuckle. "You don't trust me?" He sighed. "Fine. You drive and I'll navigate. When you get tired, we'll switch."

"Okay," Elaina said as they walked together toward the vehicle. She looked at the keys. Attached to them was a plastic fob bearing a few symbols. She pressed one of the buttons, and the front headlights lit up and the van unlocked.

She climbed into the driver's seat and pulled on her seat belt. An automated voice notified her that she had thirty seconds to enter the access code before the self-destruct sequence was initiated.

"Fuck!" Charles hissed. "Why does everything have to be so goddamn hard?"

He searched the lifeless guard for codes while Elaina rummaged through the compartments of the vehicle.

The fifteen-second warning soon delivered.

"Goddammit!" Charles shouted as he ripped at Hamilton's clothes.

Elaina glanced around once more and grabbed an armful of loose supplies from the van. Then she dashed toward the tree after Charles. Under cover of the tree, they peered back at the van, not sure what to expect.

There was a harsh shudder, and a loud pop under the hood, followed by black smoke. The two of them ducked back behind the tree to brace for a big explosion, but none followed.

Once he was reasonably sure it was safe, Charles eased back toward the van, found a flashlight, and popped the hood of the smoking vehicle.

"What are you doing?" Elaina called, coming out from behind the tree.

Charles didn't answer, but eased his hand under the hood to open the safety latch. When he lifted the hood, a fat, black cloud of smoke billowed out. Charles fanned at the smoke and squinted to see through the beam of the flashlight into the engine. When the smoke cleared, he saw a small box attached to the engine block of the van. All the wires were melted, and there was a fist-sized hole in the side of the engine block.

"Can you fix it?" she asked hopefully.

"Hell no." He slammed the hood down. "We're not going anywhere in that van. The engine's useless."

He returned to where Elaina was rummaging through the pockets of the dead officer.

"You couldn't have just choked him until he passed out?" he asked angrily. "You had to kill him? We could have forced him to give us the code first. Did you ever think of that?"

She turned to glare up at him. "Right, that's what I should've been thinking about seconds after he was about to shove his cock in me. I should've known the van was booby trapped. Should've known we'd need a fucking code." She paused and looked him in the eye. "Tell me, what were you thinking about just before Kristoff shoved his cock in your ass?"

Charles tightened his lips and turned away.

"That's what I thought," Elaina said.

~~~

With only one half-full, twenty-ounce bottle of water, they walked through the night and into the next morning, taking very few breaks. They were energized by their freedom and anxious to place as much distance between them and the slain officer as possible.

As the sun rose in the sky, Charles removed his prison shirt and used it to create shade over his head. Elaina tied her hair into a thick bun. She was lagging and unable to maintain Charles's brisk pace. He looked back at her and sighed. She spent a lot of energy in killing Hamilton.

"Twenty minutes of rest, and then we start again" he offered.

He took advantage of their respite to survey the landscape and examine the position of the sun. Bent down on one knee, Charles drew a crude map of the continent in the ground with his finger, placing an "X" in the middle. Then he placed another "X" at the northwest corner. With his index and middle finger, in even strides, he walked his two fingers from the first marking to the second.

Elaina came over to inspect what he was doing, and collapsed into the sand. She was sweating profusely.

"I don't mean to tell you how to live your life," he said. "But if you wrap your head with your shirt, it'll help keep your body temperature down."

"I'm fine with my shirt on," she snapped as she got up on her knees to view the map.

Charles shrugged and continued to perform his improvised mapping.

"If you're so concerned, maybe we should be searching for food and water," she argued. "From the looks of your map, this port city called Darwin has to be hundreds of miles away—"

"A thousand miles."

Her weary face fell.

"Give or take," Charles added.

"We're going to die out here!" she said, her voice thick with panic.

"We're not going to die," he said with unnatural calm. "We've put a good distance between us and K-City and like the warden boasted, they're not going to come looking for us. We keep moving, find water, food, and maybe some shelter. Come on. Let's go." He didn't wait for her to respond but started walking.

"You can't be serious!" she screamed. "We just sat down!"

He didn't answer. With every stride, he moved farther away from her. She yelled, but he kept on. After another few seconds, she launched herself up off the ground and ran after him.

When he heard the pounding of her boots, Charles looked back over his shoulder. She eventually closed the gap between them, but now she was out of breath, coated in a new layer of sweat, and her skin was ashen.

He stopped in his tracks, turned, and shoved a finger in her face. "Don't ever run like that again unless you actually want to die," he declared. "If I'm in sight, you're still fine. A few seconds of running, and look at how much you're sweating. That's water you can't afford to lose."

"Okay, but let's get one thing straight," she said in the sternest voice she could gather. "You are not my father." She past him, walking with purpose and looking strong despite her obvious fatigue.

"If it won't kill you, maybe just say thank you," Charles said, unable to restrain himself from smirking.

Elaina smiled but didn't let him see it. "Since you know everything, I've been meaning to ask you how is it you're able to navigate direction by the sun, speak different languages, and talk of this place as if you were born here instead of another country thousands of miles away—"

"A little less than seven thousand miles," he told her.

"You see, there it is again. You're full of random knowledge that most people wouldn't know."

Charles kept his face forward and changed the subject. "Last time I checked, you also spoke more than one language. What I know and how I know it isn't your concern. What is important is that, first, we keep moving—not running—north by northwest. Second, our priority is water and then food. We can survive three weeks without food, but it will only take three days for us to die of thirst." He paused to reconsider. "Then again, out here, we might last two and a half days at best."

Charles glanced at Elaina and saw that her expression was a mixture of awe and confusion. He also noticed that a few beads of perspiration had accumulated on her upper lip, which ignited another basic thirst in him.

Elaina saw him looking at her, took off her shirt, and wrapped it around her matted brown hair. Charles didn't mind the myriad bruises and bite marks covering Elaina's torso. He let a flash of pity slide across his face.

Elaina caught it and shot him a piercing look. "They look worse than they are, so keep your pity and get us to Darwin, I want off this continent."

Chapter 17

OR TWO DAYS, ELAINA KEPT up Charles's pace, both occasionally stumbling from exhaustion. Despite Charles's optimism and advanced intellect, they hadn't found a single drop of water. The bottle they had taken from the prison van was empty.

During their morning push, Charles studied Elaina's body. Her dead stare, cracked lips, and silence told him that she was already far into dehydration. Her face was ruby red from sun blisters. He knew that neither of them would last much longer.

A moment later, Elaina began to stray sideways. Charles turned back to help her, but it was too late. She fell to the hot ground, the fall snapping her back into consciousness just as her face blasted into the hot sand and dirt. Blood trickled from her bottom lip.

Charles held out a hand to help her up. Instinctively she reached for it until she caught herself and smacked his hand away. Through stubborn determination, she struggled to her feet, only to teeter over again. Charles attempted to help her again, but she resisted. He ignored her, plucking her up by her arm. She was burning up. He placed his fingers on her carotid artery to check her pulse.

"I said I'm fine," she slurred.

"Do you even remember passing out the second time?" Charles asked.

"What?" she said just before she vomited.

"Exactly," he said as his eyes filled with worry.

"Don't look at me like that!" she shouted.

"Like what?" *Like I'm worried about you?* He said to himself.

"Like . . . like I'm weak. Let's go. Let's just go."

"Okay by me," he said with a shrug.

As they trudged onward, he found himself again considering the thought that had flitted through his mind. Was he really worried about her? He couldn't conjure up an answer, and again he felt the inner shiver that came with the realization that, once more, events in his life were beyond his control. Even his own feelings were betraying him.

He shook his head. He was too hot and tired and thirsty to work out an answer.

Charles had hoped that they could go one more day without water, but Elaina's transition into delirium meant that they wouldn't make it. She was shivering, and Charles wouldn't be able to ignore his own dehydration and exhaustion much longer. His perpetual sensation of lightheadedness made him anxious, because he knew he would soon collapse.

Less than a thousand steps later, he stopped and fell to his hands and knees. As his nose almost touched the ground, he waited for the sick feeling to pass and his vision to clear. Then he noticed something about the sand beneath him.

Elaina must have missed the fact that he had stopped marching, for she fell over him.

"Goddammit, watch your step!" Charles yelled.

"You're supposed to be walking," she shot back, "not lying on the ground."

Charles issued a harsh, scratchy bark of laughter.

"What's so goddamn funny?" she demanded.

Charles pushed her aside and touched the sand that Elaina hadn't disturbed in her fall. He crawled forward a few more feet, breathing heavily. His dry tongue felt like cardboard as it grazed his cracked, sunburned lips. He looked off to the left, and disappointment filled his chest. After crawling a few more feet forward, he brightened as he pointed.

"There's water nearby!" he cried.

"Where!" she demanded. "Where is it?"

"That way," Charles flailed a hand to the east of the direction they had been traveling.

Elaina forced herself back onto her feet and swerved a crooked path along the course he had indicated.

"Do you even know where you're going?" he roared.

"No, but we're not getting there any faster by standing here," she yelled back as she staggered. Then she corrected herself. "Or *lying* here."

Charles scanned the ground for a few more seconds to study the small animal tracks he had discovered. He knew that wherever there were animals, there had to be water. He rose to join Elaina.

"What the hell are you doing?" she shrieked, looking back at him. "Hurry up already!"

"Slow down," he said, his voice cracking. The dry ache in his throat had become a painful throb that beat in rapid time with his heart.

Charles returned his focus to the tracks in the sand and traced them as they faded and reappeared. Each step he took was heavy, deliberate, and focused. The days of traversing the rough, uneven terrain almost nonstop had caught up with him, and now with each step, he felt as though a spear was coming up through the bottoms of his feet.

Charles looked up at the sun to study its position, but his concentration was broken by Elaina crashing to the ground, followed by her groaning. As he scanned the area in front of him, he saw only open, parched desert.

He abandoned the animal tracks and dragged himself over to where he had last seen her. She had collapsed and slid down a shallow hill. He eased his way down to her, pulled her over onto her back, wiped the sand from her face, and checked her for a pulse. Her heart was racing.

"Don't die on me now," Charles demanded.

Somehow, he managed to pull her small frame up and heave her over his shoulder. He staggered toward a collection of brush. When he reached it, he positioned her body under what little shade it provided and checked her pulse again. She was dying.

Caught up in the urgency of Elaina's condition, Charles had neglected his own wellbeing. Now he realized that his own pulse was racing as his vision faded in and out of focus. He was angry at himself for carrying her, but for some reason he still didn't feel that he'd had a choice.

Every breath he took seared his lungs. He closed his eyes and felt the world swirling around him, then cracked them open and caught a glimpse of a small brown image darting by. As he turned his throbbing head around, the world moved in slow motion. He squinted but saw nothing. His heart fell. A mirage. He was hallucinating.

He saw no signs of life, just more brush and scattered trees in the distance marred by hot, wavy lines that thickened the air. He released his grip on Elaina and she slumped down, her face now back in the sand. She was suffocating. He scurried over on his hands and knees, pulling her upright and checking her pulse once again. Nothing. He laid his head against her chest, listening for a heartbeat and again hearing nothing.

He tried to scoop the sand from her mouth. He slipped two fingers into her mouth and pressed her dry, swollen tongue to the bottom of her pallet. Its texture was like carpet. He took his other hand and lifted her neck, pinched her nose, and blew air down her throat. Elaina's chest rose and fell with the air he forced into her lungs until she jerked and coughed. Her eyes watered, and when Charles saw her tears, he couldn't help himself. He bent over and licked her eye.

"What the hell are you doing?" Elaina demanded. She tried to hit him with a fist, but her arm just fell limp to the ground. She tried to shield her eyes from the sun, then went unconscious again.

Charles looked up just in time to see something move in the distance. He steadied himself, allowing his eyes to lock onto a floppy-eared animal fifty yards away. *A dingo*, he realized.

Charles pulled Officer Hamilton's knife out of his pocket. He gripped its handle with his left hand and corralled a length of shackle chain around his right. As he staggered toward the animal, it stood still and watched Charles draw near.

"What are you up to over there?" Charles whispered. "You protecting something?"

Twenty feet separated Charles and the animal when he stumbled over a rock and startled the dingo. It didn't flee. Instead, it pinned its ears back and bared its teeth at Charles.

Not wanting to give the beast the upper hand, Charles charged. "Rrraaaaaah!" he roared at the dingo, hoping to intimidate it.

But it held its ground, growling in return. Charles roared again, louder than before, and the dingo leapt at him. It was a wiry beast, and strong, and it toppled Charles to the ground. Charles lost his grip on the knife, and all he could do was turn his head and try to hold up his arms to keep the dingo's sharp teeth away from his throat.

As the snarling dingo tore into him, Charles slither away from the attack. His back stung and burned. The dingo had its jaws around his hand. When it let go to lunge at his throat, Charles threw his forearm up in defense. He screamed as it clenched tighter. He could feel its teeth penetrate the muscle and graze the bone inside. He punched, scratched, and clawed at the animal with his free hand. The beast must have bit into a nerve, because it suddenly felt as though his entire arm had been hit by a sledgehammer.

Bloodied and desperate, Charles thrashed on the ground until he realized he had a weapon. He grabbed a handful of the chain and pounded at the dingo's skull and neck. Each blow made the animal wince, but this was the animal's natural habitat which meant it was a seasoned survivor of the desert, and it was relentless. Charles knew if he gave up, he would die.

At last, he managed to smash the full weight of the chain down into the animal's skull. After an awful shriek, it let go and ran away sideways.

Charles watched it run a ways, turn back to look at him, and loop around to come in for another fight. Charles didn't wait. He stood and swung the chain over his head like a lasso. The chain made a whipping noise as it cut through the air, and Charles's weakened body swayed with each pass.

The dingo followed the movement of the chain for a moment, then lowered its head and charged at Charles again. Charles threw the chain in the air and slammed it into the dingo's body so violently that it fell over, whimpering. Charles hit it again, and this time it scrambled to its feet and ran.

Once it was at a safe distance, the dingo paused to look back at Charles. It trotted in two large circles as if it were contemplating another attack, but at last it decided to seek easier prey and trotted away. It looked back at him several times, but kept moving away from him. Soon it was out of sight.

Once he was sure the animal was gone, Charles fell to his knees and cradled his wounded forearm. The flesh was lacerated and punctured—skin, muscle, and blood mixed in with dirt and sand. His head and heart were pounding.

Charles removed the shirt still wrapped around his head, placed one corner of it in his mouth, and grabbed the other corner with his left hand, wrapping the shirt around his bleeding forearm and wrist in an effort to control the loss of blood. He pulled on the ends once more to tighten it, which caused another streak of pain to rise up the full length of his arm and to the back of his head. His pulse raged at the base of his skull.

He pulled himself off the ground and back on to his feet, almost collapsing, but he caught himself and managed to stay upright. Sweating heavily, he staggered over to where he had left Elaina, a constant pain throbbing through his arm with every step.

The sun's heat was oppressive on his uncovered head. His eyesight was failing him, the sky, ground, and all the shapes and colors around him beginning to blur. He knew that his forearm had saturated its wrap and was dripping onto the ground, leaving a trail that any wily person or animal could track.

Then he felt lightheadedness coupled with a strange tingling sensation that ran through his body and ended on the tip of his tongue. He fell to his knees, then onto his side. His breathing became uneven as he arrived to the edge of blacking out.

He closed his eyes.

So this is what dying feels like, he thought.

Chapter 18

"MANDAWUY, I FOUND HIS WIFE," Oodgeroo alerted. "She's as hot as the ground."

"Bring her here," Mandawuy replied. "Now, splash water onto her face and then wipe water on her lips. She has to wake before she can drink."

"Come on, little woman," she coaxed. "Open your eyes. She's so hot, Mandawuy. We may have found them too late."

"No, look at her chest," he retorted. "Her breathing is shallow, but she's still taking in air. Rub more water on her. Her thirst will wake her."

Oodgeroo pursed her brow and picked up the cloth again to moisten Elaina's head and neck.

"Do it again." The man nodded encouragement while continuing to cool Charles. "You see? This one is already starting to come back. Had he been a smaller man, the dingo might have killed him."

"How is his arm?" Oodgeroo asked. "Were you able to stop the bleeding?"

"It has stopped for now, but we won't be able to give him the care he needs until we get them back to the village. There! You see? Her breathing is getting better. They're going to be all right"

~~~

Elaina watched as Charles came out of his dream. He called out in a hoarse voice and flailed about on the dirt floor.

When he opened his eyes, he found himself in a dimly lit, circular room. He scuttled backward when he saw the two dark, slender figures standing over him, also watching. Elaina maneuvered behind him, put her head over his shoulder, and wrapped her arms around his chest.

"Charles, it's okay," she said in a soothing voice. "We're safe." Her cheek grazed his face.

Charles was confused by her touch but welcomed it. The pain in his swollen forearm came to life, a harsh reminder of his scuffle with the dingo.

He looked at the couple. They had retreated a few steps and stood close to each other. The man was tall, slender yet muscular, with wooly black and gray hair, a wide nose, and forceful, keen eyes. She was thin with smooth skin, and she kept her hair tied up in a vibrant cloth. The woman spoke in their native language, stepped just behind her husband, and came back with a wet rag. Her smile was sympathetic as she moved toward Charles and Elaina.

Charles recoiled from her, so the woman paused and held out the compress to Elaina. She took it and dabbed it along Charles's brow. As he relaxed beneath the cool water, Charles felt a sudden rush of blood in his body. He exhaled and let his head fall back onto Elaina's chest. The woman tilted her head and smiled at him.

Something about her unnerved Charles. Why was she so big-hearted, given the circumstances? He looked around the modest home. They had put Elaina and him in a darkened corner of the main room. The walls were constructed of smooth clay, with one wall flowing into the next and rising up to form a domed ceiling. Behind the husband and wife stood the cooking table and utensils.

Elaina dabbed at his tight, cracked, blistered lips. His tongue was still swollen and would occasionally stick to the roof of his mouth. When their hostess again tried to approach the pair with a small cup, Charles hesitated once more.

"For Eloah's sake, just take it, Charles," Elaina said sharply. "Believe me when I tell you, this one is persistent."

He looked back over his shoulder at Elaina and surrendered to her being right. She helped to lift his head so his lips could meet the wooden cup. When Charles swallowed the water, it felt like the purest elixir of life. He tried to drink again but coughed as it shocked and revived his system.

"Where are we?" he asked Elaina with a raspy, dry voice.

"I don't know, but we're safe," she assured him. "I awoke just a few hours before you. She's been very attentive to me and seems kind. Her husband keeps to himself, but he doesn't seem dangerous, just uncomfortable. I'm guessing they found us and carried us here."

Standing nearby, their two hosts continued to speak in their own language.

Charles looked at them and then at Elaina. "Have you spoken to them at all?" he asked with a renewed urgency.

"Not really," Elaina answered. "Mostly with hand signals and broken English that I'm not sure they understood. Why?"

"Because they can understand everything you're saying," Charles revealed. "They speak English." He turned, called over, "*Wela'lin*," and smiled.

The wife nodded, put her hand to her chest, and returned the smile. The husband's eyes grew large as he gripped his wife's shoulder, but he, too, nodded.

Charles propped himself up on his elbows and then sat upright on the floor. "*Não agora*[29], Elaina," he said in Portuguese. "*Temos coisas mais importantes para descobrir.*"[30]

Elaina's mouth dropped. "*Quantos idiomas você pode falar?*"[31] She asked. "Or do you just speak all of them?"

"*Sete*," he answered, holding up seven fingers. Then he turned his attention back to their host and hostess. "May we speak English to each other?"

"Yes, English is fine," the man said. "We both speak it very well."

---

[29] "Not now, Elaina"

[30] "We have more important things to find out."

[31] "How many languages can you speak?"

"My name is Charles, and this is Elaina." Charles smiled as he spoke. "Thank you for saving our lives. Can you tell us where we are?"

"You are in the village of the Yolngu people of the Northern Territory that your people call Katingal," he said. "Your eyes have been shut for two days. My name is Mandawuy, and this is my wife, Oodgeroo. Welcome. It is a custom of our people to help those in need and to extend hospitality as if they were our family. Oodgeroo has been caring for you since we brought you here. If you need anything, she will tend to it for you."

"Yes, thank you. *Wela'lin.*" Elaina echoed the same warm tone Charles had used. "We would have surely died, had you not found us."

"You were lucky we heard your husband's screams when the dingo attacked him," Oodgeroo said with a concerned frown. "Otherwise, the two of you would have died."

Charles and Elaina looked at each other in an awkward manner. Charles touched his ravaged forearm. "I don't feel lucky just yet." He coughed out a laugh. "This hurts worse than an arm full of darts."

"You are lucky," Oodgeroo said before pausing to contemplate her next sentence. "What were you and your wife doing—?"

"Do you by any chance have any food?" Charles cut in. "We haven't eaten for days."

Mandawuy glanced over. "Of course!" She jumped up and went to her cooking area. "I should have offered you food as soon as you both awakened. There will be plenty of time for conversation later. Your child is what's important, and it needs its nourishment." Oodgeroo ladled some brown stew from a large metal pot into wooden bowls.

The news sent a sudden jolt through Charles's stomach. He rolled onto his side to look up at Elaina, but she didn't see him. She was looking down at her belly. She touched it, but her face was creased in worry.

"Você disse a eles?"[32] Charles whispered. He needed to know whether Elaina had any other conversations with their caretakers while he was recovering. He wondered how loose her lips were, and whether she might have also gossiped that they were fugitives.

"Eu não disse nada,"[33] Elaina insisted, her eyes still locked on her belly. "Of course I wouldn't say anything. Besides, it's not possible. I'm infertile. I've tried and failed at having a baby for the past three years." As she clutched her stomach, tears fell from her eyes and streamed down her cheeks.

Oodgeroo heard Elaina's sniffling and looked over. "Oh, I am so sorry." She placed her hands over her mouth in embarrassment. "I didn't realize your husband wasn't aware of your condition. We have four children of our own, and I've been midwife to over ten mothers here in my village. Babies are a regular part of our lives." She brightened before she grabbed Charles's hand. "She will bring forth a child seven

---

[32] "You told them?"

[33] "I said nothing."

or eight moons from now. Place your hands on her belly. Feel how swollen she is. Don't worry. You'll grow used to it. But it is peculiar at first. The first child always requires the most adjustment."

To maintain appearances, Charles smiled and placed his hand on Elaina's stomach. He couldn't detect any swelling, but when he felt Elaina's warm body, a chill washed over him, forcing him to withdraw his hand.

Chapter 19

AFTER THREE DAYS RECUPERATING IN the Yolngu hut, Charles had enough strength to venture outside. He had noted how eager Oodgeroo was to introduce Elaina and him to the villagers, so he decided it would be a good idea to see if they could make some more friends in the village.

Mandawuy was starting to look upon them with suspicion, and was becoming less content to not have any answers. Every day that Charles dodged his questions, he could see that Mandawuy was feeling less secure about having them remain with him and Oodgeroo. Charles knew it was just a matter of time before they would have to flee.

But Charles had also learned that his wife, Oodgeroo, enjoyed the attention her guest brought her in the village. She also relished in feeling needed. Mandawuy was the protector but his wife was the boss of the family, so they remained, and he played to her ego to ingratiate themselves. The longer he and Elaina could stay in the village, the stronger they would be when they left.

On this day, he had asked Oodgeroo to escort him for his first outing. Elaina had wanted no part of the spectacle, and remained inside. It had seemed that the moment she acknowledged her condition, her morning sickness came on with a fury. Up to the day prior, unaware of her condition, her only concern was to survive Katingal, but now, so cared for, she grew weak and was unable to digest even the blandest porridge that Oodgeroo prepared especially for her.

After making sure Elaina was comfortable, Oodgeroo emerged from her hut ahead of Charles, smiling and swinging her hips. The moment Charles, with his burgundy-hued skin, crossed the threshold, the villagers gathered to see him. But from how they eyed him, murmured among themselves, and kept their distance, it was clear to Charles that rumors had been circulating about these strangers in their midst.

What made Charles feel nervous more than anything was how the parents shielded their children and guided them away. He felt his heart racing as he wondered if somehow they had figured out who he was and the crimes he had committed.

But then he only needed to glance at his hostess, who remained near him beaming with pride, to know that he was being paranoid. Had it not been for Oodgeroo and Mandawuy, Charles and Elaina would have been rotting away, their carcasses picked over by the scavengers of the Northern Territory.

Charles considered the part that luck had played in the hand he was dealt. He wondered whether Oodgeroo and her husband would have saved him had he been alone. Maybe Oodgeroo's clairvoyant detection of Elaina's pregnancy was what had drawn her to save them from perishing in the outback. Maybe that was what had made the fugitives seem more human, the notion that they were bringing new life into the world.

The notion overwhelmed him to where he felt as if he was carrying a weight too heavy to continue walking. He squatted and sat on the ground.

"I thought you wanted to walk," Oodgeroo said.

"My legs aren't feeling so strong, but this fresh air is incredible."

Oodgeroo shrugged and sat on the dusty ground next to him. She proceeded to point out, name, and describe the character of each villager. They conversed in her native aboriginal tongue, a language Charles's supercharged brain had been able to learn quite quickly. His fluency helped assuage her concerns about his and Elaina's past.

She pointed to a crowd of children running in circles and tried to explain the complicated tag-like game they were playing. The movement of their long limbs and lean bodies mesmerized Charles. The sharp pain piercing the back of his head returned.

"What games did you play when you were their age?" Oodgeroo prodded.

"My childhood was more scholarship than play after I was sent to boarding school in West Africa," he said.

"You attended Sankoré?" she asked.

Charles was shocked that the reputation of his school had traveled to the nomadic lands of the aborigine. "Study. Eat. Sleep. Study."

"Many of our world leaders attended your school," Oodgeroo said. "Such an opportunity!"

"Yes, I guess. But I was young when they sent away there. It felt more like a punishment and that my parents were ashamed so they discarded me. Although, I did ultimately make quite a few influential acquaintances."

"Your parents must have wanted what was best for you."

"Right, the best for me. Well, they didn't attend my graduation. They sent a letter of congratulations, along with my birth certificate and the business card for a lawyer. I haven't seen or spoken to them since."

Oodgeroo's maternal kindness had disarmed him. He never opened up to others about his childhood, and certainly never spoke of this grief.

"They said I was a mistake," he continued. "That I was sick. A burden to them. I would be a burden to the whole family. So they disowned me. Put some money in a trust fund and walked away."

Oodgeroo placed her hand on his shoulder.

"Don't touch me!" Charles snapped and jumped up.

"Your parents' lack of love is not your fault," she said gently. "Every child is deserving of love."

"Yes," he said, turning to watch the children again. "I couldn't agree with you more." His anger had flared up, consuming his reason. Charles had let his guard down, and he was resolute not to let it happen again. He wondered just how resolute Oodgeroo's convictions would remain if he were to tell her what he wanted to do to those children, just how he wanted to love them.

The children's game soon brought them closer to where he and Oodgeroo were standing as they chased one another into confusing circles, exploding into laughter when one would tag the other. Charles's demon danced within. He could see the outlines of the girls' bodies through their lightweight cotton dresses, their developing curves as they bounced and ran over the hard ground.

One girl came to be his object of desire. Her perky nose and smooth forehead shone in the sun, and her long, lean, brown body made him ache. He pressed his teeth together against the pain in his head as he watched her fall after her feet tangled with another's. She sat for a moment a few feet in front of Charles and Oodgeroo and laughed into her hand.

Charles stood to offer her a hand.

Before the girl could take it, Oodgeroo stepped in front of Charles and reached down to pull the child up.

"My daughter, Abaroo, is so clumsy," Oodgeroo said, smiling with pride. She and the girl wrapped their arms around each other.

"I didn't realize you still had a child that lived at home," he said.

"She's been away with her grandmother, preparing for her womanhood ceremony tonight. It's a very sacred ritual. So sacred, she should be spending every moment preparing," Oodgeroo teased. "Where is your grandmother, child?"

"Sleeping. She and the other elders are resting in preparation for this evening. I promise, Mother, I'm ready and won't dishonor you." Abaroo bowed her head and looked at the ground.

"I know you won't, because you're going to return to your grandmother and continue your preparations. Your time for play has ended. Now go."

"Yes, Mother." Abaroo turned and ran off toward the edge of the village until she passed out of sight.

The scene had caught the attention of the villagers, and Charles felt exposed. Oodgeroo's pride in her daughter might have blinded her from noticing, but had the others seen his desire for Abaroo?

"Don't let their eyes bother you," she said. "You are my guest until you and Elaina regain enough strength. Your wife must not exert herself."

"Oodgeroo, your charity is appreciated very much. You and your husband saved us, and for that, we will be forever grateful." Charles felt the stares fall upon him again. "Perhaps we should return to your home and see how Elaina—"

"Oodgeroo!" came the voice, interrupting Charles. "Please, come here." An elder male of the village summoned the woman from the entryway of a nearby hut.

Charles had been so taken with the teenagers' play that he hadn't noticed this stern man appearing. Hearing the elder's call, Mandawuy emerged from his hut. Oodgeroo looked at her husband, her forehead pursed, and together they walked to greet the elder.

Charles watched the trio. The elder was explaining something, and his hosts listened, nodding. Everyone's faces were tight and drawn. When the elder gestured toward him, Charles knew he had been found out. The tenor of their conversation was far too dire to be about ordinary circumstances. His skin flushed cold.

When the elder finished talking, he went into his hut, and Oodgeroo and Mandawuy came back toward Charles. Without looking at him, she continued to their hut and disappeared through the threshold.

Mandawuy stopped in front of Charles. Still seated, looking up at Mandawuy, Charles lifted a hand to shield his eyes from the sun awaiting his host's message. "It is time for you and Elaina to leave. Your presence has disrupted our village." He bent down to look Charles in the eyes. "Do you think we are a stupid people? Do you think because we have remained a nomadic tribe and shun what your people call 'civilization' that we are ignorant?"

The seriousness of the moment was undeniable. "No, Mandawuy, of course not."

"We know what you are, Charles. You and Elaina." His nose flared.

Charles's blood felt electric in his veins.

"One of the customs of my people is to help those in need," Mandawuy said. "But I knew what you were when we found you, and to my mind, you and your woman did not qualify for what is expected of this custom. Had I encountered you while alone, I would have left you for the buzzards. But my wife has a good heart, better than anyone I know, and she has a strong faith in humanity. That is why you are alive now. But her heart is sometimes *too* good. Only Eloah knows what evils you've committed to earn your exile to this continent."

"Mandawuy, I—"

The aborigine raised a hand to silence him. "Our elders don't care for any of you outsiders, as you have plundered our lands and erected a city to confine the worst of mankind. If it were possible, we would have fought you all off just as the indigenous people in the western continents. Instead, we have chosen to remain true to ourselves, and we live alone, at peace. The elders and I don't know, nor do we care, what your crimes are, but we do know that nothing good will come of you two remaining here."

Charles stood motionless, shocked into silence.

"Our customary obligation to provide help has been fulfilled," Mandawuy continued. "You have to leave our village."

"Understood," Charles said. He stood, went into the hut, and sat on the floor beside Elaina, who was curled into a ball in their corner of the main room.

Mandawuy followed and disappeared into the back bedroom with Oodgeroo. Charles could tell from the tone of their whispers that their discussion was a heated one.

Elaina groaned in her sleep. He nudged her until she woke. She looked up at him angrily. Her face was very pale, her eyes unfocused.

"They know we're fugitives," he said. "They've always known. Their hospitality has come to an end. They've asked for us leave the village. Now."

Elaina's face fell. She turned away and curled back into a ball. "No," she whispered. "No."

Charles sat with her a moment, staring through the open doorway, catching glimpses of the villagers going about their business.

Eventually, Mandawuy and Oodgeroo's argument died down and they were quiet. It was apparent how much they loved one another, how much respect lived between them. Charles looked at Elaina's soft curves through the coverlet. The lust brought on by the young girl that had started in his stomach and had grown inside him returned as he listened to the children playing outside the hut. A throbbing migraine shot up from the base of his skull, matching the pulse in his genitals.

He leaned forward to cope with the discomfort, and instinctively gripped her arm.

"For Eloah's sake, Charles, you're hurting me!" she exclaimed, pulling her arm away.

He noticed that when he touched her, the pain dissipated.

"I'm sorry," he said. "I didn't mean to hurt you. It's my head."

He reached out and caressed her arm. She didn't seem to mind his touch, for she lay back down. He thought of Abaroo, and desire regrew in his stomach and groin. His head pulsed with pain. He squeezed Elaina's arm, and she reached to hold his hand. His headache subsided, but his body remained aroused.

Elaina moved away from him and avoided his eyes. "I thought you weren't attracted to grown women." She laboriously got to her feet, grimacing, and wrapped her arms around her chest.

"What does that have to do with us having to leave," Charles said. He stood and began to gather some blankets, tools, and containers for water.

Elaina, understanding at last that they were leaving, found a burlap bag and filled it with food. He nodded, and she followed him out of the hut without a word to their hosts. They walked through the village, aware of people's eyes on them, saying nothing.

When they reached the boundaries of the village, Elaina touched his shoulder and said, "I need to stop."

"Just a while longer," Charles said. "Let's put as much distance as possible between us and the village." When he looked back and saw her heading in the wrong direction, he said, "Where are you going? That's not the way—"

"Shut up, Charles! I don't feel well, and I have to pee." She squatted in the brush, out of his sight.

"What's the matter?" he said, approaching her. "I can hear you crying."

"What are you doing? Stay over there."

Charles stopped in his tracks, but could see a silhouette of her backside that ignited an aching lust for his travel companion. He sneered at himself and pushed the thoughts of her away by shifting to images of the teenage girl, her nubile body so taut and unspoiled.

He realized then that he could still get to her.

Elaina was rummaging through her sack of provisions, pulling out a rag that she used to wipe herself, followed by more winces of pain.

"Resting for a while isn't such a bad idea," Charles said. "We have plenty of provisions, and we'll make better time traveling by daylight. I'll set up camp. You get some rest, and we'll continue at dawn." He began to roll out their bedding.

Elaina looked at him as she gathered herself and threw the rag to the ground behind the brush. She pulled her clothes back on and returned to help Charles create a makeshift mattress and pillow on the ground as they had done the past few nights in the hut.

Charles organized the remaining supplies around Elaina and sat next to her. He watched over her, letting the rise and fall of her ribcage, the in and out of her breath, and the warmth emanating off of her comfort him as she fell into sleep.

Then he sat up, his hands resting in his lap, his eyes closed, taking deep breaths as the wind swirled around him. He detected a certain scent on the wind and waited, inhaling deep, to let it come to him fully. It was smoke, and moments later, the wind pushing at his back, he knew from what direction it was blowing. He opened his eyes, looked behind him, and searched the horizon.

His sight adjusted to the light, and then he saw it: a thin stream rising into the distant sky. He checked to make sure Elaina was asleep, then stood and began to walk in the direction of the smoke.

As he continued, the line of smoke grew thicker, and he began to hear the steady beats of a drum. He closed the distance to thirty-five yards and found some brush to hide behind. He remained still, barely breathing, as he watched the group of women both young and old. He counted four older women and nine younger girls, all in the midst of building several small shelters from sticks and mud.

He watched them until the older women left the girls to continue their work while they sat beside the fire and pulled leaves from satchels tied around their waists. When the girls completed the shelters, they joined the elder women near the fire and tossed the leaves into the flame.

"Sit and inhale the smoke, children," one of the women directed.

The girls did as their elder instructed, though they all began to cough. One by one, each girl was led to the periphery of the fire's light.

"Each of you lie down in the hollow we've prepared for you," the woman said. "Tonight you begin your journey into womanhood. Here will you remain with us and do as we say. Your journey will span two moons before we release you to claim your husband and perform whatever duties he bids you. Behind you are the days when you ran about as you pleased. Behind you are the days when you could sleep when the sun was highest in the sky. Never again will you sleep at night until those elder than you are at rest first. For two moons, we will prepare your food. You will remove honey from your diet for four moons. At the first light of the next day, you must rise and eat the food we prepare. When you hear a bird call, you must shake yourself all over, and make a noise like this."

Charles watched and listened, entranced, as the old woman made a ringing noise with her thick lips.

"You will do that every time you hear a bird sing. You will do that whenever you hear the people in this camp begin to talk, laugh, or sneeze. If you fail to do so, your hair will streak grey before you bear your first child. Your sight will become blurry, and your bodies will grow weak."

The elderly women motioned for the young girls to lie in the freshly dug earth. "Don't be afraid, children. Do as we say."

The other elder women walked over to the shelter, where several large pails stood. They each gripped a handle and dragged their pail toward the holes. When they reached the edges of the shallow holes where the girls lay, all the elders chanted in unison some words that were inaudible to Charles.

After a few moments, they stopped, and the leader said, "Remove your garments."

The firelight barely reached the girls' bodies. Charles watched their shadows disrobe before lying in the beds dug for them in the ground. The older women poured pails of water on the girls. They shrieked.

Charles felt a throb in his loins, which sparked the ache in his skull.

The women mounded dirt on top of the girls until only their heads poked out. They muttered blessings and stroked their faces with mud. When the last girl had received her baptism, the girls rose to approach the fire. Beige paste clung to their lithe, glowing forms. The girls whirled in a dance that allowed the flames to bake the soft mud into a hard body-shell.

The elders approached with bowls of pigment and painted red and white spots on their shoulders and breasts. They tossed sprays of white flowers and feathers over the girls' heads and adorned their chests and arms with armor made from woven hair. For the final rite, the elders pierced each girl's nose with a thin-whittled stick of birch bark. The girls accepted the pain without protest.

"You are a woman now. Go find your husband."

One by one, the girls wandered back to the village road. Charles lay in the brush, awaiting the one he wanted.

She was one of the last few to leave the fire's glow and the elder's arms. He tracked her, timing his steps to match hers. Every crunch of dirt and gravel resonated in unison. He watched her hips, her calf muscles, and her curved back. He was twenty-eight feet away, twenty-four, eighteen, twelve, six. She was so close that, if she had stopped, he would have crashed into her.

"Abaroo," he whispered.

She dropped her bouquet of Buddha leaves and looked over her shoulder.

Charles swept her from her feet. He had meant for this first touch to be gentle, but he slammed her to the ground. She lay bare and unaware before him.

Charles's migraine returned. He tried to ignore the pain. He pulled his clothing off, yanked Abaroo's thighs open, and pressed himself against the unconscious virgin.

His penis refused his desires and remained flaccid. Determined, he stroked it and fingered Abaroo's unwelcoming vagina. He pulled harder on himself, but his body refused to respond. He fingered the girl more vehemently. His forehead wrinkled, his temples tightened, and his jaw ached. The dull pain in his head intensified.

For several minutes, he tried in vain to rape the daughter of the man and woman who had saved his life.

The girl rolled her head and fluttered her eyes. Blood stained the creases of his fingers and trickled over onto his hand. She screamed, then fell back, unconscious.

The high pitch of the scream yanked Charles out of his tantric focus on his failing erection and back into the reality of the situation. He jumped on top of the young girl and covered her mouth with his hands, trapping her under the weight of his body.

The thin and panicked child again awoke and tried to fight him off, but Charles slipped his hands from her mouth to around her throat and squeezed in a rage. He looked around to see if the elder women had heard anything.

When he again looked down at the girl, he found her staring at him. She might have become a woman in the ceremony according to her village custom, but he could see in her eyes glittering at him in the dark that his molestation had removed all innocence from her soul. She gasped for air while despair and panic filled her eyes. Tears ran down the sides of her face.

Charles grew even angrier as he realized with every passing moment that, even after taking this incredible risk, he was failing to satisfy the urge undulating in his gut like ocean waves. Abaroo grew weak beneath his grip. He glared at her, furious. He needed her to fight. To get up. But she was falling out of consciousness again.

He raised his right arm in the air and brought it down hard on Abaroo's face, pulverizing her nose. He did it again and again until blood spattered in all directions.

He paused, breathing hard. Her breath had grown shallow, her chest barely rising and falling beneath his thighs. This was the first time in his life, since he'd begun making other children pay for the life he'd been given, that he'd failed to consummate an attack.

He stared down at her bloody face and realized that in his frustration he'd hit her too hard. She was no longer breathing.

Even so, his penis remained limp. He had failed. Something was different. Something had changed.

Chapter 20

W HEN CHARLES RETURNED TO ELAINA, she was asleep. As he watched her, a gust of wind swept by, carrying an odor he had detected earlier while Elaina was ducked behind the brush they were using as a makeshift toilet. He traced the scent, and the aroma grew stronger until he found the discarded rag Elaina had used to clean herself.

The odor and color of the rag revealed what Elaina was trying to conceal. Her captors had left her with not only a bastard to carry but also gonorrhea.

He dropped the soiled cloth and walked back over to their camp, gathering the supplies before shaking her awake.

"What's wrong?" she murmured.

"We have to go," Charles insisted.

"You said first light," Elaina groused. "It's still dark. Leave me alone."

"Now!" His voice was high, urgent. He hated the sound of it and loathed the fear that had knotted in his chest.

"Now? Why now?" She sat up.

"It's not safe for us here," he said, pulling her to her feet. "Stay if you want, but I'm leaving. Good luck surviving pregnant and on your own."

"Charles, what's happened?"

He didn't reply.

She sighed, shook her head, and grabbed the small bundle of clothes she had used as a pillow and stuffed them into the burlap bag.

He checked the cap on the gallon container of water he had taken from Oodgeroo's kitchen and motioned for Elaina to hurry after him into the darkness of the Northern Territory. She obliged but still looked confused. Through the pitch dark, they moved swiftly in silence as Charles led them into the vast unknown.

"We're going to keep moving north by northwest until we reach Darwin, just like we originally planned," he said. "As soon as we're safe, we go our own ways."

"What the hell's going on, Charles?" she demanded again.

He ignored her inquiries. After a while, Charles glanced over and read her expression to mean that she wasn't going to let this go. He kept a hurried pace and hoped some sense of loyalty or faith would keep her moving with him, trusting him. Since he had saved her life, maybe there was room for such a thing, even if it would surely be temporary.

~~~

They traveled all night without stopping. Charles needed to ensure that he put as much distance between them and the village as possible before the sun rose.

Between his rewired libido and the migraines, he began to wonder whether his hyper-intelligence from the KPP procedure was more of a curse than a gift. It had been so long since he had enjoyed the comfort of one of his shales, and last night's debacle increased his frustration. Hours of effort with nothing to show for it. Now they were retreating into the dark, hoping to cover their escape route. Once the girl's body was found, they would hunt for him.

When dawn crept up, purple and rose, he turned to look at Elaina. She was pallid, with dark circles under her eyes.

"We can rest for fifteen minutes," Charles said, averting his eyes from her. "Then we start again for two hours. Then we rest again."

She said nothing. Charles realized that he was also exhausted, but nonetheless, he quietly counted out the nine hundred seconds he had regimented for their rest period.

"And then what, Charles?" Elaina interrupted. "You expected us to walk around the clock? At some point, we must eat, drink, and sleep. This pace isn't realistic."

"I know. Just a little while longer, to put more distance between ourselves and the village. But until then, we rest for fifteen minutes after we walk a steady seventeen thousand and six hundred paces." He turned away from her again.

"Seventeen thousand and six hundred paces?" she mimicked him, snickering.

"Of course," Charles said. "It's ten miles."

Elaina opened her mouth but said nothing.

~~~

About halfway through the first 17,600 paces, they reached a high point on the land. As Charles and Elaina looked around the panoramic view of the landscape, they could see only dry, orange earth with specks of foliage. The best of the sparse vegetation were trees, perhaps the height of an adult, bearing only a few brittle leaves. To the east stood some small mountains. It was a bare but serene beauty, yet neither Charles nor Elaina could appreciate it.

Charles scanned the surrounding area for somewhere to rest, then looked at Elaina. The once rich tan tone of her face was now pale as she hunched over. He kept one eye turned in the direction from where they had come.

"You expect someone to be following us, Charles?" Elaina inquired with sarcasm.

Charles just kept rotating, his hand shielding his eyes. "There," he pointed. "Just a little while longer. We'll use some of our clothes and the blanket to create a canopy and get some sleep until nightfall." He resumed walking, heading toward a small collection of brush and boulders.

She caught up to him. Her stare was piercing in the opposite direction of Charles's designated area. "Why aren't we going over there?" she asked, pointing at a large hill in the distance. "We can probably find a cave to better shield us from the sun there. And why in the hell are we resting during the day when we can see where we're going? I'm tired of tripping on things in the dark."

Charles sighed. "The temperature is going to rise soon, and fast. That hill you're talking about is Uluru Rock. It's the wrong direction, and four times farther than the brush. If we travel during the day, we'll use more energy and consume more water and food. Trust me. In an hour, you'll see what I mean."

He was trying to be reasonable and keep his voice measured, but he could see she was reaching her limits of frustration.

Elaina stopped walking. After taking a few more paces, Charles looked back at her. She pursed her lips, hefted the supplies in her arms, and continued in his direction.

As he had predicted, they arrived in about an hour. They made haste creating their shelter as they raced the rising sun.

Even in scant clothing, the two perspired profusely as they struggled to sleep on the burning hot ground. Elaina was restless, unable to find a comfortable position. She rolled over and watched Charles breathing, unsure if he was asleep or just resting.

She sat up and reached for the water bottle to sneak a swallow or two. If Charles noticed a change in the level, he would be furious. When the first drops hit her parched lips, Elaina had to resist the urge to drink it all. She sipped while maintaining her peripheral vision on Charles.

Then she saw something moving in the distance. Elaina squinted again toward the horizon and saw a small band of men walking in a fan formation. They were carrying spears.

She placed the cap back on the bottle and returned it to its spot.

"Charles?" she whispered, crawling onto him while she shook his arm. Her eyes were wide and afraid.

Charles startled and rose up to a seated position to look. His heart pounded at the sight of the aborigine search party headed toward them. He leapt to his feet and began pulling their shelter apart.

"What's wrong? What did you do, Charles?" she asked. "What are you keeping from me? Whatever you did, it's on you, not me."

"If you want to take that chance, then go right ahead." He glared at her. "But the supplies come with me. If they catch you, you won't need them and I won't be coming to save you, again." He grabbed the supplies and walked off in a hurry.

She looked back at the search party to discover that they had picked up their pace and were headed right at them. Elaina shuddered from an immediate and visceral recall of the last time multiple strange men descended upon her. She scurried after him.

Charles looked back and slowed enough for her to catch up with him.

"Wait, where are we going?" she whispered. "This isn't the same direction as Darwin."

"We're headed to Uluru Rock." Charles pointed at the large hill that Elaina had spotted the day before. He glanced up to check on the search party's progress. He opened the jug and gulped down a mouthful of water before passing it to Elaina.

"What if they don't give up?" she queried.

"We'll deal with that when the time comes," Charles replied, his eyes narrowing. He didn't want to tell her that they were in for a fight. After what he'd done, the search party were not going to give up.

When Elaina was looking down, he glanced at the men's progress. Two of the fittest men from the group had surged ahead a hundred yards from the rest.

Charles explained that they needed to run the last fifty yards to the opening at the face of the mountain. She nodded. Then they shared what was left of the water and went for it.

Despite having little energy, they both dug deep and found a way to sprint. Charles entered first and pressed himself against the rock wall. When Elaina arrived seconds later, he pulled her close and positioned her out of view. She collapsed as she gasped for air. He peered through the entrance of the cavern to gauge how far back their pursuers were.

Charles noted that one of the lead men had surged ahead of the other. He looked right at Charles, and they locked eyes. It was Mandawuy. He pointed his spear at Charles and yelled something to the other men.

Charles turned back into the cavern, which opened into an even larger area, and pulled Elaina along with him. She stumbled back onto her feet as they traveled deeper into the cavern, soon disappearing into vast recesses of darkness.

"The only way they'll find us is if they fall over us," Charles said as he guided Elaina through a virtual pedestrian's puzzle of rocks, stalagmites, and stalactites.

Moments later, they entered an enormous opening in the cavern. Ancient cave markings covered the walls. These walls rose to meet a ceiling a hundred feet above, culminating in a large hole at the top that allowed a glimpse of a blue sky littered with milky-white clouds.

Charles counted five different portals that likely led to even deeper caves. *Not safe without supplies*, he determined. He surveyed the walls around and above him. There were different levels of uneven rock that led to higher areas where small crevasses and caves had been naturally forged.

"We'll hide up there," Charles said, nodding toward the upper level. He removed his shirt and threw it on his back. He motioned for Elaina to do the same. "Now, run over the entire area," he instructed. "Make as many tracks into the dirt floor as you can. We need to make them think we left. Put some that lead to those different exits." Charles ran in all directions, Elaina followed suit, and they circled back.

Charles started climbing the wall. Using the protruding rocks as hand- and footholds, he scaled to a higher level of the rock formation. He reached the ledge, turned, and reached for Elaina. The power in her grip surprised him. He couldn't help but marvel at her strength. Within a few minutes, they had reached a suitable hiding spot.

They maneuvered their way into the deep but tight cave, maybe four feet across and four feet high. Charles crawled in on his belly feet first, followed by Elaina. Charles reasoned that the darkness of the small cave provided the perfect cover. They had the vantage point to see what Mandawuy and his hunting party were doing without being seen.

Charles and Elaina each retrieved a weapon from the supplies and waited. With no room to spare, he pressed his back against the wall while she took up what remained of the cave floor on her stomach.

The lack of room forced their bodies to touch. Elaina could feel his stale breath with every exhalation, even through her thick head of hair. She heard his breathing intensify. Then she turned to glare down at him and his obvious signs of arousal as she moved away against the opposite wall. She clutched her weapon, her face full of contempt.

"I'm sorry," he whispered as he reached down to adjust his erection. "I really don't understand what's happening. Ever since the surgery—"

"Shh!" Elaina hissed.

Their pursuers had just entered the cavern. Charles moved into the space that Elaina had evacuated and peeked over the ledge to spy on the aborigines.

Mandawuy paused and knelt to analyze the tracks in the dirt. Charles listened to the conversation.

"Look at the tracks," Mandawuy said. "They lead into one of those caves exiting here. They couldn't have gotten very far." He pointed his long spear across the cavern toward one of the exits. He motioned the others to follow until he abruptly stopped to analyze the ground again.

"Their footprints lead everywhere like they've split up. You two go in that direction." He gestured. "And you two go there. I'll go in this one. Travel no more than two hundred paces and then return. Then we'll determine our next move."

"Looks like it worked," Elaina whispered to Charles.

"Maybe," Charles said. "We'll have to see what they do when they don't find us."

~~~

After about an hour, Elaina began to squirm with exhaustion, hunger, and the need to relieve herself.

"I have to pee," she said.

"Not much we can do about that now, except—"

"Don't say anything." She sighed. "I know the answer. Just don't—"

Charles heard the men and clapped his hand over her mouth. They had returned after inspecting each exit, and now they huddled in a circle in the middle of the cavern.

"Did you find any fresh tracks?" Mandawuy asked.

"We found nothing," one of the younger men said, his voice frustrated.

"Then we stay and continue to search," Mandawuy vowed. "We saw them enter the cavern. We stay and search until we find my daughter's killers. We return home only after I have killed them with my own hands."

"What are they saying now?" Elaina whispered.

Charles shook his head.

"Mandawuy, we all want to find and slay them," the younger man said. "But there is no shame in losing two people who had a day's head start. We were fortunate to track them this far. We don't have enough food or water to search for them, so we will eventually have to go back. They will surely die out here, anyway."

"You, Baju, are young and unwise about the ways of our people, our ancestors before you," the eldest of the bunch, a bald, short man, yelled. "Your generation only values immediate results. You've never been a patient person. If you wish to leave, go! I will not go back to our village carrying this shame. Do you think these strangers know our country better than we? You can leave if that's your desire but we will not return until their heads are mounted on the tips of our spears." He thrust his spear in the air.

"They're not leaving until they find us," Charles whispered. He sensed her body slumping behind him. Then, a moment later, he felt the warm fluid on his leg from Elaina relieving herself in their cave. When she was finished, Elaina moved toward the mouth of the cave to look down.

The elder was still speaking but had calmed. Having gotten his point across, the men embraced, then broke apart. The younger man disappeared into one of the caves, and returned with dead wood to build a fire.

"So now what do we do?" Elaina whispered.

"We'll wait until they're asleep," Charles said, putting together his plan. "Then we'll sneak past them. When they wake, we'll be miles away, and they'll still be searching this cavern. We'll get at least another day head start on them. By then, hopefully our tracks will have disappeared, and we'll be lost to them forever."

They watched the men build a fire, sip water, and chew dried meat they pulled from small satchels they wore on their shoulders. Elaina's stomach growled louder, and she salivated at the sight of their modest dinner. She buried her face into her dirty palms, trying to block out the longing for the nourishment her body needed.

~~~

Elaina was jarred awake by the sound of loud snoring. She reached over to cover Charles's mouth, but her hand met empty space. She scooted to the edge of their cave, and saw that the aboriginal men were asleep around the fire with the elder making all the noise. As she scanned the rest of the room, Elaina wondered whether abandoning her was part of the scheme Charles had been planning all along.

Just then, a gruesome moan came from below, followed by a scream. Elaina's heart leaped into her throat. She grabbed the knife she had stolen from Oodgeroo and scooted back as far as she could against the wall while sounds of grunting, moaning, and screaming came from the cave floor below.

Then the horrible clamor gave way to the simple sound of a single person panting in heaves. That animal-like noise was more worrisome than the fighting. She clutched her knife and battled an overwhelming sense of nausea. Elaina readied herself to slay whatever approached her.

"You can come down now," Charles said. "They're all dead."

Chapter 21

HE SUN WAS DIPPING TO the horizon, signaling the end of the eighth day since Charles's ax decided the fate of the men hunting them. The two fugitives had been lucky enough to find shelter in caves along the way to wait out the intense heat.

Each day was the same. After daybreak, they had set up camp, rested during the worst heat of the day, then woken to eat. They were adept at making meals of lizards, snakes, and rodents, and developed an unspoken understanding of how to conserve the pitiful amounts of food and water they were able to collect.

The best part of the routine was watching the beautiful orange glaze stretch along the horizon at dusk. It also meant that the evening breeze was upon them. But the unforgiving outback had taken its toll. The flies and ants were etching their persistent way into their resolve to survive. Charles and Elaina both had open sores from their constant scratching.

At the same time, the journey was softening their hardened souls. They had come to find solace in each other's bodies, the only physical comfort they had among their survival regiment. Their bodies craved the companionship that had eluded them in their former lives. It had gotten to the point where it had become a biological imperative.

"It's time to go," Charles said, gently touching her shoulder.

Elaina rolled over and squinted at Charles before the sensation of her irritated skin came to life. She scratched at the raw flesh on her arms, where insects had torn into her during her slumber.

"What day is it now?" she asked. "Day nine? We're halfway there, right?"

"Eight," Charles corrected.

"I swear, you could ruin a wet dream, Charles," Elaina complained as she shot him a piercing glare and rolled back over. "You couldn't lie to me? You couldn't let me believe in the fantasy of one extra day?"

"Stop being a child," he said as he performed the ritualistic measure of the descending sun to plot their continued course. When he turned around, she was standing a breath away from him. Caught off guard, he backed up a few steps.

"Funny!" she exclaimed with a wry smile. "Funny how you would choose those particular words. You think I didn't notice that Mandawuy was leading that search party? And maybe why we had to leave the village so abruptly?" Elaina marched past him, but when she looked back, she saw a man with a more reserved stride than normal.

"There's nothing to tell, apart from what I've already said," Charles insisted. "They knew we were fugitives and had worn out our welcome, so it was time for us to leave. Now, pay attention to where you're going. If you're going to take the point, you need to make sure we're still headed in the right direction."

Charles picked up his pace during their silent march. The only sound was the wind whipping and their boots crunching over the gravel until he finally walked past her.

"I've never been able to understand why men feel they have to think for us," Elaina said, fuming. "Or why they have this unrelenting urge to always lead, as though women are inept and need direction and saving. Maybe it's necessary for you to sustain the delusion that you're kings of your jungle," she said.

"Like the lion." Charles interrupted but Elaina retorted a snicker.

"Of course, the lion. You have the name of the animal right. However, but the large mane and gender? That part you men have all wrong. Anyone with access to the nature channel would see the flaw in your assertion."

When Charles offered no response, she gave a wide smile.

"Don't you just love those shows? All those male lions lazing around, sleeping all day? His size is all he has. Just a body to throw around to prove he's dominant. All that makes him is a bully. The female lion, however, is the clever one. She possesses the natural instincts and skill. The female lions are the ones who spot, stalk, and pounce on the prey that nourishes the entire pride. No matter how fast the prey, they run it down. No matter how strong the victim, they drag it to the ground, burying their razor-sharp claws into its body, wrapping their powerful jaws around its throat, and crushing its windpipe until it is dead. Much like how I did away with the correctional officer when we escaped.

"Wouldn't you agree, Charles?" she prodded, her voice sinister in its sweetness. "There's not much difference between lions and humans. Females are still the bearers and the nurturers of the pride, and the males are more like sloths than kings. Your sole contribution is your size. Your ability to copulate with us."

She looked at him, and for some reason he didn't understand, he stopped walking and looked back at her. In Charles's past dealings with women, he would have done any number of vicious things to end such a nagging rant.

But now he couldn't offer a single word in his defense.

Chapter 22

THE SUN'S GLOW WAS GONE, leaving the starry night sky to guide them. Elaina had adapted to the pattern of three-hour marches, moderate conversation, and brief rest periods. Hours had passed, and while Elaina was in the lead, she was feeling excited that they would be taking their scheduled break soon.

"I'm tired, Charles," she complained.

"Just a little while longer," he urged.

"I'm hungry, thirsty, and my legs and back are throbbing. I need to stop. When is our next break, Mr. Mathematical?"

"Our break time was about an hour ago."

"What?" Elaina exclaimed. She dropped her burlap bag and began to rummage through it for the little food they still had.

Charles grabbed her by the arm and pulled her to her feet.

She snatched her arm away from him. "You must have lost your mind!" she snarled. "Don't you ever put your fucking hands on me ever again!" Charles raised his hands in the air by his shoulders as he stepped back, trying to placate her.

"Look, the sun will be up soon," he urged "I know we were supposed to stop, but if we keep going, we can make it to those small mountains. Wouldn't you rather sleep under real shade instead of under our clothes?"

"I am the master of what I do and I'm willing to bet we still have plenty of time to make it to those mountains!" she screamed, her voice quaking from anger. "And if we don't, fuck it. We'll just make due but in the meantime don't you for a second think you're going to manage me."

"How many times do I have to explain this to you?" Charles rattled off without taking a breath. "Those mountains aren't as close as they appear, and the sun will rise faster than you think. Every step we take, we travel one yard. That's one thousand seven hundred sixty steps in a mile. The average person walks three miles an hour. We walk four hours, rest for a half-hour based on the sun's movement, and repeat that cycle. Then we walk another two. That's thirty-six miles every day, north by northwest toward Darwin."

Elaina continued to sit on the ground and stare at him with the same suspicious glare he had become all too familiar with. She slowly and sarcastically clapped her hands. "Congratulations, you can count like a computer. What about our food and water?" she asked, dumping out the contents of their bag. Some foraged shrubbery and insects along with the last few scraps of the dried meat from Oodgeroo lay on the dusty ground. "Can you count us up some more food? These rations will last us another day. Two days, tops!"

"You're right," he said. "That's why we have to keep pressing toward those mountains. We're more likely to find water and plants or animals there." He continued to try and keep his voice measured, but was growing irritated with her tantrum.

"Look, I told you. I'm…not…moving. Either stay here and rest with me the next thirty minutes, or you continue on without me," she announced, clutching the container to her side. "Whatever you decide though, the water stays with me." She stared at him almost to the point of taunting.

"Fine," Charles tersely agreed. "But we must ration the water. One mouthful per person per rest period. Not a drop while we're walking."

Elaina unscrewed the cap, looked him square in the eyes, and swallowed as much water as her open mouth could hold. Before draining the gigantic gulp, she raised the container to her mouth again. Wide-eyed, Charles jumped to his feet, but she had swallowed the second mouthful of water before he could intervene.

"I'm pregnant and drinking for two, remember?" Elaina said. She placed the bottle beside her and stood in defiance of Charles aggression. "Go ahead, take another step closer, and I'll send you to meet my ex-husband and his whore."

Charles looked in her eyes. She appeared to have slipped into a trance. He stepped back. Her fighting stance spoke volumes as to her intentions . . .

~~~

Elaina was twelve, pressed down on a ratty blue mat by a boy two years younger than her. He was between her legs, trying to bend and pull her into submission. She fought back as best she could, but her opponent was determined. She felt her strength was fading, she winced and grunted, fighting with every ounce of her will not to give him what he wanted.

She turned her head to the side and saw the banner in the rafters of her father's dojo. *Nunca desista!*[34] it read. *A dor é a fraqueza deixando o corpo!*[35]

From the sidelines, her father barked instructions to help his daughter fend off her brother. "Bridge your back and reverse his position, Elaina!" he screamed. "Hurry, before it's too late."

Elaina hit the mat hard three times when she could no longer endure the pain of the arm-bar submission hold.

"That's enough," her sensei and father ordered. "It's over!"

"Ha! I tapped you!" her younger brother gloated. Their father charged onto the mat and smacked his son's face.

"Quiet! Never taunt your opponent," their father commanded. "Always show respect and never embarrass your sister.

"Yes, Sensei," he replied, looking at the floor. Enduring the pain of his father's strike. He knew, from experience, that any attempt to nurse the pain would be followed by another strike. That's how his father disciplined his students.

---

[34] Never give up!

[35] Pain is weakness leaving the body!

"Now, since you have enough energy to humiliate your sister, put it to good use. Ten minutes of circuit training."

The preteen bowed, hopped up, and sprinted to the weight training area of the dojo. Elaina stood beside her father, also ignoring the pain in her arm and taking in deep breaths.

"Elaina," her father said.

"Yes, Sensei," she replied, looking at the floor.

"Sit here," he ordered, motioning at the seat next to him. She jumped to do exactly as she was told.

"Do you know why you lost to your brother?"

"Yes, Sensei. My rolling defense needs more work."

"Well, yes, your defense requires more work. But that is not why you lost. Despite your seniority, nature has designed men to be physically stronger than women. Even now, your little brother, who lacks your technique and experience, won by overpowering you. Therefore, when a man is your opponent, you cannot rely on your strength. Do you understand?"

"Yes, Sensei."

"Now, tell me, do you now know why you lost?"

"I am a girl, and he's stronger."

"No, Elaina!" he said flatly. "That is incorrect!"

Elaina looked at him, wildly confused.

"His size and strength gave him the advantage but even his execution was sloppy," he said. "But that is not why you lost." He repeated.

She stared at him.

"There's a story my father told me when I was your age," he said, his animated tone capturing her attention. "A brave

Brazilian warrior once explained to his grandson that we all have two wolves living within us. One of the wolves is selfish, controlling, greedy, impatient, restless, cruel, and desires only immediate gratification. The other is kind, unselfish, compassionate, calm, understanding, and patient. The grandson asked him, 'Which one wins?' The grandfather answered, 'Whichever one you feed.'"

Her father took her small hands in his. "Elaina, ever since you were a young child," he explained with loving but serious eyes, "you have fed the second wolf, which has made you a generous and loving person. But that wolf won't keep you from harm. So, when you find you must engage in combat, you must starve the wolf you're so fond of. Abandon it and leave it to fend for itself. Embrace the first wolf. Embrace its cruelty, release its restlessness, and nourish its greed. That wolf will keep you alive when threatened."

She felt her heart lift. "Yes, Sensei!"

"Good," he said. "Now stand up."

She got to her feet.

"Davi!" he shouted to his son. "To the mat!"

Exhausted from the circuit training drills but still wearing a smirk, Davi jogged to the mat and took a battle stance. Elaina assumed her spot on the line opposite her brother. Her face was stony.

Elaina's father spoke to her. "What wolf is feeding now, Elaina?"

His son glanced between them, confused.

Elaina lowered her stance and re-clenched her fists. "The first, Sensei!"

"Good. Now, fight!"

~~~

Elaina raised the gallon of water to her lips to defy Charles's authority.

"I'm warning you!" Charles threatened.

"Fuck you, Charles. Who are you to warn me, coward. You prey on children. Why were Mandawuy and the others tracking us?" Her lips quivered and her brow darkened. "Did you say or do something to his wife. . . or the children in the village?" Elaina took another long drink from the jug. Her cocked hip and widened stance gave her an air of assertiveness he had not noticed before.

"And what if I did?"

Elaina dropped the jug and charged him, tackling him and driving him to the ground.

"Are you nuts?" Charles yelled, sandwiched between her and the ground.

She elbowed him in the nose, sending his head smacking into the ground. He tried to get up, but she had straddled his chest and pinned his arms. Charles rolled to unbalance her, then thrust himself up from the ground. Elaina tumbled with his countermove and sprang to her feet.

"You want to fight, huh?" he challenged. "Come and get it, bit—!"

Before he could complete his insult, she delivered a blinding roundhouse kick to his face

"You talk too much. Bitch!" she retorted. He vision doubled and starts danced everywhere he looked. Elaina circled him, bouncing on her toes like a prizefighter. Still gathering himself, Charles admired Elaina's strategy of forcing him to keep moving as his equilibrium recalibrated itself. It kept him a step behind her attacks.

She sprung into the air, kicking him again in his jaw. He lifted his arms in defense a split second too slowly and tasted the sole of Elaina's boot once more. She did relent and followed with a right cross the moment her feet touched the ground, smashing his nose. He crashed to the ground. The back of his throat filled with the same blood that was filling the palms of his hands. He could barely breathe. Charles thrust defensive kicks at her while lying on his back, but Elaina bounced in and out of range, delivering low, sidewinding kicks of her own to his thighs.

Charles scuttled back like a crab, hoping to gain a few seconds and regain his composure.

Elaina pursued. Jab, step, spin, kick—her every move seemed to build in momentum and strength to end with a climactic ax-kick. He watched her left leg rise parallel to her torso before descending toward his head. He crossed his forearms to protect his face. Elaina changed the trajectory of her blow and directed the heel of her foot to his ribs.

Charles rolled onto his side, writhing in pain, leaving his back exposed. She delivered more snapping kicks, targeting his neck and shoulders.

"Elai—" He pleaded, before she landed another kick to his stomach, the fury on her face deliberate and intense.

"Tell me how it feels! Having your ass handed to you! By a woman!" Elaina antagonized.

Charles fought his way back to his feet, but he was barely able to stand upright. His legs were knotted from the numerous kicks his thighs. He'd reached full rage and through trying to reason with her. He tossed a few meaningless jabs to measure off his striking distance, followed by a powerful right hook she blocked but the force threw her off balance. His front snapping kick that followed found its mark in the middle of her chest, knocking her to the ground.

But she rolled backwards with her own momentum and sprung back onto her feet to immediately charge back at Charles again. Like a dancer, she leapt into the air with one leg extended. Charles threw his arms up to protect his broken nose, but at the last second Elaina bent her leg back under her and landed gracefully on the ground. Charles braced, ready to absorb her kick until the flash of her uppercut snapped his head back. The sun's bright smile greeted his gaze until Elaina swept his legs from under him turning his world upside down.

The course terrain mixed with the blood pouring profusely from his nose. Dust and gravel coated the side of his face, nose, and lips. Elaina continued her rhythmic defensive bounce, chin down and fists clenched.

Charles sneered. He was finished letting her have the upper hand. No woman was going to beat him into submission.

They circled each other, and through the piercing pain in his nose, dust filling his lungs, and the throbbing pains over his body, Charles willed himself into a new attack. He bull-rushed Elaina, using brute strength tackling her to the ground. She immediately wrapped her legs around his waist, creating a defensive posture to protect her from the barrage of angry strikes to come. Charles's attacks were sloppy. She was dodged or blocked the majority of them with her forearms.

"You fight like shit!" she taunted him. "You strike like a bitch!"

He looked down at her body, and her eyes grew wide. She instinctively threw her arms in front of her abdomen. Charles threw a punch with all his might aimed at the mouth degrading him. She dodged that one too and listened to it smash into the hard earth. The pain stunned his entire body.

Elaina shot her legs from around his waist to his throat, as she had done to the correctional officer. The panic is his eyes were instant. He had already witnessed how this scene would end. He knew she could kill him.

"Confess, pedophile," she raged. "What did you do? At the village?"

Charles couldn't speak. Foamy saliva gathered in the corners of his mouth as she tightened her grip around his neck with her thighs. His vision dimmed to dark shapes and shadows before he collapsed.

When he went limp and crumpled to the ground, Elaina lifted her face and screamed up to the heavens in victory. She let go and kicked him away from her, discarding him to the wasteland where he belonged, exhausted. She looked at him lying still, limp, kicking him once more to the back of his head. He didn't move.

She stared at his body for a moment before bursting into tears. She put her filthy hands to her face and sobbed, her whole body heaving. She'd won a victory, but it was short-lived. Now she was alone.

Chapter 23

HARLES WOKE ON THE GROUND—NOT the dry, red dirt of Katingal, but the clean, white brick of an unknown land. A pair of fresh dungarees, a short-sleeved button-up shirt, and black dress shoes had replaced his dusty, blood-stained prison uniform. He felt well and jumped up.

He turned in a slow circle, amazed by the open, flat land stretching in all directions. All that disrupted the emptiness was a large white building so well-camouflaged that it seemed almost like a mirage.

He approached and looked through the glass double doors etched to catch the sunlight. No one milled in the lobby. He pulled the door's golden handles and a sterile, interior breeze passed over him as he took the first few steps inside a long white corridor.

The doors shut behind him with a definitive thud. He turned to look, but the doors had gone. In their place was another corridor identical to the one on his other side. He hesitated, lost. A brief memory of his fight with Elaina flashed in his mind and blood began to pour from his nose. He cupped his hands, but they filled in seconds overflowing into a puddle on the floor.

A woman in a white coat and stethoscope dashed through one of the halls into a room. Charles yelled after her for help. She did not turn.

"Doctor? Anybody?" His voice echoed off the smooth white walls.

He found a room with swinging doors that led to a surgical theater, metal table, white sheets, and tools perfectly aligned. There was no sign of the doctor or anyone else. He returned to the hallway and bumped into a desk that had not been there before.

"Is anyone here?" he yelled, tearing off his blood-sticky shirt. He balled it up and held it against his nose while banging the shiny silver bell on the desk with his other hand.

"God, no!" a woman yelled from the operating room he had just left. Only a few seconds had passed, but somehow the room had filled with several doctors, nurses, and orderlies all working on a young female patient lying on the table. Bloody footprints and bandages lined the floor. Charles watched the commotion through the round windows of the swinging double doors.

"A liter of epi, wide open, and hang another liter of O-neg," the doctor said as she pressed on the little girl's chest and looked at the monitor. "Charge the paddles!" she ordered.

The young girl's peasant clothing lay in shreds on the floor. She was naked on the table, and the doctor and nurses did not notice or, perhaps, did not care about the blood, dirt, and body tissue smeared over their white coats.

"Clear!" the doctor shouted as she placed the defibrillator paddles on the girl's chest and squeezed the buttons to release the electric shock.

The girl's body jerked violently.

"Charge to one twenty! Clear!" The doctor delivered another jolt of electricity.

The girl's body arched again into the air and flopped back down. Charles inched as close as he could. Her eyes were closed, and her body was limp. Her skinny arms fell off the sides of the table and glistened under the strong lights.

The doctor climbed on top of the girl and continued CPR. Charles moved into the room. Reddish dirt filled the creases on the bottom of the girl's feet. Her knees were skinned raw, and scratches and abrasions hatch-marked her thighs.

Charles stood silent behind a crying nurse. The doctor hung her head and began to weep, too. A steady flow of blood bubbles pulsed from a deep laceration in the girl's throat. With every compression, air exited the slit that ended her life prematurely. The monitor's steady, shrill flatline gave undeniable proof that the patient was dead. An elderly nurse fell to her knees, mumbling and chanting in an aborigine dialect.

"Look what they did to my child," the doctor cried out. "Open your eyes! Open your eyes, or I'll take a switch to you."

She began beating her daughter's chest, harder, then harder, until the surgical tools on the gurney crashed to the floor. The small child's body began to rock faster and faster. Her head tilted to the right, and her fixed, lifeless eyes targeted Charles. The doctor stopped, her face in full recognition of what had happened.

Charles suddenly recognized that the doctor was Oodgeroo.

"I curse the demon who stole you away from your father from me. Speak their name, child. Tell me where they are, and I'll hunt him to the ends of the earth!"

The child's right arm shifted, her finger was limp but fell at rest in Charles's direction.

Silence fell over the emergency room. The nurse ceased her murmuring. Everyone looked at Charles.

"Abim!"[36] The doctor screamed. "You butchered my child after I saved your life? Abim! Abim! Abiiiim!"

Oodgeroo lunged toward him. He closed his eyes, ready to accept his fate at the hands of the mourning woman.

~~~

His eyes fluttered open under the blazing sun, and in its ferocious heat, Charles became aware of a dull ringing in his ears. His head pounded and his neck was stiff.

He lifted his head from the hot ground and rolled over, looking all about him to get his bearings. His memory felt dull

---

[36] Satin!

and cloudy for the first time since his surgery, but sharpened and focused as he tried to stand. Each ache and pinch of his stiff body reminded him of another detail of his battle with Elaina. He inspected his bruises and wounds, noting the collage of bite marks that Katingal's insects had left on the exposed parts of his body.

He had no idea how long he had been out. Charles struggled to stand, stumbling about like a punch-drunk boxer. Eventually, he gathered himself to brush away the pebbles and dust imprinted to the side of his face from being pressed against the ground for so long. His tongue was as dry as the earth falling from his clothes with every wavering step he took. His thirst was peaking again. He swung his heavy head, looking for the supplies he so desperately needed.

It's all gone! All the water and food, gone. She took it all.

He noticed one of the T-shirts that he and Elaina used to carry food tumbling in a distant gust of wind. He dashed toward it, flailing to catch it, until he trapped one sleeve under his foot. His body teetered as he bent, and the desert twirled around him. He rested one knee on the ground to restore his equilibrium.

He inspected the shirt for food but found only dust.

She's left me for dead.

He rummaged through his jarred memories and salvaged a memory of the mountains. He oriented himself until he could see the mountain's peaks poking above the wavy heat lines twisting the air above the sand. His rubbery legs wobbled with each step, like a toddler learning to walk. He held out the palms of his hands and watched them shake beyond his control. Nausea swelled inside him. He steadied his breath, in through his nose and out through his mouth.

"I may have a concussion," he told the air.

His blood boiled and his hands shook as more memories of the fight he lost returned to him. His steps became more rapid, and the feeling of nausea returned.

"Focus, dammit! Keep your head. Breathe in through your nose and out through your mouth."

For two hours, Charles stumbled toward the mountain range, where he had hoped to find shade, water, and salvation. Bugs and spiders, children's laughter and crow calls, pools of water and drifts of snow, all manner of hallucinations danced in his brain as he struggled to stay on his path.

He realized that he was the closest he had come to greeting death since his battle with the dingo. He chanted the word *persevere*, hoping his mind could convince his body that the situation was not as dire as it seemed. He looked up at the sky, squinting at the sun with contempt, but the sun's hypnotic rays cursed him back.

His face-off with the sun caused dizziness to overwhelm him, and again he fell to the ground. He broke his fall with his hands, but couldn't stop the momentum of his head before it cracked against the earth. The sun was heavy as it pressed its weight upon his back.

"Damn you and your creator," he cursed at the sun. "My soul isn't yours to take." he shifted his attention to the ground beneath him, squinted his eyes as if he could penetrate the numerous layers beneath him until he could see Hell and all its inhabitants. "My soul isn't is yours, either!"

A hissing sound broke him out of his rant. A four-foot-long serpent writhed before him. Charles froze, and the serpent stopped slithering to stare at him. It exhibited no defensive or offensive posturing, but maintained its eye contact.

Charles placed his hands on his knees and peered closer at the reptile. His heartbeat slowed and his breathing returned to normal. The serpent remained still, flipping its tongue at Charles as the two creatures remained motionless.

Even baked by the heat, Charles's brain scanned until he was able to identify the snake as *Antaresia/Liasis perthensis,* a nonpoisonous pygmy python.

He circled the serpent, anticipating that his movements would encourage the snake to slither away. The python defied Charles and stared back at him as if they were kindred spirits.

Charles stepped onto its head with his boot heel and grabbed the serpent, pulling and twisting until it detached from its head. The still-slithering body coiled around Charles's wrist as he lifted it to his mouth to drink. The warm, wet snake blood stained his lips and teeth red as he squeezed every drop of moisture from this creature that was both sacrifice and his savior.

Fortified, he tucked the serpent's skin into his belt and continued his march to the mountain range. For the moment, his focus was clear. He looked up at the heavens once more.

"Not today," he mocked with a bloody sneer. "I'm not finished with your world."

~~~

Charles had reached the mountain while the sun was still perched in the sky. The small crevices he found provided enough shade so he could rest, but it would be only a matter of time before the earth's rotation changed the sun's trajectory to where its glare returned to him.

The shade was a relief, but there was no salvation from his thirst or the swarms of insects hopscotching the length of his body. He had given up on the effort of shooing them away.

He scanned the area for any sign of water. He scavenged among the large rock formations, searching every crevasse and cave for the substance he needed most to sustain life.

The search seemed to last as long as the walk to the mountains. He continued around large rock formations that seemed to never end. Eventually he scaled the mass, hoping an elevated view would bare more fruitful results, but all he found were the same cloned rock formations that began to blend into one large collage with no foreseeable end.

His mind tormented him, returning the fear that he might never find water, and that the blood he drank from the snake still swinging from his belt was a fleeting triumph. He shielded his eyes and noticed that, not too far from him, buzzards were circling.

He scowled once more at the heavens. "You send them for me?" he said with outstretched arms and clenched fists.

One of the birds broke from the flock's aerial formation and dove toward the earth. Charles marched to the open ground the buzzards were stalking. Then he positioned himself on a rock formation that overlooked open ground about a hundred feet below. The flock of buzzards circled fifty feet above him. One by one, they would dive to the ground.

Charles approached the ledge. Below, he saw the rotting carcass of the animal the buzzards were pecking. From the condition of the rotting meat, he could see that this feast was fit only for the birds. He had no idea what the corpse had been in life.

Exhausted from his long trek and the rocky climb, Charles watched the circling scavengers. Another buzzard dropped out of formation and headed toward the ground. This time, it descended more, lower and lower. Charles watched its descent, observing the vulture's hesitant approach.

Then, in a flash, it struck the body of the dead animal with its powerful beak, ripping and tearing away at its flesh. It threw its head back, swallowing the pieces whole before two more buzzards soared in for their share of the meal. Now all three were on the ground eating, and at times flapping their wings and pecking at each other as they laid claim to their share of the carcass.

Charles's stomach growled at the sight of the trio's feast, and he salivated at the idea of stomaching the same disgusting flesh.

Then the outcry of one of the buzzards snapped Charles from his daydream. He looked down at the ground and saw two of the three buzzards bouncing away from the carcass, opening their large wings and taking flight. The third buzzard was lagging behind, bouncing away, trying to fly with one wing open. It fluttered on the ground, screeching in pain.

In defiance, the buzzard fluttered its way back to its feet, only to be met by a long, wooden spear impaling its body. The buzzard summersaulted backward in reaction to the violence before landing on the ground. Charles realized that it wasn't a broken wing hobbling the buzzard, but instead, another wooden spear protruding from its body. The second spear ensured that the buzzard wouldn't get away from whoever was hunting it.

Charles pressed his body against the rock cliff, hiding himself from whatever hunting party he feared might truly be tracking him.

The dying buzzard lay on the ground for a few moments, fluttering its wings. Then, from out of a cropping of shade, Elaina emerged, dressed in her prison jumpsuit. She charged at the dying bird, carrying another long wooden spear in both hands. She stabbed it once, putting it out of its misery. Then she flashed the buck knife she had taken from Charles and decapitated the bird.

Even from Charles's elevated position, he could see the ground grow dark from the blood pouring out of the buzzard. She grabbed the dead bird by its two tethers and dragged it back into the shaded area from where she had come, leaving a trail of blood to the entrance of her cave.

Chapter 24

CHARLES SPENT THE LAST ILLUMINATED moments of the day watching Elaina travel back and forth into the cave, preparing the buzzard she had killed. She hung the animal upside down, draining what blood remained in its body. She ripped the feathers from its flesh by hand and scraped away the feathers with the buck knife as a barber would shave a customer's hair. Once finished, she impaled it and positioned it over an open fire to cook.

While she labored over her fresh kill, Charles plotted on the perfect time to descend the rocky formation. He had been ignoring his hunger and thirst, as well as the screaming urge to kill Elaina and take all her food and water. He would drift off into daydreams of what he would do to her for besting him, taking their supplies, and leaving him for dead.

She broke into a sweat as she labored. Eventually she removed the top portion of her prison uniform and tied it around her waist. The excess material fell along her hips, accentuating their curves. Her skin glistened from her perspiration.

His heart rose in parallel with his loins. Confusion set in, precipitated by his sudden arousal at the partially clothed woman who had emasculated him in combat.

His thoughts swooped back to his abduction of Abaroo, and how he'd failed to ravage her like his countless previous victims. Since the surgery, his body had betrayed all the natural instincts he had cultivated up until his capture.

To avoid Elaina's seductive femininity, Charles rolled over to lose himself in the clouds drifting above him, but his heart continued to race. He closed his eyes, hoping to make sense of it all.

His meditation was broken by Elaina's voice screaming out in pain and terror. He turned around to find that the area where Elaina had been slaughtering the bird was vacant.

Charles pulled his weakened body from off the ground. As he navigated toward her cave, he could hear the echo of her voice, but her words were inaudible. To remain undetected, he paused outside her cave as he waited for his eyes to adjust. When his pupils dilated, the contents of the cave became clear.

It was shallow, with the small fire Elaina had lit flickering close to the entrance. The two wooden spears she had used to slay the buzzard were propped against the wall with the freshly cooked meat stuffed into a satchel. Scorpions and rodents circled the area beneath the satchel, feeding from the discarded scraps of carcass. A few feet away was the nearly full jug of water.

She found water? His heart leapt at the sight, and he crept toward it.

As he moved closer, he discovered Elaina in a kneeling position, her back to him. She was swaying in every direction with her outstretched hands in the dirt. The light of the fire revealed that she was gripping the metallic blade of the knife in her hand as she mumbled to herself.

Charles watched as she continued to pick and fumble through her hair as if trying to remove something from the messy mane. Then she moaned and clutched at a section of her head, then her neck and shoulder.

Charles had reached the jug of water, and crouched down to pick it up and raise it to his lips, making sure he didn't alert Elaina to his presence. His tongue and throat rejoiced as the container's cool contents saturated his coarse throat. He could feel the path the water flowed down the back of his throat, past his tonsils, down his esophagus, and into his stomach. The sensation was orgasmic as it shot outward and the energy expanded through his body. It was rejuvenating, giving off an opiate-like rush.

"Get off! Get off of me!" In the far corner, Elaina stabbed at the earth with the blade.

Startled, Charles coughed. Some water shot from his mouth and fell down his chin, mixing in with the dried snake blood he had drunk hours earlier.

Elaina swung her head around to face her intruder. Charles placed the jug down and rose to a defensive posture, readying himself for Elaina's attack.

The dim light from the fire illuminated the right side of Charles's body and face. His feet disturbed the insects and rodents foraging on the discarded meat, sending them scurrying. Charles saw Elaina's eyes widen at the sight of him, but it wasn't a look of surprise that he had survived, or even of familiarity. It was as if she was looking upon him for the first time.

Charles remained silent and grabbed one of the spears propped against the wall behind him, pointing it at Elaina. She turned around to face Charles, but remained kneeling.

"I figured you'd come for me, eventually," she slurred, her head swaying as if she were intoxicated.

She grimaced and reached for her scalp and neck again to comfort it. The muscles in her face twitched and took exaggerated blinks with her eyes. When she removed her hand from her neck, Charles could see a swollen, burgundy welt. Large beads of sweat ran down her face, and her clothes were saturated. She stuck the knife into the ground around her a few times, then held it up for Charles to see three impaled scorpions. Then she pointed at what remained of the snake dangling from Charles's belt.

"Of course, now you reveal yourself after first sending your minions poison me!" Elaina said. "I see the stained remains of the souls you devoured on your face. Have you come with your serpent to feast on me, *Diablo*?[37] Why didn't you reveal yourself when they raped me, one after the other? Only you could plant seeds of hate so deep where we would even need this place called Katingal."

---

[37] Devil?

Charles stared at her for a moment, then said, "Who do you think I am?"

"I *know* who you are!" she snarled. "You know who you are!"

"Then speak my name," Charles demanded.

"*Encarnado. Satanás! Você é o Diabo!*"[38] she responded in her native Portuguese.

Charles took a step back and tilted his head in disbelief at the accusation. He looked her over the best he could in the dimly lit cave, and what troubled him was what rested at her feet. The remains of at least a dozen scorpions were piled up all around her. Most were at least two inches long, their lethal tails still curled up over their backs as though poised to strike.

Charles realized all at once that the scorpion stings were the reason for her screams and accusations. Their venom had infiltrated her system to cause her delusion.

He watched her paw at her tangled hair to rid herself of any remaining scorpions. He kept his distance, unsure of what Elaina would do next. Her head began to bob as if it had become too heavy for her to hold. Her grip on the knife she wielded was growing weaker by the second. Even though she was in a seated position, she struggled to maintain her posture while perspiration coated her skin, bringing it to a glowing sheen with the help of the dancing light of the fire.

"Elaina, you're very sick right now," Charles warned. "You've been stung by scorpions. You have to let me help you."

---

[38] "Incarnate. Satan! You're the devil!"

"Stay away from me, *Encarnado*," she spat.

"I can't do that, Elaina," Charles said in measured tones. "Now, I'm going to walk over toward you. Don't do anything foolish."

"I said stay away!" She tried stumbling to her feet but was unable to maintain her balance. Her head swung around, heavy like a drunk, and the knife fell from her hand. Her eyes rolled into the back of her head as all her weight leaned to one side, ready to collapse.

Charles dashed toward her as her body fell towards the red earth beneath her, and managed to catch her before her head slammed into the hard ground. She was unconscious, eyes fluttering. Her breathing was uneven, but she was alive.

Chapter 25

WO DAYS LATER, CHARLES WAS still watching Elaina pass in and out of consciousness from the scorpion venom. During every fleeting moment of her coherence, he would force-feed her and make her drink. He had smoked the buzzard meat and had even managed to kill another one with one of Elaina's spears. Roasted buzzard wouldn't have been his first choice in a fine restaurant, but he preferred it to roasted rat.

He was chewing on a tough, stringing piece of buzzard meat when Elaina screamed, another nightmare jarred her back to awareness. Her eyes fluttered open until they grew steady enough to scan the dark cavern, eventually falling upon Charles.

For the first time in days, Charles could see that she recognized him. He watched as she processed her surroundings, then scurried backward to reach for the knife in her belt. Charles removed the knife from his belt and stabbed it into the ground before resuming eating his meal.

"Looking for that?" he asked. "Only the owners of an unclear conscience would reach for a weapon upon seeing an old friend. No food, water, or weapon." He paused, watching her as he chewed the stubborn meat. Then he swallowed and said, "No chance of survival. That's how you left me."

She sat on the ground and against the wall, remaining silent.

"You left me for the buzzards," he continued to lecture.

"Just like you left the girl Abaroo!" Elaina shot back. "Had you died, it would have been a deserved death, because you are an animal, Charles. Just like the one rotting outside this cave."

"And what are you!" he shouted. "Where are we? This is Katingal. We fight, maim, and kill, and we're content to do so."

"So if that's all we are, then why am I still alive? You've had plenty of opportunities to kill me."

Charles's anger subsided for a moment. He stared back into her eyes as he pondered. Then he could do little more than offer a half-shrug. "I've thought about it many times over the last couple days," he confessed. "But I didn't because I need you. Rather, we need each other to get off this continent, whether we want to admit it or not."

When she remained silent, Charles looked over at her. He was taken aback, as this was the first time in the weeks he had known her that she didn't have a pithy reply.

"Yes," he admitted. "I need the woman who left me for dead three days ago, and now you need me."

He reached down and pulled the knife from out of the ground. She watched him as he surveyed the dirt around him. Then, in a flash, he pierced the torso of another scorpion and held it up for her to see. Its legs moved frantically through the air, as though it still had hope of escaping the blade.

"Urodacus manicatus, or the scorpion," he informed as he placed the scorpion over the fire. *Its legs grew still as it blackened.* "We need each other to survive this place."

"How did you find me?" Elaina said, her voice oddly hushed.

"I found you two days ago, babbling and delirious inside this cave," Charles said. He watched the scorpion as it charred and shriveled, and eventually fell into the fire. "This is the most lucid you've been since I tracked you down. See the large blisters on your shoulder and hand?"

Elaina inspected her body. She winced when she touched the burgundy and blue whelps. A look of confusion swept across her face when she looked back at him. "Why can't I remember?"

"The venom in your body induced a fever, delirium, and hallucinations," he explained. He took a sip of water and handed the container to Elaina.

She reached up to accept the peace offering without question.

"Now get some more rest," Charles said. "We leave at sunset."

Elaina swallowed a mouthful of water before rolling over and surrendering to faith that she would be safe to sleep. To warm up, she untied the arms of her jumpsuit from her waist to pull it back onto her upper body.

She stopped when she saw large, dried bloodstains near the inner thighs of her clothes and put a hand inside her pants to investigate. When Elaina saw blood on her finger, she looked at Charles for an explanation.

"I'm sorry," he said, and realized with more than a little surprise that he meant it. "I wanted to wait before telling you. You miscarried. I'm sure it was the scorpion venom."

Her expression went blank, and she closed her eyes for a moment as she released a small sigh. Elaina leaned her head back, face pointed toward the heavens before opening her eyes again.

"Thank you, Eloah," she said as the smallest of smiles formed on her lips.

Chapter 26

As THE SUN SET, CHARLES and Elaina made their final preparations for what he believed to be the thirty-first night spent walking across Katingal's Northern Territory. They could see the lights of Darwin's skyline, and the terrain's transition from the desert landscape to fertile, green foliage. Charles was more than a little relieved to see that his efforts at rudimentary navigation had paid off.

Since Elaina's scorpion attack, the two of them had retreated into the recesses of their minds and conformed to an automatic and even pace. Gone was their mutual resistance or quarreling. When supplies ran low, they both foraged the landscape for sustenance.

After a month of rationing food and water, they had grown accustomed to surviving on bare minimums. They were both physically spent from the traveling and sleeping on whatever patch of land they happened upon when the sun rose.

With each passing day, Charles grew more confident that they would see the horizon of the port city. He knew that they would see signs of the city soon, and so, at every sunrise, he kept his eyes peeled for Darwin.

He looked over at Elaina once more as she tied off the satchel containing what few dried-out scraps of food they had left. She caught a glimpse of him observing her and returned the stare. Charles thought it foolish to break the silence, even though he was starved for conversation. He reminded himself of how Elaina's Brazilian Jujitsu had rendered him so close to death.

He gathered his load, took a deep breath, and continued the hike on swollen feet and tortured legs, determined to reach Darwin.

They were oblivious to the landscape, and to its insect inhabitants and their distracting noises. All Charles could hear was the monotonous crunching of rocks and earth under their boots. Elaina looked at Charles from time to time, but didn't utter a word.

Then finally she paused and called out to him. "Charles, I need to rest," she said.

"No!" he replied. "Keep walking."

"I'm not asking your permission," she said without moving. "I'm informing you of my intentions."

"We don't have time for this, Elaina," Charles said. He continued trudging forward without as much as a glance back at her. "We've already lost three days."

Elaina stared after him. "You're one special type of psycho!" she yelled. "What happened to all that 'we need each other' bullshit you fed me?"

Charles didn't break his stride as he continued in the direction of Darwin. With the prize almost in sight, he couldn't stop.

Elaina kept after him. "It's no wonder to me why your parents abandoned you. They obviously realized they brought a monster into this world but I wonder, when did you realize you were an abomination?" she asked.

Still, he kept moving without pause. "What is this, Elaina? Another attempt to start a fight so we stop and you get what you want? Is that how you maintained order in your home? Feeble tantrums to manipulate your husband when things aren't going your way? No wonder he had a mistress."

"You are so fucked up," Elaina shot back. She had started walking again and was ten paces behind him.

"Me? You're judging *me*?"

"Yes! I want to know why you're the way you are, Charles!"

Charles took a quick glance over his shoulder to see that her face showed no sign of her relenting from her inquisition.

"I want to understand it!" she demanded.

"It? What *it*, Elaina?"

"*It!* How and why you and I became monsters."

He made no reply to that. She paused for so long he thought that perhaps she had tired of the conversation. But then she spoke again, and her voice carried bitterness.

"Back in Brazil, I didn't have to kill them. I could have just left my husband. I could have married again and been happy. You have the answers to everything else, so tell me why I had to kill them and. . . and their child." She drew a ragged breath. "I can't stop seeing their faces. I want to stop seeing their faces whenever I close my eyes."

"You'll never stop seeing their faces," he replied. "That's the price we pay for being who we are. I don't have all the answers, but that I do know. You can't, won't, or ever understand why I'm the way I am, just like I'll never understand why you ripped an unborn child out of its mother's womb."

Through all of this, he never slowed. His boots thumped steadily over the hard ground.

"I'm sure it would be ideal to sum up what we are in some neat, novice psychological diagnosis," he continued as though warming to his subject. "But life's not that simple. I'm sure there are plenty of behavioral scientists who would *love* to poke and prod at me like a lab rat, deciphering what makes me this way."

"What's her name?" Elaina asked.

That surprised him so much he stumbled a bit before resuming his march. "What do you mean? What's whose name?"

"The woman who broke you."

Charles scoffed. "You can't be serious."

"Someone did this to you," Elaina persisted. "And the way you hurt girls and take pleasure in doing so tells me it was a woman."

Charles made no effort to hide his frustration. "So you're my psychologist now?" He issued a harsh bark of laughter. "This heat has you convinced you're Sigmund Freud? Just keep walking. Save your breath."

"Why do you hate women so much? And why children? You and your Duenno have destroyed so many daughters, nieces, and granddaughters. You're all failures as human beings!"

He stopped suddenly, turned toward her, pulled out his knife, and grabbed her by the throat. Elaina didn't resist. Instead, she allowed the razor-sharp blade to graze her cheek as she stared him in the eyes with a resolute glare.

"Okay," she said flatly. "You have a knife pointed at me, and I've witnessed you slay men with ease. But we both know I'm not afraid of you, Charles."

"You don't want to understand me," Charles said. "These are the questions you want answered about yourself." When she blanched, he kept on. "What about the hate inside you? You ask me the *why* like you're some child, ignorant to the ways of the world and the people who live in it. People like us aren't exiled by accident. We've earned it. *You've* earned it!" A slight smile of condemnation crossed Charles's face.

"We're not the same, Yäbälay," Elaina mocked. "I'm not a notorious child molester."

He grew furious and threw her hard to the ground. Elaina's eyes fluttered to regain her focus, only to face Charles's blade still pointed at her face, reflecting the sun's light.

"You're right, you just cut them from their mother's belly. Then you mutilate the corpse with cigarettes burns."

She spat in his face. He slowly pressed the blade into the skin on her face. The tip of the knife pierced her skin drawing blood that ran down her cheek. "Go ahead. Do it!

Do the only thing you know how to do well. Which will it be? Rape me? Kill me? Or both, you coward!" She forced a condescending chuckle. "Do you even know how to give pleasure to a woman, Charles?" A single tear escaped from her eye, mixing with the blood trailing down her cheek. Then she allowed the tension from her body to release as she lay flat and spread her arms and legs in surrender to him. She grabbed his hand and uncurled his fingers until the knife dropped. "You don't need that today," she said. "I'll take my clothes off for you and let you inside me."

Charles couldn't make sense of the pinwheel of emotions Elaina had demonstrated in the last few minutes. His arms shook as his eyes danced from her face to the surrounding landscape. Elaina pulled his chin around to face her as she undid the buttons of her jumpsuit until her exposed body lay beneath him, her legs spread.

"Can you do it, Charles?" she said. "Can you be with a female without forcing her into submission? Without forcing yourself inside her?"

He looked down at her and back into her eyes before pressing his body on top of hers. Like a novice, he fumbled to unfasten his pants as he buried his head along her shoulder to avoid eye contact. As he ground his hips into her pelvis, she felt the head of his warm penis touching her labia.

Just then, his body tensed while he shivered like a lost soul. Elaina remained beneath him and positioned her head to look at his face, but he was insistent on looking off into the distance.

She put her hand along the side of his face. "Thank you, Charles," she whispered. "Thank you for revealing the real you. A scared, powerless, little man in the presence of women." Now she placed her other hand on the side of his face and pulled him toward her, forcing him to look her in the eyes.

Charles struggled to hide his embarrassment.

Elaina leaned in and kissed him on his forehead.

Lightheaded, Charles jumped to his feet and pulled his clothes together. Once dressed, he gathered his portion of the supplies and marched off in the direction of Darwin, visibly shaken.

Elaina rose, and as she pulled her jumpsuit back up past her thighs, her hand brushed against the semen Charles had released before even entering her.

She looked up and watched him marching away, rubbing the back of his head.

Chapter 27

HE BRIGHT STARS THAT HAD illuminated the desert sky were dimming, a signal that the sun would soon reveal itself. Charles wondered if this would be the last night they would spend traveling Katingal's outback. The thought triggered a memory of the book about the continent's geography and population distribution. Darwin was a small city with a population of 124,818, by far the largest and most populated city in the Northern Territory.

Charles halted their march just past Mitchell's creek so they could bathe for the first time in more than a month. The bath was without soap, but submerging themselves in a clean body of water was refreshing all the same. Charles hadn't realized how a thick layer of dirt could cling to the human body. The crystal clear water became murky the moment they waded chest high into the cooling stream.

Afterward, Charles and Elaina sat naked on the bank of the creek to air dry. While Elaina worked her fingers through her wet, tangled hair, Charles watched the Eastern sky, trying to determine how much time they had before the sun would rise.

The cloak of night would help them covertly enter the pristine cul-de-sac of houses a half mile or so away. He had played this scenario countless times in his head for the past four and a half weeks.

"You see those houses there?" he asked. "That's where we're headed."

Elaina peered in the direction Charles pointed.

"There we can get a change of clothes, a few hours' rest, food, but most importantly, a car."

"But you said Darwin was a port city and we needed a port city. Now I may not be some genius like you, but I know cars don't work well on water."

"Darwin is Katingal's largest port city," he replied. "That translates into a necessity for border control, which means KPP detection. Our stop in Darwin is out of necessity."

He reached into the satchel and removed some articles of women's and men's clothing he had stolen from Oodgeroo's hut weeks ago. He tossed some at Elaina. He put on a pair of dungarees and a green tank-top shirt on himself. Elaina held the dress up in the air and then next to her body before looking at Charles in disappointment. The garment was made for a slender, nomadic body, and despite how much Elaina had thinned, she remained too curvy to fit the dress.

"You can calculate how many miles we traveled the past month in a single breath," she said, shaking her head. "But you haven't reserved a single brain cell for artistry or creativity. Give me your knife."

Elaina took the knife he handed her while biting a small tear at the front neckline of the dress. She cut the legs of her prison uniform half way up the thigh and removed her shirt. When Elaina pulled the dress on, it fell down her waist until her hips prevented it from sliding any further, so she cut a straight line down the front and pulled the two sides around to her back. She turned around, facing away from Charles.

"Now, tie it into a knot or a pretty bow, if you can," she instructed.

The tight fit of the dress and the slit just below her breasts with a secured knot in the back propped her breasts like any sports bra. Her handiwork had transformed the rustic apparel into a lusty outfit that would distract anyone.

"Your turn," she said, moving toward Charles with the knife.

Within a minute, she had cut off the legs of his dungarees two inches above his knee. She stepped back to admire her creation. "Come on, turn around for me," she said, speaking in a playful tone for the first time since they had been together.

Charles performed a half-turn without moving his feet much until she gave him the nod of approval. Then he gathered their spears, satchel, and other items, and threw them into the deepest part of the creek. They watched the heavy items sink and the ragged clothing float until the current carried them out of sight.

They turned and faced the peaceful cul-de-sac before them.

"It's been two months since I set my feet on a paved street and smelled fresh flowers and grass," Elaina said. "I'd almost forgotten the beauty of a city."

Charles was fixated on the neighborhood, its residents, its closed-circuit televisions, or any other potential threat to his freedom.

"Now would be a good time for you to share how you plan to get us off this continent without our implants alerting the peacekeepers," Elaina quipped.

"I can't explain every detail to you, Elaina. Sometimes you're going to have to just trust me. For now, let's just keep walking. The sun is almost up."

They closed in on the edge of the city, the cul-de-sac just a stone's throw away.

"Trust you?" she said. "I didn't suffer the last month just to get captured the moment we make it back to civilization."

The dirt perimeter bled into a cement street.

"Not now, Elaina!" he said, putting his arm around her shoulders.

Elaina pulled away from him, but Charles cupped her far shoulder and yanked her back in closer to him. "Look and walk as normally as possible, and follow my lead. We're just a local couple out for some morning exercise."

They had officially breached the city limits. The soles of their boots touching paved ground felt odd to Charles, just as Elaina had said, and the smell of fresh-cut flowers wafted in the air as the sun rose higher in the sky.

"The first empty house we find," Charles said, "we break in, find a change of clothes, take the vehicle, and then we're headed to Channel Island."

"You expect to find a car at an empty house?" she challenged. "If the house is empty, won't that mean that its residents have taken the car?"

Before Charles could reply, they spotted a young couple leaving a house. The couple hadn't noticed Charles and Elaina. The husband was lugging two laptop bags to their car while his wife carried an infant.

"Quick, start jogging." Charles said as he shoved her into a slow trot.

Within seconds, they were within sight of the couple, and the husband took a full glimpse of Elaina's frame. Every curve bounced to the stride of her soft trot and drew attention away from Charles's less-convincing jogging attire.

"Greet them." Charles whispered to Elaina.

"What?" she questioned.

"Just do it! Greet them!"

"Peace be onto you," Elaina said with her Portuguese accent while both of them raised their palms into the air and then set them over their left breast.

The husband returned the smile while placing the bags into the car. "Peace be onto you," he replied, reciprocating the hand gesture.

His wife's forced smile melted into a jealous gaze as she stepped in to break her husband's line of sight on Elaina and shoved their child into his arms.

"Keep going and don't look back," Charles instructed as they continued their farce of a workout.

A few seconds later, he heard the engine of the couple's car starting.

"Now let's cross the street and head back toward their house," Charles ordered.

They crossed the street and slowed their jogging pace to a near crawl on the same side of the couple's home. The couple's modest car pulled out of the driveway, and the husband stopped to ensure that there was no oncoming traffic. His wife glared to deter him from stealing another glance at Elaina.

He turned away from Elaina and Charles's direction and headed down the street.

Charles and Elaina finished their jog back down the street toward the unsuspecting couple's home and up the walkway until they reached the driveway. There, Charles grabbed Elaina by the arm and darted to the back of the house. When they arrived at the back door, Charles removed his shirt and wrapped it around his fist. Elaina stepped in front of him, stopping him from smashing the window. Then casually she turned the doorknob.

"It's open," she said, looking disappointed at Charles. "Had you surrounded yourself with normal people rather than pedophiles and other degenerates, you'd know that people rarely lock their doors anymore."

Elaina walked in ahead of Charles as he unwound his shirt from his hand, embarrassed. He hurried in after her, then immediately crouched down and closed the door behind him. He pressed his back against the wall and pulled Elaina down next to him near the back door facing into the home's kitchen. Then he turned around to peek through the wooden blinds covering the windows next to the door, surveying the nearby houses for any neighbors who may have witnessed them entering the house.

"I think we're okay," he said, but out of the corner of his eye, he could see that Elaina had already gone.

When he looked up, he saw that she had shuffled further into the kitchen and was standing at the sink. She turned the knobs of the faucet, cupped her hands below the stream of clear water, and lowered her lips into the pool she had created, swallowing large gulps.

"Not so fast," Charles warned. "You'll make yourself sick."

Elaina replied by removing one of her hands from under her mouth and extending it to Charles, its middle finger pointed toward the ceiling. She splashed water on her face before she made her way over to the refrigerator and pulled the door open.

Elaina gasped with delight and started rummaging through its contents, eating whatever she found that didn't require cooking. Charles took up a space next to Elaina and plunged his dirt encrusted hand into a bowl of mashed potatoes that she had moved on from after having her fill. He devoured what remained of the creamy dish until there was nothing left but the bottom of a large green bowl. Elaina had emptied another plastic container of food and let her eyes roll to the back of her head in satisfaction.

The moment Elaina swallowed her last mouthful, she jumped up to inspect the remaining shelves of the refrigerator. Before her stood more food, condiments, and beverages she had been deprived of for the last month. They plowed through meatloaf smothered in gravy, a bowl of mixed vegetables, and an assortment of fruit in the bottom drawer.

Then Elaina's eyes bulged as she grabbed for a can of Foster's beer. Charles almost knocked her over to seize one for himself. They both pulled the tabs back, and Elaina gestured, holding her beer in the air, awaiting Charles to return the sentiment. Elaina took a mouthful, swallowed, and released a large belch that would have made any man proud. Charles's throat bounced up and down with each gulp until he had guzzled every drop.

"Oh my God! That was good," Charles rejoiced, taking a few deep breaths and releasing one last short burp before he could feel the effects of the alcohol coursing through his system.

Elaina continued to take single mouthfuls of beer until she finished at her own pace. Charles sat back to enjoy the gradual sense of euphoria that was overcoming him. He was content for the first time since before he had been arrested. Elaina continued her sacking of the refrigerator until Charles broke the silence.

"Did you see the laptop bags they were carrying?" he asked. "They won't be back until after work hours. We'll be better off waiting for them to come home to steal their car rather than trolling the neighborhood looking for one to break into. So, in the meantime, let's get cleaned up, acquire some real clothes from their closet, and squeeze in another meal before they get home."

She nodded acquiescence, and he was grateful that at last he'd made a suggestion that she agreed with.

He rose from his place on the floor, the alcohol causing a pleasant swirl in his head. For the first time in months, he felt free.

Then Elaina jumped up from her place on the floor, nudged past Charles, and ran up the stairs. "I'm going to take a bath," she called back over her shoulder.

"That's not a bad idea," Charles said. He walked the length of the house on the first floor in search of a second bathroom he could claim as his own. He went from room to room while Elaina's footsteps upstairs had come to a halt and the sound of running water traveled downstairs.

There was no second bathroom to be found, so Charles took up a spot in the master bedroom while Elaina continued filling the tub.

On one side of the room, there was a set of double doors, and on the other side was the bathroom. Charles had barely stepped into the room before the soft fragrance of bath salts greeted his senses. He leaned in the threshold of the bathroom door, watching Elaina rummage through the medicine cabinet in a white cotton robe.

She stopped, grasping a small plastic container of antibiotics in the palm of her hands. She turned the nobs of the faucet, and water shot from the spout. With hurried and fumbling hands, she twisted the childproof top from the bottle, shook three pills from the container, and threw them into her mouth. Then she shoved her open mouth under the running water, gulping mouthfuls until the lack of air forced her to stop.

She dropped the container of pills into the pocket of the robe and hurried over to the bathroom's linen closet. She paused once the doors swung open, and a wide smile graced her face—wider than any smile Charles had seen from her before. For the first time, he glimpsed the true beauty she had possessed before the ravages of men and the harsh sun had stolen it from her. She popped open every beauty product and smelled the contents of each one before snatching the shampoo and conditioner of her choice.

Then she retreated to the bath.

"*Oh meu Deus, sim!*"[39] she sang from the bathroom. "*Eles têm uma Jacuzzi!*"[40]

Charles headed for the king-size bed in the middle of the bedroom. It was encased in a wooden frame, draped with a burgundy bed linen, and topped with a collection of oversized pillows. Charles placed the pillows in a perfect formation before lying down.

Seconds later, the rumble of the Jacuzzi jets sounded. Elaina's melody and the constant rumble of the Jacuzzi lulled Charles into a brief but deep slumber until his appetite

---

[39] Oh my God, yes!

[40] They have a Jacuzzi!

wakened him. He headed back downstairs to riffle through the cupboards for any delicacy left behind from the first feast.

He had searched all the cupboards and found only nonperishables and other items that required cooking, so he returned to the refrigerator, hoping to find something that he and Elaina had overlooked in their haste. He shuffled and shoved the containers they had already emptied, then spotted it in the back: a large Tupperware container. He slid it out and pulled it open to find the leftovers of an Aussie meat pie.

I'll only eat a small piece, he thought.

Forgoing any eating utensils, Charles scooped a modest piece of the Aussie pie with his index and middle finger before stuffing it into his mouth. He chewed the cold meal and savored every morsel before washing it down with a can of soda. He belched, took another scoop of the food, and finished the can of soda before returning upstairs to the master bedroom.

There, he took his place among his pillow formation with plans to retire until Elaina finished her bath.

Charles closed his eyes and relaxed to the sound of the Jacuzzi jets from the other side of the door. He felt himself drifting away toward what he expected to be the most enjoyable sleep he'd had in ages.

That euphoria was broken when the buffet of food and drink he consumed began a loud rumbling inside of him. His eyes shot open and he sat up on the bed. His feet were hanging off the sides while he patted himself on this chest. A grotesque belch erupted through his esophagus. Along with it came a foul stench that reeked of a muddied combination of the beer and all the foods he had eaten since breaking into the house.

He could sense that his body was displeased with the sudden collage of food and beverages, and already it was too late. He darted to the bathroom door and turned the knob, forgetting that Elaina had locked it. He pushed and slammed into the door as it refused to give way to him.

"Elaina, I'm going to be sick," he pleaded through the door.

"I'm sorry to hear that, but I'm not moving," she calmly responded. "Find another bathroom to be sick in. I'm not going to let you ruin this for me."

"Open the door," he replied, violently shaking the handle. "I'm about to shit myself."

She laughed. "Now I'm definitely not opening the door. The last thing I want is to be in the same room with you while you're releasing whatever projectiles are set to shoot out of your ass. Sorry."

His stomach grew angrier by the second. He clenched his buttocks, hoping to trap the buildup of gas and excrement that had already worked its way down from his colon. He turned in circles like a confused dog. Hot flashes rushed through his body, and he began to sweat. An overwhelming feeling of nausea hovered over him. The pressure in his stomach had reached its breaking point.

He stopped in his tracks, took one last scan of the bedroom, and spotted a ceramic wastebasket in one of the corners. He lunged at it, yanked down his pants, and sat down. His toes clenched the thick carpet, his fingers mimicking the motion against his belly.

Charles let the robe he had taken from the closet fall off of his shoulders and settle on the floor. He had barely had time to position himself over the top of the wastebasket before everything came out of him in a rush. Some of his waste spilled over the sides as he evacuated everything he had consumed within the last hour.

A few seconds into his humiliation, the bathroom door swung open. Elaina peeked around the open space, looking baffled first by the sound and then by the sight of a naked, shivering, and flushed Charles hunched over with his backside hovering over the wastebasket.

He watched in shame as she released the largest smile and burst of laughter he had ever seen from her. He moaned as his backside sounded off like a tone-deaf trumpeter.

Elaina's smile gave way to a look of disgust. Despite the embarrassment, Charles's backside continued to empty into the small basket to the point that he began to fear it would overflow before he was finished. He looked over at Elaina, embarrassed, his thighs burning from the torturous position and his rectum transformed into a violent fountain of feces.

"Now that's just disgusting," Elaina said before slamming the door and returning to her perfumed bath.

Chapter 28

"**W**AKE UP! THEY'RE HERE!"

Charles awoke to the sensation of Elaina shaking him. He found himself in the bedroom, curled up on the formation of pillows he had sculpted on the bed while Elaina took her shift on lookout for the returning couple.

He snapped to attention and leapt from the bed, disoriented by the nearly forgotten amenities of civilization.

"We have to hurry," Elaina said, rushing downstairs ahead of Charles.

In the far corner of the living room stood the luggage they had packed with a new, stolen wardrobe for themselves. Next to that was a trash bag full of groceries they had sacked from the kitchen.

Just as they had planned, Charles hurried down the stairs and took his position behind the front door, waiting to set the ambush.

"That's not going to be a problem, is it?" Elaina asked, nodding to how Charles was shaking the sleep out of the arm he had slept on for too long.

"I'm fine," he assured her.

Elaina nodded, then opened her mouth as if she had more to say, but hesitated.

"What's the matter?" Charles whispered while keeping an eye on the couple as they gathered their belongings from the car.

"We're going to just tie them up, remember?" Elaina reminded him. "You aren't going to—"

"Shhh, they're almost at the door," he whispered forcefully as he brandished his knife.

Both their backs were against the wall, where the door would swing open. He reaffirmed his grip on the handle of the dagger and whispered in her ear. "If they cooperate, there won't be a problem. We'll just do it the way we talked about. By the time they free themselves, we'll be long gone."

Charles took one last peek out the small window to see the approaching couple fifteen feet away. He looked back at Elaina standing beside him and put his index finger to his lips. He could hear the couple's feet approaching the door, the baby crying, and the husband turned the doorknob.

They didn't lock the front door either, he thought, and he wondered, as he had for perhaps a thousand times, why people were so trusting.

The latch of the door released, and with the palms of her hands, Elaina cushioned the impact of the door swinging open. The couple took a few steps into their house before Elaina slammed the door shut.

Without hesitation, they charged their targets. Elaina toppled the wife and child, sending them both to the floor. Charles subdued the husband and had his knife up against the frightened man's throat before the man even knew what was happening.

"Don't you even think about fighting back!" Charles ordered.

"My baby!" the mother cried out, struggling to her feet with the child in her arms. "Please don't hurt us."

"Nobody's going to hurt your baby," Elaina told her. "Just relax."

The frantic crying of the baby heightened the tension.

"We don't have much money," the husband pleaded. "But whatever you find, you can have."

"If you two follow our instructions," Charles said as Elaina struggled to control the protective mother, "we'll be out of your home and on our way."

"Just take what you want and leave!" the mother demanded, her tone sharp. It seemed that Elaina's words had somehow given her courage, and her fear had morphed into indignation. She slapped angrily at Elaina's hands as Elaina reached for the thrashing baby. "Don't you touch me or my baby! Is that my blouse you have on?"

"It'd be wise for your wife to relax," Charles advised the husband.

"Honey, please don't!" the man begged. "There's no reason to—"

"Why aren't you doing anything?" she interrupted.

The man stared at her, then glanced at Charles. His face had gone paste-white. With the knife at his throat, he seemed too terrified to speak further.

"You're such a fucking coward," she said venomously. "My father warned me not to marry you. What kind of man are you that could see his wife and son treated this way? Fight back, you fucking loser!"

Charles's expression went cold as the wife's emasculating words echoed in the canyons of his memory. A scowl developed on his forehead, and before he quite knew what was happening, he had driven the blade into the man's neck. A short gurgle emanated from the husband's mouth before spurts of blood gushed over the wooden floor.

Elaina and the dead husband's wife watched in horror.

"Why would you do that?" Elaina questioned after she had found her voice.

The man's wife was making little gasping sounds, as though unable to find her breath. She shook in terror as she stared into the face of Charles's demon. Her legs betrayed her and she sank to the floor, still holding the screaming baby.

Charles rose out of the bloody mess with Elaina and the wife's eyes following him. He walked over to both of them and crouched down, the knife dripping blood from its tip and onto the forehead of the young woman he had just made a widow.

"Happy now, you loudmouthed bitch?" Charles asked with a snarl. "No need to worry about being married to *a fucking loser* anymore!" He kneeled next to her and wiped the blood from his knife onto her yellow blouse.

"Charles, that's enough," Elaina said, her voice strained.

The wife's trembling grew stronger, which sent shock waves of fear into her child. His howling escalated. Charles looked down at the child.

"Quiet this damn baby before you personally witness a *really* late term abortion," he warned.

The wife clutched her child close to her bosom. She seemed to have run out of insults and invectives.

"Where are the keys to your car?" Elaina said.

The woman stared dumbly at her.

"The keys!" Elaina smacked the woman in the face.

"My husband has them," she said, still gasping. "They're in his pocket."

Charles still had a sinister smile on his face. "You stay there and keep her in check," he instructed Elaina while he returned to the body.

He pulled the man up from the blood-drenched floor and started searching his pockets.

"You're probably smiling down on me from heaven, grateful I saved you from this raging bitch," he said to the dead man. He continued his search for the keys, getting more frustrated with each empty pocket. Then finally he heard the jingle of metal. "Of course they would be in the last pocket I checked," he said with a chuckle. He pulled the handful of keys from the dead man's pocket and relocated them to his own.

"You have the keys . . . now just go," the wife pleaded through her sobs as Charles walked over to the strips of bed linen they had shredded to use as restraints and blindfolds.

"Such a terrible hostess," Charles said to Elaina with a tone of disapproval. "Nothing like Oodgeroo."

Elaina crouched down next to the whimpering widow and tied a blindfold around her head, then began tying her hands. "Start counting to a thousand," she ordered. "If any peacekeepers trail us, we'll make sure to finish what we started."

Sobbing quietly, the woman nodded.

Charles gave Elaina the remaining strips of material and reached out for the baby. The woman sensed what he was doing and recoiled from him. He touched her cheek with the tip of the knife.

"We can't tie you up if you're holding a kid," Charles explained with exaggerated patience that didn't match the demented look on his face. "If we don't tie you up, then we'll have to kill you. You decide."

Elaina jumped in to defuse the standoff. "Give me the child, and I promise I won't hurt him."

Still the mother refused. But then, as Charles touched her cheek again with the knife, she relinquished her grip and quickly handed the baby to Elaina.

Charles watched as Elaina cradled the child and looked upon its face as if in a trance. "Come on and hand him over while you finish tying the mother up,"

Elaina complied with obvious reluctance. Charles patted the crying child on its back and carried it over to the bloody remains of its father. He then propped the baby up against the dead man, and the baby stopped crying.

"Will you look at that?" Charles quipped as the child sat in the puddle of his dead father's blood, smacking at it with his tiny hands. "Daddy managed to stop the little one from crying."

"Eloah, deliver us from this evil and wickedness," the blindfolded mother prayed in fear.

Charles rolled his eyes at the mother's prayer and motioned for Elaina to grab the suitcase and trash bag of groceries. After peeking out the window, he opened the door. Elaina extended the retractable arm of the wheeled suitcase and shuffled past Charles toward the car.

"Remember now," Charles said to the wife. "Count to a thousand before trying to untie yourself. I'd hate to make your child an orphan because his mother couldn't follow directions."

Then he took one final look at the infant, whose onesie was now saturated in blood.

"When you hear the door shut," he said to the wife, "start counting. Don't move until you reach a thousand. Got it?"

She nodded. He could see that she was trembling all over.

He closed and locked the door between him and Elaina, who was waiting outside. She whipped her head around to peer through the windows at the top of the door. Charles pressed his index finger against his lips, signaling her to be silent. She dropped everything onto the ground and stared through the glass at him.

The mother was counting aloud. ". . . five, six, seven, eight, nine, ten. . . "

Charles could see the concern on Elaina's face.

". . . eighteen, nineteen. . . hello? Are you there?"

When the blindfolded and restrained widow received no response, she started to struggle against her bonds. "J. R., Mommy's right here. Don't you worry. Mommy's coming."

Charles watched as she writhed and jostled her body around the floor, trying to break the strips of material that bound her hands behind her back. She rolled onto her back and tucked her knees into her chest so she could slide her arms under her body and bring them to the front. Now she could use her hands to remove her blindfold.

The moment she pulled it away, Charles bent down to greet her face to face. He muffled her scream with his hand clamped over her mouth. He shook his head in disappointment.

"What happened to the other nine hundred and eighty-one numbers?" He asked.

"I'm sorry! I just wanted my baby." She cried the last of her muffled words through his hand.

"Excuses, excuses," Charles said as he pushed the restrained woman over and climbed on top of her.

She tried in vain to fight him off as her eyes danced about the room. When she saw her child playing in her husband's blood, streams of tears fell from her eyes.

"Why do you shed tears over a *fucking loser?*" Charles asked, throwing her own words back at her as he positioned the knife outside the soft tissue between the open space of her ribs. "'You fucking loser,'" Charles repeated as he looked down at her ring finger. "Those were the last words he heard from the woman he loved so much that he put a diamond on her finger. Just another ungrateful, spoiled bitch."

She offered no defense. To be honest, Charles didn't think she would have been capable of speech. He continued his condemnation as more tears flowed from her eyes.

"You know what he should have said to you before I opened his arteries?" He forced the blade to pierce her flesh just below the skin. "Fuuuck. . .youuuu," he said in a slow and exaggerated tone. "That's what he should have said. Fuck you." He pressed forward so the weight of his body thrust the blade through her left breast and into her heart.

Gradually the widow's screams subsided to low moans as her face and body writhed through the pain.

"Fuck. . .you," Charles repeated as she groaned from the blade shredding the tough tissue of her heart.

Several seconds passed before her body went limp. He climbed off her and looked over at the baby, who was still busying himself finger painting with his father's blood. He had crawled back over toward his mother, leaving behind him a trail of bloody hand- and knee-prints on the floor.

Charles looked up toward the door at Elaina, who was still watching from the window. Her face was pale, and he had no doubt that she would be offering her opinion of his latest actions.

As he stood and exited the house, Elaina stared at him, clearly repulsed. He cared little. He pulled out the keys to

the car and pressed the button to unlock it. He scanned the
street once more and opened the driver's side door. Elaina
remained standing by the door to the house, mystified, the
stolen luggage and groceries still lying on the ground where
she had dropped them.

"Breaking into their home, stealing their clothes, food,
and car wasn't enough?" she said. "You had to take their
lives, too?"

Charles picked up the luggage and garbage bag and put
them in the car before jumping into the driver's seat. "I spare
the kid didn't I? Now, get in the car Elaina. We don't have
time for another philosophical discussion about the meaning
of life."

Elaina dragged herself to the passenger side of the car,
but even after climbing in, she pressed against the closed door
trying to stay as far away from Charles as the confines of their
stolen vehicle would allow.

"Your philosophy is not of life," she muttered, as though
to herself. "Your philosophy is only of death. Torture and
death."

Charles slammed the transmission lever into reverse and
backed out of the driveway. "What did you think was going
to happen after they'd seen our faces?" he demanded. "The
only reason that child isn't bleeding out next to his parents
is because he can't identify us. Otherwise, I'd have slit his
throat, too."

"You might as well have. What do you think is going to
happen to him now that his parents are dead? Killing him

would've been more humane than leaving him there alone to waste away from thirst and starvation."

Charles didn't reply. He hadn't actually thought about that, and he decided she was probably right. As an act of mercy, he should have cut the boy's throat. His foot eased up on the accelerator as he considered turning around, then decided it wasn't worth the risk. They had to get out of the area before some nosy neighbor saw them driving the couple's car and called peace keepers. He pressed down on the accelerator, and the car picked up speed.

"You're a maniac, Charles," Elaina said. "How can you save me one moment and kill others the next? For such a smart man, your reasoning is handicapped. We could've taken the child with us instead of leaving him to perish."

Charles remained silent as he concentrated on his driving.

"What's the purpose?" she pressed, as though she actually wanted an answer. "Why would you do that, Charles? Why?"

Charles looked over at her with self-righteous contempt. "Why not?"

Chapter 29

IFTEEN MINUTES OF SILENCE HAD passed since the vicious killing of the young couple. As Charles steered onto a narrow, metal bridge connecting to the smaller Channel Island, Elaina spoke.

"When we get off this continent, I wish to never lay eyes on you again," she stated in a quiet voice as she gazed at the water flowing beneath the bridge.

To Charles, it was as if she didn't exist now that they were into the last stretch of their trip. He'd reached his destination and was now scanning the coastline for one particular boat. With his neck perched like a crane, he scanned from side to side until his eyes stopped on a specific spot.

Charles made a quick turn onto a dirt and gravel path that led onto a modest dock, where ships of various sizes and names bounced to the ocean's rhythm.

One vessel was much larger than all the others in the dock. An older man with a thick white beard, glasses, and a ragged captain's hat was tending to the vessel. The sound of trampled gravel grabbed the captain's attention. He shook his head, pointed to a sign stating the dock's hours of operation, and flagged them away.

Charles ignored him and drove as close to the vessel as the dirt road allowed. The beautiful, pearl-white vessel bore the name *The Egression*, its bow standing two stories high with a twenty foot-long Katingalian flag.

The captain again shooed them away. As Charles stepped from the sedan and walked toward the ship, the captain took hold of a large wrench.

"Put the wrench down," Charles said.

"Who the hell are you to give me orders?" the captain retorted. "Either both you and your lady friend are fucking illiterates, or you're up to no good. Either way, I suggest you turn around and be on your way before I introduce you to the business end of this here wrench."

"I tell you, Captain Bradshaw, if I weren't such an understanding man, I'd kill you where you stand," Charles threatened. "Then I'd toss your worthless body into the water and just take my boat as easily as it was given to you."

He stood resolute, still brandishing the wrench, but hearing his name had taken some of the wind out of his sails. "Do I know you?"

"Yes, you do. I was hoping our meeting one another would have been much more constructive. Maybe a, 'Thank you, Yäbälay' for the new boat." Charles smirked as he kept walking. "I'm sure business for you must've picked up since this dandy new vessel fell into your lap."

"Did you say Yäbälay?" the captain asked, his face taking on a confused expression.

"I did," Charles replied before revealing the abstract tattoo on his wrist.

The man stepped closer, studying Charles's face. The wrench fell to the deck. "Yäbälay, I'm so sorry. I didn't realize—"

"Quiet," Charles cut in. "I'm sure, having never met face to face but now that you do know it would behoove you to escort my friend and I onto this vessel as soon as possible. We want off this continent." His tone had gone from cordial to deadly serious. He looked back at the car where he had left Elaina and signaled for her to join them.

As Elaina approached, Charles could see the captain sizing her up as his demeanor grew softer.

"Yäbälay?" the captain whispered as he took a few steps closer. "Is she going down below with the rest of the shales?"

"She's not to be touched," Charles ordered. "And you will not mention the cargo to her."

The captain cowered. "Yes, sir, of course."

"Also, send a message ahead for Mr. Adi so he will be expecting us."

"Yes, Yäbälay," the captain responded.

"So this is how we get off Katingal?" Elaina asked, looking around and clearly impressed with what she saw.

"Yes," Charles replied. "My boat, my captain."

The captain relieved Elaina of her bags and scurried off to take them to the master's cabin. Charles extended his open palm at the boat, inviting Elaina aboard. She paused as she stepped onto the platform that led to the boat's deck.

"What about our KPPs?" Elaina asked. "What's to stop peacekeepers from greeting us at the next dock?"

"Have I failed you yet, Elaina?" Charles questioned, leaving her to ponder his interrogative.

"Failed? No. Disgusted? Yes."

"Your disgust is not important," he replied, unmoved by the insult. "Soon, you'll never have to lay eyes on me again." He couldn't tell whether the thought bothered her.

"And where is our destination?" she asked.

He smiled. "Indonesia."

Chapter 30

LESS THAN AN HOUR LATER, Charles, Elaina, and Captain Bradshaw departed from the docks of Channel Island. Captain Bradshaw was at the helm of the vessel, accompanied by Charles, navigating through the Indian Ocean toward Indonesia.

Elaina continued sequestering herself from the two men. Charles watched as she found a place along the bow, clutching the railing and staring out at the sea as the sun descended into the darkness of the distant waters.

Since her bath in Darwin, she had let her hair out, allowing the wind to bounce off the water and whip through her long, golden mane. She threw her head back and closed her eyes, and Charles saw the water glistening on her cheeks. From this distance, he couldn't tell whether it was salt spray or tears. The wind and salt water mist was like a baptism, he thought, but it would never absolve her of all the sins she had committed.

"That's the loveliest criminal these old eyes have ever seen," the captain observed, drawing Charles's attention from the note he was scribbling on a small piece of paper he had found among the mess in the captain's helm. "Where we're headed, a woman like that is a rare commodity," the captain concluded.

Charles chuckled as the captain's choice of words reminded him of what the warden had said about women in K-City.

"Our so-called civilization is no different from Katingal," Charles said quietly. "All of you just don't realize how similar and interchangeable those worlds are."

The captain nodded, though Charles knew he had no idea what Charles was talking about.

"I called ahead to Mr. Adi, as you requested," the captain said. "I left a message with his assistant. Not sure how familiar you are with Banyuwangi, Indonesia but—"

"The Regency of Banyuwangi has an estimated population of one point six million, and is located at the easternmost end of the Indonesian island of Java." Charles sighed without lifting his pen. "It serves as a ferry port between Java and Bali. It's surrounded by mountains and forests to the west, and by sea to the east and south. The city of Banyuwangi is the administrative capital. The name 'Banyuwangi' is Japanese for 'fragrance water.'"

The captain was staring at him. "You memorize an encyclopedia?"

"Yes," Charles replied with a serious face. "But that information came from a travel book, not an encyclopedia."

The captain stared at him, mouth agape.

"So how long have you been working for Adi?" Charles asked.

The captain made a visible effort to collect himself. "Almost three years. I make his runs and drop off his cargo of shales to a few islands in Indonesia."

"And how did you manage to accumulate a debt that usually would cost a man his life?"

The captain looked down at his hands. "On my old ship, there was a carbon dioxide leak, and I lost an entire transport of shales."

"And you're still alive?" Charles scoffed. "The Adi I've come to know was so understanding and would have had you chopped into fishing bate." Charles said to the bitter man.

"I'm the only captain in Channel Island willing to do this type of work," he admitted. "None of the others from my port are equipped to do what's required in this profession."

"Any reason you left a message instead of requesting to speak with Adi considering your special fugitive cargo?"

"Mr. Adi doesn't speak directly to anyone anymore," the captain explained, prompting Charles to pause from writing his note. "As of late, I've only communicated with his assistant."

Charles frowned. "When did he start using this flunky as his middleman?"

"Not long ago. One or two months ago, maybe."

Charles pondered that last bit of information for a few moments before returning to his note, jotting a few more words. When he was finished, he stole another glance at Elaina. The force of the winds blew the loose fabric of her stolen dress around her body, leaving little to the imagination. Just then, Charles squinted his eyes.

"You're looking as if you've never seen her before," the captain observed, watching him.

"It's not Elaina I'm concerned with," Charles said, folding the finished note into his pocket. "It's the little girl staggering up from behind her that alarms me."

Charles bolted out of the door, down a metal railing, and landed on the deck. One hundred feet ahead of him, Elaina was still captivated by the sea air, oblivious to the mystery girl behind her. With every step, he closed in on the wayward adolescent while Elaina rocked to the rhythm of the boat.

Then the girl made a whimpering sound, and Elaina whipped her head around to be greeted by the terror-ridden girl with auburn hair.

"Help—" the girl pleaded. Then her legs gave out and she collapsed to the deck just as Charles arrived. He took a mental inventory of her dirty, tangled hair, stained jeans, bare feet, and the small tattoo on her shoulder blade.

"Who is she, Charles?" Elaina asked while the filthy girl writhed on the floor and sobbed uncontrollably. "That tattoo is the same as yours," She shot him an accusing glare as the significance of that hit her. "Did you know about this?"

Before Charles could reply, Elaina turned back to the young girl. The girl reached out for Elaina in desperation. The terror in her eyes was obvious as she continued to gasp and sob.

Captain Bradshaw came running toward them with a pistol in one hand and rope lassoed around his torso. "I'll get her, Yäbälay," the captain shouted.

"And you want me to trust you?" Elaina looked down at the young girl, and saw the terror in her eyes, the unkempt hair, the dirty clothes, and the abrasions around her ankles and wrists. They served as stark reminders for Elaina of what she, herself, had endured just a month ago.

She pulled the young girl up from the deck and held her close in defiance of Charles and the captain.

The captain rushed up to the girl, but Elaina took a stance that dared him to take one step closer.

"This is none of your concern," the captain said as he reached to grab the girl. "Step aside."

Elaina took hold of his arm, restrained him, and delivered a series of kicks to his ribs and face. The young redhead scampered away while the outmatched captain bore the brunt of Elaina's attack.

"Yäbälay, please make her stop!" the captain yelled.

Without hesitation, Charles punched Elaina from the side, which knocked her into the steel railing of the boat.

"No!" the young girl cried as she watched Elaina crumble to the deck. She raged out of her mind, lunging at Charles, kicking and punching at him until he grabbed a handful of her auburn hair with one hand and smacked her across the face with the other, bloodying her nose and subduing her rage.

"Captain, come do your job." Charles snarled, tossing her by the hair onto the deck.

"Of course, Yäbälay," the captain acknowledged.

Elaina remained on the deck, unconscious.

"What about your curly-haired friend?" the captain asked. "She still not for sale? She's not young like the others, but we can still get a couple thousand for her."

"The next time you question a decision I've already made," Charles said, glaring at him as if burning a hole through his soul, "you'll find yourself at the bottom of this ocean."

"Yes, sir, Yäbälay." The captain offered a slight bow of submission. "I'm sorry, sir."

"When you're finished with her, tie up my friend. We'll keep her below deck with the others for now."

Moments later, they were each carrying one of the restrained girls through narrow corridors to the back of the vessel, where the cargo was kept. Charles wrinkled his nose in distaste. The area smelled of perspiration, urine, and feces.

Charles walked by the metal dog kennels the captain used to hold the captives. He counted ten filthy juvenile girls restrained in chains in the cages. They were all petite, and looked particularly vulnerable from their fetal positions as they struggled to remain as comfortable as possible.

While the captain adjusted the redhead onto an old, dirty mattress, Charles walked over to inspect the rope from which the redhead had escaped.

"I figured the rope would keep her, but this bitch must be half rat," the captain reasoned, gnashing his teeth to mimic a rat. "There's much better profit in trafficking pussy than those damn fishing tours. Especially white women like these.

The redhead is the prize of the bunch. She's the youngest, a natural redhead, and a virgin. I'll collect five to six grand, easy, for her alone."

"Do you typically have them wallowing in their own filth?" Charles asked.

"Oh, of course not, Y-Y-Yäbälay," he stuttered, suddenly realizing that Charles's mood was not as jubilant as his own. "I was about to let them shower and clean themselves up just before you showed up."

Charles stared into the captain's eyes, and knew the dirty old bastard was lying. He had just finished restraining Elaina to the redhead when Charles noticed that the young girls were pretending to sleep. It was a tactic he had witnessed hundreds of times from captives who wished to avoid unwanted attention.

The tears in their shirts were evidence of the captain's frequent visits. The prettiest of the group was balled up in a kennel, shirtless and shivering. Fresh bruises and welts laced her arms and back. Charles turned toward the entrance.

"Clean them up before we continue our trip," he ordered. "The last thing you will do is deliver disgusting product to Adi."

"Yes, Yäbälay," the captain responded.

He unlocked the cage of the shirtless girl and pulled her through the opening by her bruised arm. She winced, but didn't resist. As they reached the cargo hold entrance, Charles grabbed her by the other arm and placed her face-first against the wall, exposing the Duenno tattoo on her shoulder blade.

"Once these girls were daughters and nieces that belonged to their families, even if for a short span of time," he said softly. "But the moment their bodies bore the ink of my mark, they became a shale of Duenno. So long as they bare my mark, you will ensure their quality."

"Yes, Yäbälay," the captain responded before he dragged the girl down the corridor to shower and clean her.

Chapter 31

ITHIN A FEW HOURS, THE florescent lights of the city of Banyuwangi were visible from the captain's helm. Charles and the captain traveled the last few minutes in silence, sharing the tranquility of the night sky, a thermos of coffee, and a sandwich.

As they neared port, the captain drew back on the ship's throttle and navigated the shallow dock.

Waiting on the wharf with a big smile was Adi, a balding, pot-bellied gentleman with glasses. Behind him stood two much larger men who seemed to be doing their best to look dangerous.

Charles left Captain Bradshaw and made his way down to greet the entourage. He waited as the vessel drifted closer to the wooden dock. Captain Bradshaw rushed to tie off the boat and lay out the long, metal plank.

Charles stepped off first and was greeted by Adi's open handshake.

"It's good seeing you again," Adi said. His smile looked painted on. He made no effort to introduce the two larger men who stood behind him. Charles knew they were Adi's bodyguards. "When I heard of your capture and exile, I wondered if I'd ever see you again."

"Understandably so," Charles reassured him. "But any person with a minimal amount of common sense knows the authorities will knock down the door of every criminal. The question is, will you be prepared when *that* day comes?"

"This is true. Luckily for you—"

"It was not luck, Adi," Charles corrected. "Careful, proactive planning. I cannot afford to rely on luck."

"That's what I meant," Adi responded, head bobbing.

"Is this one of the surgeons?" Charles questioned, directing his attention to the nervous individual who had come up to join them.

"Peace be unto you, sir," the doctor greeted Charles, placing his right hand over his heart. "I'm Dr. Cavalcanti, your plastic surgeon."

Charles returned an expressionless stare, rebuking the universal greeting. "And where is the other doctor?" he asked Adi.

"The moment I received word from the captain that you were on your way," he said quickly, "I contacted your attorney, and he placed her on the first flight from Ethiopia. She'll be here in the morning."

"Excellent. And Duenno?"

"Duenno is in disarray." Adi hesitated for a moment as though thinking about the best way to break the bad news. "It's splintered into a few feuding factions. In every country, you'll find someone declaring themselves Yäbälay. Governor Negesso initiated a massive campaign against Duenno after the kidnapping of his son. Every day, multiple times a day, there's a raid. If he hears the slightest whisper that even one shale is in a building, his task force hits it, arrests everyone, and burns it to the ground."

This was not so much different from what Charles had expected.

"Speaking of my insurance policy, how is the governor's son?" Charles inquired.

"He's still tucked away with plenty of security, and out of the shale circulation, as you ordered. Only the members of the council know his specific location."

"Good. Now let's address the business at hand." Charles looked at the physician once more.

"We are prepped for surgery on the top floor of one of Banyuwangi's premiere hotels," Adi assured him. "You will have the entire floor to yourself, and I will personally oversee your travel and meeting with the council. Whatever you need, just ask and it's yours."

Charles nodded in acknowledgement.

"Captain," Adi said, rubbing his hands together as he got down to business. "Go fetch the girl and bring the shales along with her. We've yet to negotiate a price for them."

As the captain turned and headed back for the ship, Charles glanced at Adi in disappointment. "The shales are cargo below deck on my boat," he said, making no attempt to keep the threatening tone out of his voice.

Adi's minions looked at each other, on alert and ready to pounce at the order of their boss. A smile formed on Adi's face as he waved them to stand down.

"Your profit is now my profit," Charles said. "Or have the most rudimentary rules of business changed while I was away the past couple months?"

"They have not," Adi agreed. "And you are absolutely correct."

"Perfect." Charles smiled, then turned quite serious. Despite his words, the expression on Adi's face did not offer the level of submission Charles was looking for. "When did we become equals?" Charles asked, his voice suddenly soft and dangerous. "Have you miraculously ascended Duenno's ranks to become a member of the council of which I am the sole Yäbälay?"

A sly smile crossed the other man's face. He glanced around, making sure his minions were still attentive.

"In truth, I suppose it must be obvious that things have, indeed, changed in your absence," he said to Charles. "The moment you were placed under arrest, "you forfeited your control over Duenno. Furthermore, the moment another man bent you over a chair and treated you like an ordinary shale, you lost the title of Yäbälay. A lot can happen in two months, Charles."

This public outing froze Charles in humiliation and fury.

"To be honest," Adi went on, as though he cared nothing about the rage that was growing on Charles's face, "when your attorney contacted me, I didn't take your plan to escape very seriously. But here you are. It matters not, however, for Duenno is no longer yours, and in Indonesia, I am Yäbälay."

Charles clenched his fist at this last announcement, a move that Adi saw and shrugged away.

"Did you know there is a ten-million-dollar reward for the safe return of the governor's son?" Adi said with a grin. "And fifteen million for any of his captors. Lucky for you, though, I'm not a greedy man, and my obligation to this arrangement ends with the safe delivery of your fugitive beauty to the Brazilian who is awaiting her with great anticipation."

"But I must admit, an extra ten million dollars is enticing," Adi mused, interrupting Charles's thought process. "So why don't you tell me where the governor's son is? Then you and the girl can continue with the surgeries you need before going on your way."

"I'm going to enjoy killing you," Charles responded, causing the bodyguards to stir.

"Kill me? Is this my reward for facilitating your new lease on life?" Adi questioned. "Look around you. The snap of my finger and you'll find yourself bent over again like you were in K-City," Adi said as his brow crumpled and his nostrils flared. Without waiting for a response, he snapped, "Bagus, kill him."

Before Adi's last word hit the air, the brute named Bagus launched a series of jabs and kicks upon Charles, who blocked most of the blows with his forearms and ducked the rest. The enforcer reared back and charged at Charles, but he sidestepped the raging bull, grabbed his wrist to absorb the man's momentum, and cast him off the edge of the dock. The clumsy henchman flailed in the air until he crashed into the side of a neighboring boat and dropped into the water, where he lay motionless with his neck twisted at an impossible angle.

Charles turned toward Adi, who looked at him and smiled.

"Gema, kill him!" Adi ordered his remaining bodyguard.

The two men locked into combat while Adi, the surgeon, and the captain, who had just returned with the shackled captives, looked on. The two skilled fighters punched and kicked at each other with precise ferocity. Charles was holding his own, but was slowing from exhaustion. Gema landed a solid kick to Charles's midsection, and followed by tackling him to the ground.

"That's it!" Adi barked. "Break his neck!"

Charles pulled out his buck knife and sliced at the crease between his opponent's forearm and bicep, causing a stream of blood to pour from the severed artery. The fight in Gema poured out of him as quickly as the blood leaving his body. When the big man pulled back to clasp a hand over his bleeding arm, Charles thrust the knife up under his ribcage and into his heart. Gema stiffened and fell to the side.

Adi shook his head in disappointment at Charles's disposal of his second bodyguard.

"I'll do you the old-fashioned way," Adi said, his .357 magnum handgun pointed at Charles.

Hands up, Charles froze in place, a smirk blooming on his lips. A shot rang out—*bang!*—followed by a look of shock on Adi's face. The usurper's body thumped to the ground.

The captain lowered his rifle. "I never did like that son of a bitch," he said.

Next to him, Elaina and the young shales cringed into the background. Charles went to Adi's dead body and retrieved his cell phone, the plastic hotel key, and the handgun, while the captain directed his captives to join Charles on the dock.

"What are we going to do now?" Elaina asked.

"Nothing's changed," Charles said. "When Dr. Peña arrives, she'll remove our KPP devices, and Dr. Cavalcanti will change how we look. After that, you can do whatever you'd like." He paused, watching her, then added, "But there are very important people who went to great lengths to make sure you arrived here safely."

Her brow furrowed as she tried to make sense of what he'd just said. "I don't understand."

"You will soon," Charles promised.

Chapter 32

AS THE RISING MORNING SUN shone through the large windows of the Indonesian penthouse suite, Elaina woke to find one of the nurses checking her bandages and recording her vital signs.

"Sorry for waking you, ma'am," the nurse said. "I'll be done in a few minutes. Try to go back to sleep."

"I'm fine," Elaina replied. "The doctor said my bandages could come off today. It's been two weeks. Tell him I'm ready to see my face."

"Both doctors are with Mr. Gravo," the nurse explained. "They'll be in later today. Going to give you a sedative to get you some sleep, ma'am."

The nurse removed a syringe from the pocket of her scrubs and stuck the head of it into an IV receptacle. Elaina looked over at the digital clock on her right as the nurse gave her the injection. In a matter of seconds, the numbers became blurry, and her eyes and head felt heavy.

~~~

"Mrs. Souza, it's time for you to wake up," Dr. Cavalcanti said to rouse Elaina from her slumber. "*Sra. Souza, é hora de tirar os curativos.*"[41]

As she fought through the drug-induced haze, she realized that she was still in the hotel suite. Two physicians in white coats stood over her. Behind her doctors was the nurse, who held a mirror in her hands. Elaina grew anxious to see her new face.

Cavalcanti and an aide helped Elaina sit upright, and he pulled a pair of surgical scissors from his white coat pocket and went to work cutting off her bandages. Elaina felt the tension of her wraps loosening with the progression of each cut. When he was done, the cool, sterile air of the room graced her skin like a boyfriend's first kiss. She watched the doctor nod in approval.

"Nice, very nice," the doctor assured her with a broad smile. "You're a fast healer, Mrs. Souza."

"Elaina Almeida," she declared. "My husband is dead." She noticed the two surgeons regarding the other in an odd manner.

"As you wish, ma'am," one of the surgeons responded. "Now, you have some minor swelling, but everything looks good."

"Give me the mirror," she demanded with an extended hand towards the nurse. Her doctor nodded and Elaina snatched it from the nurse. But then, before looking at her

---

[41] Mrs. Souza, it's time to take the bandages off.

new face, she closed her eyes and took a moment to gather her courage.

After a single deep breath, Elaina raised the mirror in front of her face and opened her eyes. She turned her head to inspect her profile. Her cheekbones were more pronounced, and her nose thinner, more pointed. The crows' feet were gone from the corners of her eyes, and her facial lines were sculpted to be more symmetrical. Had she looked at herself her entire life, she could have easily mistaken the reflection for someone else. She smiled.

"Ah," the doctor said with obvious relief. "So you are pleased?"

"Yes, very much. What about the chip, Dr. Peña?" Elaina questioned.

"Yes, ma'am," Dr. Peña said as she approached her. "Everything is fine. And the fact that you remembered my name after meeting me once is a great sign that your memory hasn't been affected."

Elaina closed her eyes again and suddenly started weeping quietly.

"Is there something wrong, Mrs. Souza?" Dr. Peña inquired.

Rage washed over Elaina at hearing her married name again. As her teary eyes opened, she was ready to unleash the building fury until she saw the familiar man flanked by several men in suits standing behind the doctor.

"Gabriel?" Elaina uttered through a trembling voice.

"Everyone, could you please give us a moment?" the handsome man requested.

Everyone in the room complied—even the two bodyguards.

As the man whose face she knew so well walked over to Elaina's bedside, she dropped the mirror and clutched two handfuls of the bed linen in the palm of her hands.

"May I sit, Querida?" he questioned.

Elaina didn't respond. Instead, she shook her head in disbelief as the machines monitoring her vital signs spiked. "Q-Querida," she whispered. "Only Carlos called me 'Querida.'"

She jumped back as he reached for the glass of water on the nightstand. He dipped his index and middle finger into the water and smeared them against his left temple. The water washed away some makeup on his face, revealing the small scar that Gabriel had left him on the schoolyard. Elaina knew that this was the sole and discrete differentiation between the twin brothers.

The alarms on Elaina's heart monitor evidenced the recognition with a dramatic jump in frequency.

"*Breath meu amor,*"[42] he instructed as he took her hand into his, comforting her.

Elaina's chest rose and fell. "*Como?*" she asked, thinking that none of this could be real. "*Este deve ser um inferno. Eu matei você—*"[43]

"My love, it is me, your husband Carlos," he said. He paused with apparent shame before continuing. "The day

---

[42] Breath, my love.

[43] This must be hell. I killed you—

the police arrested you . . . well, it was Gabriel you shot, not me."

Every alarm on her monitors went into a frenzy. Elaina's eyes opened and closed sporadically.

"Doctor!" Carlos shouted.

Both doctors and their nurses rushed into the room and moved Carlos from the bed.

"She's going to need another sedative," the lead doctor ordered. "Only a moderate one, nurse. I need her calm but awake."

The nurse pushed a small dose of sedative into Elaina's IV, which caused her vitals to level out, along with the alarms. She felt groggy.

"Will she understand what I'm saying?" Carlos asked.

"Yes, sir," the nurse replied. "She may not remember everything, but she can comprehend."

Everyone left the room again. Elaina struggled to concentrate as Carlos took his place alongside the bed. With all the things that had happened to her over the past few weeks, the news that her husband Carlos was still alive was the most incredible.

"Elaina? Can you hear me?"

She nodded.

"I need you to pay close attention to what I'm about to tell you," Carlos continued. "You need to understand that no one else has heard what I'm about to say, and you may never repeat it."

"W-what, why?" Elaina said, confused.

"Focus, Elaina," he urged. "With a revelation like this comes dire consequences to anyone who betrays its trust. Do you understand?"

"Yes."

"You killed my brother," Carlos explained as he looked deep into her eyes, "the man you helped rise to the office of president of our beloved Brazil."

The heart monitor acknowledged another spike in her heart rate, but it soon leveled out as the medication she'd been given reined it in.

"I've never been unfaithful to you, but I have been deceitful," he confessed with a sad tone. "I loved my brother, and just as our father taught us, family is everything. It was no surprise to any of us when Gabriel rose as the leader of our country. But despite being loved by so many, he was not a perfect man. I was never strong enough to steer him away from the vices that led to his demise."

"What do you mean?" she asked, shaking her head as she tried to make sense of what he was telling her.

He inched closer to Elaina and lowered his voice, talking closer to her ear.

"*Meu amor*, we're all puppets upon their stage," he admitted. "We're manipulated by the strings they pull. Our freedom is a farce, peddled to us with smoke and mirrors."

"You're speaking in riddles," Elaina said as she pulled away. "I don't understand."

Carlos looked over his shoulder at the closed door and lowered his voice to an even softer whisper. "What I can tell you will still leave you with many questions," he said. "But I need you to listen first to what I have to say from beginning to end."

Elaina nodded in agreement.

"As twin children, my brother and I made a habit of amusing ourselves by deceiving others to think I was my brother and he was me. It started as childish fun to pass the time, though we did sometimes use it to escape trouble or punishment. Never did I think this mischief would spill over into our adult lives."

Elaina pulled her hand away.

"*Meu amor*, I've never betrayed the vows of our marriage," Carlos said urgently with a slight tremble in his hand. "It was my brother who you discovered having affairs with these women."

"All this time, I thought it was you sneaking around and lying to me," Elaina said in shock. "I thought you were with other women, but it was him?"

"Yes, and I'm so sorry, Elaina. Part of me wished that you had confronted me the moment you had doubts. We may have been able to prevent his death, your conviction, and me from continuing to live the lie. But the truth is that I should have been strong enough to tell my wife what was really going on. I should have honored you and the vows we took before Eloah."

"Do you realize what you've done?" Elaina chastised Carlos. "Why would you keep something like this from me?"

"You don't understand, Elaina," he protested, albeit weakly. "I couldn't speak of it. Not to you or anyone."

"You're speaking of it now," she rebuked, the fury rising in her heart. "Why is it okay now? After I've killed, been exiled? Do you know what happens to women there? Do you realize what I've seen, what I've done? Dear God, do you realize what that cursed city has done to me?"

"I don't dare imagine what you've endured. I, uh, and, um—"

"Spit it out!" Elaina seethed. "Explain how it could ever make sense that I had to become a murderer before you could be honest with your wife."

Carlos looked over his shoulder again and gestured for Elaina to lower her voice.

"Stop looking over there, Carlos! You look here and face what you've done!" she shouted.

He covered her mouth. "You can never say that name aloud," he snapped back. "Not even when you think we're alone. I'm Gabriel now. I want you to understand it all, but I can divulge only so much for now. My hands are tied, and they've allowed me to tell you only so much."

Her brow furrowed. "Who the fuck is 'they?'"

"'The Society,'" Carlos blurted. "Gabriel and I have been members for some time now, and that's all I can or will ever be able to tell you about it and its members."

Elaina rolled her eyes. "The Society? You're fucking kidding, right?"

"We are not to be taken lightly, Elaina," Carlos said, his tone changing to one of authority and condescension that she had never seen in him. "I can't deny the role you played in managing my brother's campaigns," he conceded. "Your assistance in his climb up the political ladder was flawless. But behind the scenes, where it mattered, the Society was pulling the strings that ensured Gabriel's narrow victory. You ever wonder how Gabriel, a political nobody a few years before his first run at a political office, could declare his candidacy for such influential political offices and win? Year after year and term after term, his election to office never faltered.

"The Society you mock had been watching Gabriel for years, and when they decided it was time . . . well, that meant it was time. They had no interest in me. But Gabriel is my brother, and where he goes, I go. He insisted they bring me along, as well, or choose another candidate."

"*Meu Deus!*[44] Carlos? Have you and Gabriel been taking turns being president, like a game children play?"

"It's not as bad as you make it out to be, Elaina," he argued, but still averted her probing eyes.

"Carlos! Answer me!"

"I have stood in for him, *physically*, when it was deemed necessary."

"When is it ever necessary for anyone to impersonate the political leader of a country, Carlos?"

"We'd played each other so many times throughout our lifetime, it was almost second nature. We could turn it on and off whenever we wanted."

"What you two did was reckless and illegal. Have you ever made decisions in his stay?"

---

[44] My God

"No, I haven't."

"Have you ever viewed classified information?" she demanded.

"God no."

"Now, please tell me the two of you have *never* done that with me . . . in our bedroom or elsewhere."

He looked startled by her question. "No! Never! I swear it! It wasn't a game to us or the Society. I only sat for him when he was summoned by the Society to secret meetings with their chief council. It was my obligation—"

"Your obligation? Couldn't you both just say no?"

Carlos's face grew cold, straight, and stern again. "Elaina, I truly don't expect you to understand, but as members of the Society, and as twin brothers, we were always obligated to one another. The Society meetings were more important than the daily cabinet meetings with his most trusted advisors. The Society determines the direction of the entire world, and Brazil is a mere cog in the machine. Nobody in their right state of mind rejects the Society unless they wish to be made to disappear.

"Virtually no one knows about our membership, what we are called, our methods, or that we even exist. You are literally one of a handful of non-members to be made knowledgeable of our existence."

"I refuse to believe it," Elaina snapped, shaking her head. "This can't be happening."

"I know. I struggle, too. But what am I supposed to do? Should I fail my brother and country? Or should I continue to fail my wife, who's caught in the middle of these lies?"

She remained silent, as though she had no answers for him.

"I've had to mourn the loss of my brother and remain riddled with guilt about you," Carlos continued. "I didn't realize that someone had discovered that Gabriel and I were trading places, or that you were being sent anonymous pictures to twist your mind."

"Looks like your Society isn't as powerful and all-knowing as you give it credit for," Elaina taunted. But her words seemed to make him ponderous instead of furious.

"Whoever it was didn't want Gabriel's vision to be realized. They put all the pieces in play and crafted the perfect scenario where you could commit murder."

"But, why me?"

"Only they know for sure," Carlos said earnestly. "But my guess is that they hedged their bets that you'd confront Gabriel and expose the secret. The scandal alone would have been enough to impeach him. I've been meeting with the Society, and we've come up with a way to protect the legacy Gabriel was forging for Brazil."

"I'm listening," Elaina said, though she was still a bit befuddled by all this news being dumped on her at once.

"They used you, but you may also be our salvation. There are two years left in my brother's term to govern a country on the edge of an economic boom. You, unlike me, understand the environment and the players after managing his campaign. You know his platform and policies as well as anyone among his cabinet. You can help me by guiding my governance as I take his place."

Elaina shook her head. "Are you insane?"

"*Me amour*,"[45] he said unabashedly, "we've always supported each other regardless of the circumstances. You continued to love me, and worked to start a family even when you thought I'd been unfaithful to you. Stand by me now!"

Elaina broke eye contact and remained silent to deliberate the points he had made. After a few minutes of mental gymnastics, she looked at him. "How would you do it?"

"I will continue playing the part of Gabriel," Carlos said. Then he dove into the details with a glimmer of madness in his eyes. "Since the plastic surgeon has altered your appearance, nobody will suspect you as Elaina. When we return to Brazil, we'll announce our engagement to marry. You're intelligent, beautiful, and personable, so the country will love you. But, erring on the side of caution, we'll keep you behind the scenes as much as possible. To the public, you'll be my unassuming first lady, but behind closed doors, we'll usher in my brother's legacy."

"You are my husband, but you are not a politician," Elaina declared. "It'll never work. But more importantly, just admit that all you want is to continue to preside over Brazil. Admit that it has nothing to do with Gabriel's legacy or your love of the country."

"If I did so, I would be lying," Carlos said. "The only admission I'll make is of my selfish intentions to finish what my brother began and to bring my wife home. If you're by

---

[45] My love

my side, I can endure anything. I didn't have the courage to do what was necessary to prevent his death or your exile, so I owe at least that much to you both."

Elaina went into deep contemplation. She questioned how she never had gotten the slightest hint that something was afoot, and she marveled at how quickly her initial joy of seeing her husband was swept away by his true deception. Elaina loved him, but Carlos's revelations bred a doubt that challenged whether the man she loved was really the man who stood before her.

Tears welled in her eyes, and she pulled at the sleeves of her gown to wipe away her tears. Upon doing so, she caught a glimpse of what remained of the discolored bruise that marked one of the scorpion stings. A flood of emotion rolled over her as she wondered at Charles's whereabouts.

"How did Charles come to play a part in all this?" Elaina asked her husband.

He paused for a moment to consider the question. "I'm not entirely sure," he admitted. "As perverse as it sounds, I wanted to thank him for bringing you back to me, but he had already gone by the time I arrived a few hours ago."

Elaina scoffed at the blind praise of the depraved, murderous pedophile she had come to know over the past month. "You speak so graciously of a wicked and soulless man," she said, clenching her teeth.

"Absolutely!" Carlos said with sincerity. "He brought you back to me, and that's all that matters right now."

"Carlos, you've made a bargain with the devil."

"That's a debt to be paid in the afterlife," he replied bluntly. "Being right here, right now, in this place and time with you, makes it worth an eternity in hell."

A tear fell from Elaina's eye as his words melted her heart. Her new distrust in him faded, and she knew she would learn to forgive him. She believed only a man pure in heart could wield such blind naivety but she also knew she could protect him from himself.

"Tell me how I made it here," she said as she reached out for his hand.

He nodded. "At first, I was useless. All I could do was grieve. In one fell swoop, I'd lost my brother and my wife. You hadn't even reached Katingal yet when I received a letter. It simply demanded that I meet the sender, since they knew my secrets.

"I went to the address to meet the author of the letter. When I arrived, I met with a man in obvious disguise who proclaimed his undying love for Brazil. He described how a scandal like this could derail everything Gabriel had done, but he wanted Brazil to continue to thrive despite being governed by an imposter. The man threatened to expose our secret unless we helped him bring you back from exile. He didn't explain why, but once I heard him say you would be home, the reason became unimportant to me."

"Did you know this plan required the participation of WICC's most wanted fugitive?" Elaina interrupted.

"Not initially. I knew it involved an inmate on the same prison transport as you. It wasn't until later that I learned it was Charles Gravo. From that moment on, the man I met knew everything about you and Charles down to the minutes and seconds of every day. He had a man on the inside.

"I knew when you entered the headquarters gates, the moment you and Charles were banished to the outback, and when you escaped after killing one of the correctional officers. Apparently, your KPPs were being tracked by K-City's dedicated satellite."

Elaina struggled to comprehend the significance of that. In their trek across the outback, for every moment of every day as she and Charles struggled to survive against impossible odds, watchers in air-conditioned rooms and comfortable chairs were monitoring their progress.

"When the warden reported that you had died in K-City, we knew that was a cover-up. We ensured that a vessel would be available to you once you reached Channel Island so we could smuggle you into Indonesia and change your identities. The rest you already know."

"You think these people who helped you can be trusted?" Elaina fired back. "All that for love of their country? You can't be that naïve, Carlos."

Carlos stood up from the bed and looked down at Elaina.

"Ask yourself," she said. "What are they getting out of this that buys us their loyalty?"

"Charles Gravo goes free," he responded. "That's the price I paid for him bringing you back to me. The both of you are ghost now." Carlos looked at her intensively, sensing her hesitation. "Elaina, I fly back to Brazil tomorrow morning.

Come back with me so we can have the family we started before all this madness took place." Carlos reached down, placing his hand on her stomach.

Elaina recoiled from his soft touch. "Don't touch me like that!" she snapped. "The last thing I need to be reminded of is how I'm unable to give you a child!" She watched the slightest smile grace Carlos's lips as he reached into his inside jacket pocket and pulled out two sealed envelopes.

"The first letter is from Charles, and the second from me," he explained. "I'll leave you alone so you can read them in private. Take your time."

When he leaned in to kiss her tender lips, another tear traced a trail down her cheek. She watched him leave the room. Once the door shut, she ripped open the letter from Charles.

Elaina,

By the time you read this, I'll have gone. I'm sure by the end of this day, you will have many questions, many of which will go unanswered. Although our time together on Katingal has ended, it will not be our last encounter. We will meet again.

Now that you are free, do not squander the opportunity before you. Death comes for us all in its own time, but we are two of the lucky few who have managed to delay its final summons. This delay will be temporary, so until it comes calling

again, never forget that you have endured while
cowards died alone. Peace is merely assimilation
in disguise!

-- Yäbälay

Elaina placed the letter neatly back into its envelope before she picked up the much thicker one from Carlos. She pried it open with her finger and looked inside to find medical forms and a single photograph.

Her memory shot back to the anonymous manila envelope that had sent her life spiraling out of control. With hesitation, she unfolded the forms to discover the letterhead of the fertility clinic she had used for her *in vitro* procedures. She scanned the documents, confused as to why her husband had chosen to give her this now. It read:

> *Mrs. Souza,*
>
> > *We are pleased to inform you that your latest round of in vitro insemination was successful. As of the date of this letter, you are four to five weeks pregnant, placing your expected delivery date to be December 5, 2017. . .*

Elaina couldn't read anymore. She clutched her fists with the form letter inside her palms. Her rage had returned. The child she had been carrying was Carlos's child, and not the product of the string of rapists who had ravaged her body in K-City. A gambit of emotions swirled in her like a tornado.

She had thanked Eloah for terminating her pregnancy in the cave. Guilt washed over her, followed by sorrow and despair.

Tears streamed out of her eyes, and her mouth stretched wide as a silent cry poured from her soul. She collapsed onto her side, clutching her stomach and trying to comfort the pain of losing the child she had longed for. Now that she knew that her wish had been granted and taken away, she wanted to disappear. She wished that she had fought harder to remain in the tube and accept the chemical-induced death alongside the Japanese prisoner. At least that would have spared her this pain.

She pulled herself from off her side and looked around the room through tear-soaked eyes. She dropped the letter to the floor, then crushed the envelope still lying on her lap. The stiff resistance inside the envelope reminded her of the photograph inside. She straightened the envelope out and removed the photograph. She looked at it, discovering that it wasn't a photograph, but a sonogram.

Her head spun. She hadn't taken any sonograms following any of her insemination procedures. But there in the top, left-hand corner of the picture was her name, and under it, the name of the hospital to which the machine was registered. In the right-hand corner was the date and time, May 2, 2016, 8:18 a.m.

Elaina scanned the room and found the digital clock hanging on the wall that displayed the date and time. *May 2, 2016, 10:23 AM.*

"This was taken today?" Elaina asked aloud. She pulled up her hospital gown and pressed against her stomach with her fingers. Tears of joy streamed down her face, rejoicing at the rush of love that filled her the moment the weight of the surprise hit her.

"Car—" Elaina caught herself. "Gabriel!" she shouted.

The door swung open.

"*Querida.*"

"We're having a child."

"Yes, *meu amor*. We are."

Elaina looked at her husband, and for a moment, everything that had happened for the last month washed away. All that mattered to her in this moment was the flood of love she was experiencing, knowing the man standing before her would be sharing the child growing inside her. She looked down at her belly again, caressing it.

"Are you okay?" Carlos asked, rushing to her and taking her hand.

"*Sim, meu amor. Tudo está perfeito agora. Leve-me para casa.*"

"Our driver downstairs is waiting to take us to our plane," he said with a smile.

"But you didn't know I would say yes," Elaina said, smiling wide.

"*Ah, querida, meu amor,*" Carlos replied, pointing to the heavens. "You belong with me, and I with you. It is not for us to tamper with fate. It is for us to let Eloah's will be done."

As Carlos walked out the door of Elaina's room, she sat perplexed at her husband, who had just recited the same phrase as the beauty queen the moment before Elaina fired a bullet through her eye.

Chapter 33

THE SUN STOOD HIGH AND strong over a small, bustling marketplace in Indonesia. All around, countless merchants were peddling their merchandise while customers haggled for better deals.

At a small makeshift café, Charles Gravo sat alone, sipping his green tea. With his oversized hat, sunglasses, and unassuming attire, he should have blended well with the locals of the city, but most people couldn't fight the urge to stare at the large bandage covering his nose.

Charles scanned the crowd from side to side until his gaze fell upon a young, petite woman who looked even more out of place than he. He set his cup of tea on a wooden table beside him and raised his hand to gain her attention.

Upon seeing Charles, a bright smile graced her face. She traversed the busy marketplace with skill, bouncing around any person that impeded her path and arriving almost out of breath.

"Good seeing you again, Dr. Peña," Charles said with a subtle hint of affection.

"I thought our paths would never cross again," she admitted. "I'm so excited to be wrong, though." She took a seat then fired off a barrage of medical questions at Charles about side effects and intellectual aptitude.

Charles smiled in amusement at her enthusiasm. "Well, there weren't many deep, intellectual, or stimulating conversations on Katingal." He then shifted his weight on the wooden stool and crossed his legs, followed by a slight wince that reminded him of his prison hardships.

"Are you in pain?" the doctor dutifully inquired.

"I'm fine now," Charles said, eager to change the subject. "Did you bring the passport?"

Dr. Peña observed his shoulder slump and watched him cross his arms. When it became apparent that he had no more words to share, she handed him a new passport. The new credentials bore a computer-generated photo of his new face and one of the many aliases he had used to successfully evade capture for many years. He pried at the plastic corners with his thumbnail to test the credibility of the lamination, and nodded in approval.

"So our agreement stands?" she asked.

"You get your lab rat back for six months and not a day longer."

Dr. Peña pulled her wooden stool closer to Charles and slid her hand under the table while Charles continued to bend and fold pages of the passport to break it in. When her hand grazed his upper thigh and reached for more, he recoiled.

"What the fuck are you doing?" he hissed. "You've read my rap sheet and know my interests."

Dr. Peña looked Charles up and down before shifting away from him in her stool. She placed her hands on the wooden table. He could feel her observing him, not as a man, but as a subject in an experiment.

Just then, a merchant pushing a cart lost his grip, and his merchandise came crashing onto the dirt road. When Charles swung his head around, Dr. Peña reached for a handful of the bulge forming in his pants.

"Yes, I read your rap sheet," she said softly, holding his genitals. She positioned her other hand at the center of his back.

Charles wanted to resist, but the chills running through his body compelled him to remain in her grasp.

"Your body hasn't caught up with your mind yet, but it will," she promised. Then she pulled herself so close that she could smell the tea on his breath. "You'll soon see what I already suspect is happening to you. Your physiology is changing."

They both looked at the burgeoning erection in his pants.

"How else can we explain my ability to arouse you, when all you've lusted for previously are children?"

Charles broke eye contact. The experience of shame over his desires had never affected him this way.

"Originally, I told the warden that I suspected you might become intellectually flawless," she said, hitting peak excitement. "But I may have spoken too soon. Never did

I consider that we may have unlocked the key to a human becoming flawless in totality."

Charles looked at her, feeling insulted and demeaned. "You think you can fix me, my desires?"

She smiled and gave him a soft squeeze. "I've brought you this far, haven't I?"

To be continued . . .

www.ingramcontent.com/pod-product-compliance
Lightning Source LLC
Chambersburg PA
CBHW020436270626
47155CB00022B/439